To Sharon,
Enjoy the story!
Lorelei Brush

UNCOVERING

A Novel
Lorelei Brush

www.mascotbooks.com

Uncovering

For more information, please contact:
Mascot Books
620 Herndon Parkway, Suite 320
Herndon, VA 20170
info@mascotbooks.com

Library of Congress Control Number: 2018911243

CPSIA Code: PRFRE0419A
ISBN-13: 978-1-64307-283-8

Printed in Canada

UNCOVERING

A Novel

Lorelei Brush

1

A river of eligible men flowed through the house that summer after the earthquake, weekend after weekend. Abu had opened the floodgates, and though Shahnaz argued it was too soon, there was no stemming this tide.

Tonight she peeked through a slit between the living room door and the hallway wall to see Naseer Khan and his family. The young man faced her, displaying springy black hair, deep-set eyes, a tidy beard, and a slender body comfortably balanced on the edge of the sofa. Not bad, at least on the surface. His thick moustache spread with enthusiasm across his top lip. The neatly trimmed hem of hairs showed that he had cut it that very day.

She sighed and leaned her head against the doorjamb. Why couldn't her father understand that her passion was making sure Kashmiri children were born healthy? There was none left for marriage. It was so unfair. He'd raised her like a son, encouraged her to ask questions, taught her to negotiate for privileges, and bragged to his friends when her grades topped the class. Until she was twelve and her brother Tahir was born. Then the world revolved around a different sun.

A hiss in her ear made her jump. "C'mon, Shahnaz, move out of the way. If you're not going to look, let me see him."

Shahnaz shook her head as she backed away from the door. That was Rabia for you, two years younger than Shahnaz's twenty-three years, and already wrapped up in the idea of marriage.

"Ooh," Rabia said from the side of her mouth. "Full lips, gentle eyes, long lashes. And Western clothes. You'll like that." She twisted her head this way and that to capture every possible detail.

Shahnaz watched her sister's ponytail bounce as she contorted her body. Kohl ringed Rabia's deep brown eyes; her lips and fingernails matched the red in her flowered tunic. So much energy packed into that lithe form, and all of it aimed at claiming a husband. Like there was gold in that living room, a nugget to be plucked from the couch and treasured—or used, who knew how. Why couldn't Naseer be for her?

Shahnaz paced the hallway, her face free of make-up and her nails of polish. Her life, her energy, was devoted to the people who lived in those mountains surrounding Muzaffarabad, the hardy Kashmiris who eked their existence from stark hills cut sharply by glaciers and oozing pebbled streams. That was where she belonged, clad in her favorite verdant greens, climbing steadily up the path to the house and clinic of one of her Lady Health Workers. Her mood blossomed with happiness every time she topped the rise and saw Bibi's children hopping from foot to foot and chanting her name. All except seven-year-old Kameela, whose foot had been crushed in the quake. She crouched and waved one of her crutches.

At least her Abu had chosen a potential husband from Muzaffarabad. The Khans lived on its eastern hills and, as she did, walked its rutted streets where little shops, hardly bigger than a bathroom, huddled side by side, facing lanes barely wide enough for a single car. A town working hard to rebuild after the earthquake.

Rabia waved her back to the door and cupped her hand over

her mouth to speak. "Abu's asking about his job. You'll want to hear this."

Shahnaz settled her right eye in the opening. Rabia was correct; she needed to know details if she was going to argue about this prospective husband. Hmm. Her sister was also right about Naseer's clothes. The long-sleeved white shirt, open at the neck, pleated pants, and belt with its shining silver buckle broadcast his openness to the dress of another culture, and perhaps its ideas.

"Yes, sir," Naseer said. "I'm a subject specialist for the Ministry of Education in Kashmir, and my subject is English. Now that our teachers must introduce English in Class 1, I do a lot of training and tutoring to improve their skills."

Shahnaz imagined her Abu, leaning forward in the chair just a few feet from her on the other side of the door. Today he had worn the white shalwar kameez she loved, the one with the elaborate filigree on the collar points and down the facing and alternating shiny and matte vertical stripes that shone elegantly in dim light. It made him look successful yet still a traditional Pakistani. But she worried. Would it give the Khans the idea that they were more religious, more fundamental, than was true?

Abu cleared his throat. "And where does one go from that sort of position?"

Ah, yes. If Naseer had few options for advancement, her father would be discouraged—and she might be as well, truth be told.

Naseer slid back into the couch and rested his hands on his thighs, as though relaxing for an exchange in which he knew all the proper answers. He didn't seem to mind the inquisition. In fact, the smile that Shahnaz saw in his eyes suggested he was enjoying it.

The young man's father chose to answer the question in place of his son. As he was blocked from Shahnaz's view, she had only his soft musical voice to go by. "I've seen talented young men rise from subject specialist to become Minister of Education. I myself started in a comparable role in Forestry and made a similar transition, as you know." He went on to cite the steps his son might take on the ladder of success, and Shahnaz found herself drawn to this earnest speaker, now Minister of Forestry. His listing of possibilities for his son could have sounded arrogant yet came across as gentle gifts given for another's pleasure. If she married Naseer, she'd be a part of a prestigious family. Not exactly her goal, but nothing to argue against.

If she had to marry—and obedience to that parental requirement seemed inevitable—perhaps he'd do. Maybe this Naseer, with his education, fluent English, Western dress, and job for life, would believe in her work. She studied the young man more intently. He did have a shy smile, an element of lurking humor, a comfortable respect for his father, a confident set to his shoulders. Was he the one?

Remembering one of her mother's many lectures on proper family life, she turned her head to focus on Naseer's mother. As her mother-in-law, this woman could forbid Shahnaz from leaving the house. Thankfully, she didn't look the forbidding type. The tunic of her shalwar kameez was a fine beige lawn decorated with pale yellow flowers. Its long sleeves and high neck showed a conservative orientation, though the wrinkles in the bodice that hugged her plump body suggested she didn't care too much about personal appearance. Her dupatta, shading from beige at the top of her head to yellow at her bosom, covered most of her hair, but allowed a few loose curls to flutter in the breeze of the air conditioner. Would she allow a daughter-in-law to go out to work? Would she want Shahnaz to cover her face as well as her hair? Shahnaz ran her fingers through her own thick tresses, now free from any constraint.

"Lovely tea set," the prospective mother-in-law said. Her keen gaze wandered the room from behind gold-rimmed spectacles.

Shahnaz watched her appraise their furniture, carpet, and wall hangings. Did this small woman detect the fraying fabric of the red-plaid living room set? Did she spot the purple stain on the carpet next to her chair? A slight flush crept up Shahnaz's face. That was where she had dropped a glass of grape juice when she was eight and first knelt to serve her elders. With surprise, she realized she cared a great deal that this woman find her home acceptable.

"Thank you," she heard her Ammi say. "That tea set was my mother's. We so appreciate the old things that tie us to family. You know, my father was born and raised in Rawalakot, my husband's father in Bagh, so, like you, we're Kashmiri. My husband works for the government, so we must live here in Islamabad, but we often return to our villages."

That was so like her mother, connecting people, drawing family together, and pleasing others. She had kept Shahnaz in her room for a half hour deciding on what the mother of a soon-to-be bride would wear to this meeting with the Khans. Suspecting conservative leanings, her mother had eschewed her bright vee-neck kameezes, choosing instead a green and brown long-sleeved tunic that buttoned to the neck but still outlined her slender figure. She'd even drawn the matching dupatta over her short salt-and-pepper hair. In a fleeting moment, Shahnaz wondered what the Khans thought of her mother. She hoped they picked up on the un-dyed hair and fitted tunic and saw her as the open-minded woman she was.

Rabia pulled at her arm. "My turn again."

Shahnaz shook off her sister's hand. It bumped the door and pushed it open another few centimeters. Horrified at announcing her presence in this way, Shahnaz clasped Rabia's wrist and whisked them both across the hall into the TV room, closing its door quietly behind them.

"Stop pulling." Rabia yanked her hand away. "Look what you've done. Now we'll miss a lot of the good stuff."

"Your dupatta's trailing on the floor."

"Oh, pooh." Rabia flipped the offending material back over

her shoulder.

"Come on, sit down. Maybe there's something good on TV." She curled into the blue cushions of the sofa. "You'll be happy to know I think Naseer is better than any of the others. He seems polite, modern, well-taught, and he has a good job."

She ticked off more pluses on her fingers. "He's twenty-seven, so he knows the world a little. He works in education. He doesn't look too religious." She dropped her hands. "The big question is whether he'll let me work."

"Pfuh." Rabia dropped into the softness of her mother's favorite chair. "You better forget this work thing; it's not going to happen. What you should worry about is his pathetic government salary." She paused, draping her body across the chair. "I want a husband who earns good money, gives me beautiful jewelry, and treats me like a princess. I want a house with ten bedrooms in F-6 near all those high-level officials, and servants to make whatever I want for dinner. I mean, Muzaffarabad—way too 'small town' for me."

"You're so shallow. It was a complete waste for Abu to send you to City School. You don't care about anything but money and prestige." They'd had this exchange any number of times before. It was like a mantra, automatic in its repetitiveness.

Rabia swished the end of her dupatta back over her shoulder. "Yes, I do. I love my friends—and I want excitement in my life!"

Shahnaz dropped her head against the sofa, unwilling to continue the boring script. She sighed. Small prickles of sweat gathered on her forehead, under her arms, and down her back; no A.C. in this room. Too bad. And she knew the pressure on her would escalate when the Khans' visit ended. Abu was bound to approve of Naseer's family and prospects. Ammi would like his soft-spoken voice and gentle manner.

Rabia switched on the small color television and clicked through the channels.

Closing her eyes and ears to the noise, Shahnaz pictured Kameela in the blue-and-white clothes of a school girl, sitting with others on the concrete slab that, before the earthquake, was the floor of the local primary school. Without walls and a roof, the girls pulled their dupattas forward to shade their faces from the relentless sun. Kameela sat with her legs crossed, her missing foot tucked under her other leg so no one could tell she was different. Bibi, Kameela, and Shahnaz all prayed for this to happen, but just last week Bibi's husband had refused again to allow Kameela to go to school. He was sure her loss of a foot was a sign of God's displeasure. Shahnaz vowed to talk to him again, to persuade him to accept a prosthesis for her. It would be free, and Shahnaz knew she could find help for them to travel to the capital for fittings. Just what should she say to this man who thought that providing a prosthesis was challenging God's will?

Long moments later, Shahnaz heard the scrape of the heavy gate across the driveway to their walled property. She peeked out the TV room door to see who had arrived, but it was just Tahir coming home. Closing the hall door quietly—there was no point in talking with an eleven-year-old boy about marriage prospects—she noted that Rabia had settled on a rerun of *East Enders*. Not her thing. She dropped back onto the couch, and ignoring the clamor of those complicated British accents, wondered how the Khans' house had fared in the earthquake. What would their bedroom be like? Was the house safe? Would he be gentle with her? Could she work when she had a baby? Should she agree to this marriage?

When her mother opened the TV room door, a scowl of disapproval marred her usually placid face. Shahnaz snatched the remote and turned the program off. Rabia leaped up from Ammi's chair and made for the couch. In the sudden quiet, Ammi perched on the edge of her chair and straightened the skirt of her kameez. "I believe they're going to make an offer, Shahnaz."

"All right! You'll be off and married by spring, and it'll be my turn."

"Rabia," Ammi said, "calm down, please." She rested her eyes on each daughter in turn. "This exuberant bouncing and banging doors is not the behavior expected of young women thinking of marriage. There I was, describing how mature Shahnaz is, and I was forced, yes, forced, by the noise to get up and shut the door."

Shahnaz hung her head. Rabia rushed to hug her mother, and taking her hands, knelt at the side of her knee. "Come on, Ammi, don't keep us in suspense. What did you think of the Khans?" She bumped against her mother's knee. "You aren't really angry at us. I can tell by the smile in your eyes."

Shahnaz could only admire her sister's ability to sweet-talk Ammi out of disciplining her daughters. Once again, Rabia turned their mother's anger and persuaded her to talk while Shahnaz was still feeling chastised. And it was *her* future they were going to hear about, not Rabia's. She was the one who should be asking the questions.

Taking back her hands, Ammi cupped Rabia's chin and shook her daughter's head. "All right, but don't embarrass me again with that childish behavior."

"We promise," Shahnaz said. She crossed her feet, sat up straight, and ignored Rabia's look of triumph. "What did you think of them?"

Her mother smiled and leaned back into her chair. After pulling a misplaced pillow onto her lap, she folded her hands. "Naseer seemed nice, competent. Your father will check with a friend in the Chief Secretary's office who knows people in the Education Ministry to make sure he's a good employee and has a secure job." She paused. "You know he's the second son. I do think we need to meet the eldest, Raja Haider. He's a city planner in Muzaffarabad." She played with the folds of her dupatta.

"What is it, Ammi?" Shahnaz perked up. Perhaps her Ammi had seen a reason to refuse this suitor.

Her mother hugged the cushion. "Did you notice what Naseer's father was wearing?"

"I couldn't see him. He was behind the door."

"Ah, well...He has a very long beard—which he may never have cut—and wears a taqiyah. The hat was modest, not overly decorated, but I'm afraid it says he is more conservative than we thought."

"Naseer didn't look conservative. His beard is short and he wore Western clothes."

"True, but as the newest wife in the house, you'll have to obey the father, the older brother, your husband, his mother, your sister-in-law—oh, you know. They could ask a lot. We need to look into this, be sure they accept the way you've been raised."

"Yes, please, Ammi." Shahnaz drifted back into worries. This father-in-law could mean no job for her, never looking a man in the eye, being tied to the house. Her nightmare. It wasn't that she didn't understand the requirement of obedience. Hadn't she obeyed her parents' requests to serve people drinks, fetch and carry for guests, and help with meals? Hadn't she accepted her father's decree about marriage? God said in the Qur'an that men are made responsible for women; she accepted that. Well, to be honest, accepted *in theory*. In practice, she was happy to surrender to God in prayer five times a day, but she wasn't as ready to surrender to men.

"I remember when I married your father, and we lived with his parents." Ammi smiled wistfully. "I thought it'd be glorious to have several sisters—his younger sisters were still at home then, and I thought his brothers would soon marry. I pictured six or seven of us young women, sitting together like girlfriends and chatting over endless cups of tea, all about our fiancés, husbands, children, in-laws, friends. Loving each other. But it wasn't that way. There was a lot of work to do, and as the youngest wife, so much fell to me.

One sister was so sloppy I often had to redo her jobs, and another was never around when assignments were given. I got her work, too. And then there was Zeenat, who whined about everything and made the rest of us uncomfortable. You remember her, right?"

Shahnaz and Rabia both nodded. When they were still in primary school, they had avoided Zeenat at family gatherings. She had a penetrating voice and a heavy tread, and each of them would duck out an opposing door when she entered a room, determined to miss the endless criticism.

"We'll have to look into this. So many things to think about." Her mother stroked the pillow, ironing out all the wrinkles in its surface.

Shahnaz nodded, pleased at her mother's train of thought. "Yes, Ammi, lots of things."

Ammi scrutinized her elder daughter. "Are you sure you don't want to marry your cousin Hamid? He's a good boy, and you've known him all your life."

Shahnaz met Rabia's eyes and then looked at the floor so she wouldn't unloose the laughter that bubbled into her mouth. Hamid was short and had a paunch from too much greasy food, and he was already losing his hair. He had had few friends growing up and sat on the periphery, like one of those sloppy dogs with its tongue hanging out wanting to play. Largely, the girls had shunned him, as had all the cousins. She couldn't imagine marrying him and remembered cringing when her mother had said his parents were inquiring. Shahnaz took a large breath. "No, Ammi, I don't think so."

Rabia had her face buried in her hands, but Shahnaz saw her glee.

"Perhaps he'd be more suitable for Rabia?" Out of the corner of her eye, Shahnaz watched for a hurtled pillow.

Instead, it was Ammi who shifted a pillow—the one she had been hugging—and tucked it into the corner of her chair as she stood up. "Ah, well, there's no decision yet. We'll see what we find out about Naseer's job prospects and the family's religious leanings." Smiling, she wagged her finger at her elder daughter. "At least he's not like that young Usman whose family did nothing but bicker when they were here. Or that Ahmed who stuttered, blushed, and stared at his feet most of the evening."

When the door closed behind her mother, Rabia grabbed the tassel on the nearest pillow and flung the plump missile at her sister. "How dare you suggest Hamid for me!"

"It was too perfect to pass up."

"Right. Like this Naseer. He's pretty close to perfect for you, but I notice neither you nor Ammi brought up your work. You coward! Are you planning to refuse him?"

Shahnaz rested her chin on her hand. "I don't know. He may be okay."

Rabia rammed her fists into her sides. "C'mon. Make a decision already!"

———•◦•———

The next afternoon, Shahnaz dropped her purse on the bedside table of her hostel room and melted onto the bed. The four-hour bus ride north from Islamabad to Muzaffarabad had been especially bad this Sunday, with the driver pounding the brakes as he approached each switchback. Just short of the Kohala Bridge, he'd bounced passengers off their seats on a stretch of potholes. With each lurch, Shahnaz had felt her stomach pummel her heart. The unwashed condition of the man in the seat in front of her had added to her nausea, and she thanked God that she had not thrown up.

Feeling a drop of sweat roll down her neck, she unwrapped her dupatta and kicked off her sandals, the open window beckoning. Her kameez stuck to her stomach, and she pulled at the damp material. Its tightness across her bust caused another flash of annoyance: the family tailor didn't seem to believe that a young woman could have larger-than-average breasts. One deep breath and she'd have to re-sew some seams. As she leaned on the sill, the lights of the sector on the far hill flickered on, creating a map of streets and houses. With concentration, she could make out the roaring sounds of the Neelum River, bringing icy water from the glaciers down past the town. Would that a bit of that iciness wafted into her room! She flipped the switch for the overhead fan. No luck; it must be a load-shedding hour. Insh'allah, God willing, by bedtime when her roommates had returned, their electricity would be on.

It did get hot here, even with mountains and glaciers close by. Having four girls share a room contributed to the dense air, but aside from the heat—which was everywhere—they were very lucky that the International Program for Peace subsidized a place for its staff.

A lilting voice called from downstairs. "Shahnaz?"

"Be down in a minute." Thank goodness that hunger had replaced her earlier nausea. It smelled like goshtaba tonight, and she did love those chunky meatballs in their thick gravy. What a blessing it was to have their own cook.

Shahnaz slid into her chair at the long wooden table and nodded to the others. Arjumand, the youngest of the group and a perpetual complainer, had the floor. In her whining voice, she announced she was scheduled to visit a Lady Health Worker in Kangard the next morning. "Two hours it'll take to climb to her house from the road," she said. "Every time I go there, I get blisters." She jabbed at a meatball with a chunk of roti, breaking off a bite. "I already know what she's going to tell me: no progress on birth control in her hamlet." Arjumand pointed her food at Shahnaz. "You know, she's got one 30-year-old woman who's pregnant with her thirteenth child. The lady is exhausted—I've seen her and even tried myself to talk to her husband. He seems to think it's his job to populate the world with Muslims, all by himself."

Shahnaz tilted her head. "Insh'allah, you'll figure something out. Maybe another family, relatives of that one, will agree to use birth control, and the idea will snowball like it did in Marak Baian."

Irum, Shahnaz's closest friend in the group, chimed in. "Isn't that Dr. Irshad's area? Maybe he'll talk to the men or to the imam."

Others added suggestions, and then they all focused on eating. Shahnaz fretted over the long list of tasks she'd set herself: organize the polio campaign, call again about the back order on immunization serum, and talk to people in Rawalakot to recruit a new health worker.

When they finished the meal, Irum and Shahnaz wandered out onto the terrace to spend a few minutes alone. Irum was one of the few people Shahnaz knew who had blue eyes. With her round face, unblemished skin, and gold earrings, she was as pretty as a model. The dangles in her ears sparkled in the twilight, reflecting the gleam in Irum's eyes.

Irum prodded Shahnaz's arm. "So, what happened? Come on, tell, tell."

Shahnaz was glad the sun had set behind the mountains and Irum couldn't see her confusion. "I'm afraid the family is too conservative. You know how that goes. First it'll be fully covering, then giving up my work, then not leaving the house. I don't want to give up my freedom." She wiped sweat from her forehead. "I have excellent training, and we've got to eradicate polio. I know I can convince people to get their children vaccinated."

They strolled along the boundary wall. Shahnaz followed a seam with her finger. "Even if the Khans let me work, I'll be expected to get pregnant right away, and that could end it all. Oh, Irum, I don't want to marry now. It's too soon." She blinked away tears. "My parents think this is the best offer they'll find for me."

Irum stopped at the corner farthest from the house. "You do have access to birth control."

Shahnaz sucked in her breath. "I couldn't do that. If I agree to this marriage, I have to enter it honestly."

"You could ask Naseer. Perhaps he'll agree."

Shahnaz shook her head. "You're a radical in conservative clothing. Maybe he'd agree after I had a son."

"You'll work this out. I know you will."

Shahnaz took both of Irum's hands in her own. "And what about you? Did you speak to your parents again?"

Irum pulled her hands away and turned toward the river's muted roar. "Oh, yes, and the answer was the same: I should not think of marriage now." Her fingers played with an earring, rolling the dangles between her fingers, and Shahnaz was reminded that these were all Irum had left of her much-beloved sister, who had married just two years before and died in childbirth. Her parents were afraid of losing another daughter and were holding tightly to Irum. "You'll be in this position one day, Irum, insh'allah. Only, you'll be sure it's the right thing."

Wiping a tear away with the edge of her hand, Irum nodded and then smiled. "At least they let me move into the hostel. I didn't think that would happen, but Abu was kind and saw how much I wanted it." She grinned suddenly. "Either that or he got tired of arguing with his brother—the one I stayed with in Muzaffarabad— about allowing me to work." They walked around the walled garden, back to the hostel doorway. "And perhaps he'll also see how much I want to marry."

—•—

Early Thursday morning, Shahnaz and Irum shared the back of a double-cabin pick-up on their way to a far-flung area near the

Neelum Valley. They guessed at the number of minutes it would take for this newly washed white vehicle to get splashed with mud. Seven? Ten?

The Lady Health Workers they supervised were running an Immunization Day, and the community had been hostile to these in the past. Their Health Workers wanted backup. Irum hated confrontations, but Shahnaz was energized by debate and looked forward to the day's possibilities.

As the truck pulled up to the small cluster of "homes," Shahnaz was once again saddened that a jumbled mixture of tents and a hut made of tin roofing, stones, mud, and rubble constituted the homes for several families. The structures occupied a narrow strip of land between the road and the mountain with two tents' walls bordering the road and a third at the end of the cliff on the right, a sort of declaration that the yard ended there. Each of the tents had a solid roof and sides that ruffled in the wind. Someone had cut windows in the best-preserved tent, which made Shahnaz wonder how the families would deal with the harsh gusts of winter storms. Of course, they needed some relief from the suffocating heat of the summer, but why not roll up the sides? She shook her head. Stupid idea. Families wanted privacy. As she moved closer, she could smell rot from the other two tents: their sides no longer reached the ground, and black mold streaked the khaki. The ragged bottom edges flapped in the light breeze and slapped against the metal tent poles. The rain must rush across the tent floors, making everything muddy. How did anyone keep clean? She shook her head.

Shahnaz held her dupatta close under her chin, watching where she placed her feet on the short climb from the road to the compound. The steps were merely a series of stones, some of which wobbled. With mud on either side of the path, the chances were good that her toes, sticking out of the sandals, would end up filthy. At the top of the stairs she offered her hand back to Irum, whose sandals kept slipping. They both stared at the yard, bordered by the tents and the scruffy greenery of the rising mountain, now transformed for their event and already busy with people. This area was often muddy, but today half of it was spread with red, green, and yellow straw mats for children to sit on as they waited their turns. On the right, beyond the mats, sat a cluster of adult-sized chairs. On the left, someone had pitched a tarp over a table and four chairs and had even found a piece of red cloth to brighten up the "clinic" area.

With a sweep of her arm, Shahnaz turned to Irum. "Look at this. It's so welcoming." The sun made the colors of the empty mats sparkle. A number of boys crowded around the table, pointing at needles and vials and plying the Lady Health Workers with questions. Several girls gathered near one tent and whispered to each other. Three or four mothers and babies were already seated. "Looks like a good group. I wonder why the Lady Health Workers wanted us to come? These people all seem willing enough, or they wouldn't have been here early."

Irum stopped to survey the adults, raising her hand to shade her eyes. "One clean-shaven man, the rest with beards, just one beard colored by henna. I see lots of taqiyahs, simple ones." She prodded Shahnaz with an elbow. "There's a man just inside that end tent. I'd guess he's the reason we're here."

"Maybe. I'm sure our Health Workers are bursting to tell us."

As she and Irum started toward the table, her mobile rang, showing her mother's number. "Ammi, what is it?" A shiver flew up Shahnaz's spine. Her mother was good about saving calls for the evening.

"Oh, nothing bad, dear, not to worry." Her mother sounded relaxed. "Your father just had a call from Sohail, Naseer's father, and he'd like to bring his eldest son, Raja Haider, to meet with you tonight. The young man and his wife are in Islamabad today."

With a wave of her hand to Irum, Shahnaz slipped to the side of one of the tents. Why, she wondered, would her mother make such a request when they both knew Shahnaz was working and many hours away? She stuffed down her annoyance. "Ammi, haven't you told the Khans that I work during the week in Muzaffarabad?"

This time Ammi paused before replying. "Abu did mention that you'd taken a job, but he didn't go into detail. They are so pleased with you. I didn't want to bring up troublesome things." It sounded like pleading.

Shahnaz's chest constricted with her rising anger. Why was working to help others "troublesome?" How come these marriage arrangements ignored what was so important to her? Couldn't Ammi be more supportive? Goodness, even if Shahnaz persuaded the driver to take her back to Muzaffarabad, she'd still have to get to the bus station—and then wait for the next bus. It would be at least six or seven hours of travel, exhausting to contemplate, and she'd be letting the team down. Not possible. "Ammi, please, could you explain that I'm up north, in the mountains?" Insh'allah, Ammi would find a compromise.

"Your father's pleased with this marriage arrangement. The Khans are well placed in the Kashmiri government and may also be able to help your brother find a job, when the time comes."

This was definitely a warning. Even though Tahir was more interested in cricket than any job prospect, Shahnaz knew her father had big plans for him. Her eye caught movement at the edge of the tent, where Irum was waving at her, urging her to come. She signaled one minute with her index finger and then turned to face the vista spotted with trees along the single-lane road winding down to the river. "Ammi, I can't. I'm nowhere near a bus, and anyway, I can't leave until we've finished here."

Her mother sighed. "All right. I told Abu this wouldn't be easy."

Tears came to Shahnaz's eyes. At the sound of clicking sandals, she turned to see Irum's anxious face. "Ammi, please tell them I'm working up here. And that I love my job?"

"Shahnaz," her mother said with another sigh, "Abu found out that Naseer has excellent prospects, his father is well regarded as Minister of Forestry, his mother is known in the highest circles, and neither parent holds extreme religious views. He feels it's important to demonstrate your commitment to the home."

Shahnaz let her shoulders slump. "Please, Ammi, if not the whole truth today, could you at least say I'm far away? Or could I meet the family when they return to Muzaffarabad?"

"Oh, no," Ammi was quick to reply. "Abu would have to take a day off work to travel up north. Not possible."

What to say? She ground her teeth at the implication that her work was not important. "Could you explain to Abu that I'm so far out of town I can't make it today? He'll know how to reply to the Khans." She brought Irum's hand up to her cheek.

"Perhaps."

Irum pulled her toward the yard. "Ammi, I have to go. Call me when you've talked to Abu, okay?"

And then Shahnaz put her mobile on vibrate and slid it deep into her purse.

Shahnaz glanced at Irum's anxious face. "It's okay. It's not an emergency." Sending a small prayer to God, she consigned her marriage to a walled-off part of her mind for later. There were vaccinations to attend to.

Three Lady Health Workers stood around the table organizing their materials. Bibi, whom Shahnaz supervised, was at the far end of the table with stacks of folders and forms laid out in front of her. The other women, who worked under Irum, greeted their supervisor and nodded at Shahnaz, then continued to unpack the vials of sera, alcohol swabs, and assorted paraphernalia.

Bibi hissed for Shahnaz to come close. She kept her fingers moving and spoke softly. "The imam's in that end tent." She tipped her head toward the opposite side of the yard. "He's full of fire, burning for an argument. Hates people from outside. Tells the men they aren't like us. He's got several of 'em in with him now, and I'll bet he's stirring them up."

"Well, then, I think that's where Irum and I should go." Shahnaz turned to Irum. "What do you say, Irum? We can take on an angry mob of men, right?"

Irum shrank back, her mouth hanging open. "If we have to..."

Shahnaz reminded herself that Irum was a Hazara, not a Kashmiri, and definitely not from a nearby settlement. "I'm sorry. That was mean. I know you hate scenes. I'll talk—but it's better if there are two of us. Okay?"

"I guess. You lead."

As they walked around the mats and greeted the women and babies, Shahnaz felt her excitement grow. She'd convinced tough opponents before, and she could do it again. A glance at Irum suggested her friend regarded the upcoming conversation more as a form of punishment. "Insh'allah, it'll be all right. Please don't fret."

The imam was pontificating. A tall man with a commanding presence, his eyes swept his listeners, as though he were probing for sin in each face. Most of the eight or nine men in the tent looked up at him with rapt faces. A couple stared at the ground. Shahnaz bit her lip. Bibi's husband, who supported immunizations, looked up just then and nodded to Shahnaz. Okay, she thought, one man on her side anyway.

When the imam completed a lengthy paragraph, Shahnaz stepped toward him, put her hand on her heart, and bowed slightly. "Bismillah, ar-Rahman, ar-Rahim. In the name of God, the most compassionate, the most merciful. Sir, I am Shahnaz Ayaz, a supervisor of Lady Health Workers, and this is my colleague Irum Eid, also a supervisor."

The man lowered his head slightly and opened his

mouth to speak.

Shahnaz hurried out her words. "Sahib, we are honored that you have come to Immunization Day. This is such an important time for us in Kashmir as we recover from the earthquake. Living as we do in tents and makeshift houses, it is more important than ever to do all we can to keep our children healthy. Think of the horrors we'd face with an epidemic of measles this winter. So many babies and toddlers, the children of our future, would die in the cold. I imagine you remember the epidemics when you were a child."

"Yes, yes, I do. I lost a brother, and—"

"Oh, I'm so sorry to hear that. Insh'allah, a child of yours will never suffer like that cherished brother." She paused to glance out the tent flap to the table. "I see the Lady Health Workers are about ready to begin. Will you honor us with a recitation from the Holy Qur'an to start the day?"

He opened his mouth, preparing to object.

"Please, it would mean so much to all these mothers, and insh'allah, it will ease the nerves of these anxious children." Again she bowed and then took two steps backward to allow him plenty of room to precede her out of the tent.

Bibi's husband followed Shahnaz and cleared his throat. "Nice job. He's trying to figure out how he got manipulated into this and probably how to get out. Wonder what he'll choose to recite?"

The imam stalked to the table and stood, looking stern, until everyone quieted. Then he chanted a long verse, which Shahnaz thought came from a later sura: "God created you from dust, then from a tiny drop, then He causes you to reproduce through your spouses. No female becomes pregnant, nor gives birth, without His knowledge. No one survives for a long life, and no one's life is snapped short, except in accordance with a pre-existing record. This is easy for God."

Shahnaz chewed on a fingertip. It was good of him to talk

of babies as gifts from God. That made them especially precious, beings to care for and hold from harm. If he'd stopped there, she'd have thought he valued things like immunizations. But he went on to issue a warning of sorts: God decides who shall live a long life, not Lady Health Workers and their vaccines. Well, of course, but didn't God want them to do all they could to treasure these gifts from Him? That tricky concept of free will again, and the one of giving up ego. Was he saying this choice of immunizations suggested the parents were usurping the right of God to decide how long their children lived? She wasn't going to hang on to that idea. It was just wrong.

With a smile, she again bowed to the imam and turned to the families. "Thank you all for coming today. It's a pleasure to see so many healthy babies and children." She looked around and waved at a small boy who was waving to her. "Now, feel free to come with your children. Check in with Bibi, and then move around the table for the necessary immunizations." As her eyes swept the table, she noticed the women had brought juice boxes—a rare treat. They must have spent their own money to buy them. She raised her voice above the movements of the mothers and children. "It seems we have a special treat today: orange juice in small boxes for the children."

For a few minutes, all went well. No one liked the shots, but Shahnaz made sure to speak to each mother and child and hand a juice box to the mobile children. Between the new marvel of straws poking into packages and sucking from a box, they forgot their tears and wandered off.

The imam towered over the small ones and hovered around the table, watching each injection. About twenty children into the day, a boy of four or five who had needed polio drops took a drink of his juice and spit it out. "It's bad!"

The imam sauntered over, demanded the box, and tried some. "Stop, stop, all of you! I suspected you from the start, you foreigners, now I know." He pointed at Shahnaz and Irum. "You are feeding our boys drugs to make them infertile. Under this guise of a treat, you've put something in these boxes. This is evil. Now, get out of here." He swung his long arm from the women to the truck, righteous anger suffusing his face.

Shahnaz froze. She and Irum hadn't brought the juice boxes, but that was irrelevant. She swept the remaining juice boxes into the backpack they'd come in and stood up facing the imam. "I'm so sorry that the juice doesn't taste good. I think it must be today's heat. We'll stop giving it to the children." She stepped a little away from the table and signaled for the health workers to continue with their immunizations.

The imam followed her, like a shepherd herding a sheep. "What have you put in those vials? Have you poisoned them, too?" His voice was loud enough to carry to the men, as well as everyone in line.

"No, sir, not at all. In fact, I brought pictures of all of the vaccine bottles, pictures that show the shapes of all the bottles and the colors of the proper liquids. Please, do check each vial against its picture." She rummaged in her canvas bag for the right handouts and then picked up the vial of Hepatitis B vaccine. Holding the picture in one hand and the vial in the other, she looked up at the imam's face. "See, Hepatitis B, same shape bottle, same color liquid."

His face was a mask of confusion.

She blushed, realizing he probably couldn't read the label and now she'd embarrassed him in public. Sure that he didn't believe her and wouldn't trust any of the other women, she called Bibi's husband over. "Please, would you read what is on this bottle and what is pictured?"

The man did as instructed. "Looks right to me."

The imam's eyes narrowed. Shahnaz could imagine the argument in his head: to trust or not to trust? He looked from Shahnaz to Bibi's husband to the women at the table. Other than a hushed crooning to a squalling baby, the table was silent.

The imam again pointed at Shahnaz and Irum. "You will not touch any of our children, and you will take away those evil boxes you call juice."

"Yes, sir. Right away." She picked up the backpack and headed for the car, followed closely by Irum.

Their driver met them at the top of the rocky steps. "I'll take that for you."

"Thank you. I'm going to return to the table."

Irum wrung her hands. "Shahnaz, you can't. He sent us away."

"Not exactly. He said we couldn't touch the children, and I won't. But I will not slink away like a beaten donkey." She smiled. "Go on, you can stay in the truck. It won't be long until we're done for the day."

——••——

Less than an hour later, Shahnaz climbed into the back seat of the double-cabin next to Irum and dropped her head against the backrest. "All done. Every child immunized."

"Oh, Shahnaz, I don't know how you do it. I'm exhausted. I was scared the imam was going to decide we'd doctored the sera as well."

Shahnaz shook her head. "It was close, I admit. But look at the number of children immunized. Makes me feel better about their making it through this next year." She pulled herself up off the seat to smooth the skirt of her kameez just as the truck bumped over a deep hole. Bile rose into her throat. Better sit quietly and watch the road. In settling herself in the seat, her foot slid against her purse and she could feel its insistent vibration. Uh oh. She shuffled through the pens, scraps of paper, and assorted necessities to locate her mobile. With a finger in her left ear, she answered her mother's call.

"Ammi, I'm so sorry. We just finished the immunizations—"

"Shahnaz, you must be here. Abu says to come immediately." The sound of a sob came through the mobile.

Shahnaz glanced at her watch. It was nearly one-thirty, and she'd had no lunch. Dropping her chin in defeat, she shifted roles from successful professional to dutiful daughter. "Ammi, please don't cry. I'll do my best, I promise."

"No, no, not your 'best.' You *must* get here."

The catch in her mother's voice stirred competing emotions: guilt at being the source of her mother's pain, elation and fatigue from the morning's drama, and anger at too much being asked of her. "Ammi, I'm still an hour out of Muzaffarabad. I'll go right to the bus station when we arrive, I promise. And I'll call you to say when I'll get to Islamabad."

Shahnaz closed her eyes and scanned a list in her mind: call Amir, her boss, to get permission, call for the bus schedule, go to the ATM for cash. Would she have time to return to the hostel to pack a few things? Ignoring her resentment at her orders, she phoned Amir (who was annoyed but allowed her to leave) and found the time of the next bus, which would barely leave time for a visit to the ATM. She would have to rely on her sister for a clean shalwar kameez. Surely Ammi would see to her clothing before picking her up. Aware that her breathing was shallow, her heart racing, and her stomach forming little knots, Shahnaz let out her frustration to Irum.

2

Shahnaz stole glimpses of each of the assembled guests as she passed the tray of cold juices and sodas. A phalanx of men from Naseer's family had commandeered the couch: a line-up of thick heads of hair, full moustaches, and sweaty brows. Sohail, the white-haired, white-bearded father, nodded his head and smiled as she knelt at his knee. A compact man in body, he exuded a calm assurance; she was immediately drawn to him. Raja Haider, the oldest son at thirty, brought his stormy eyebrows together as he selected a middle glass on the tray (as far from her hands as possible). Jamil, the next younger son, just looked bored. She hated these events, the awareness of being constantly evaluated, like an animal being assessed for sacrifice.

She moved to the loveseat, shared by Maryam, her prospective mother-in-law, and Noshaba, Raja Haider's wife. When Shahnaz approached, Maryam tilted her head like a bespectacled bird examining the offerings and then selected a glass of pomegranate juice. With the same tilt of her head she examined Shahnaz, who returned the obligatory smile, trusting that her well-tailored clothes provided the image she wished to project. She'd had time only for a quick wash, a change of shalwar kameez, and a swipe of kohl before hurrying to the kitchen to finish the dessert for the evening. Thank goodness Ammi had set dinner for nine o'clock, or she wouldn't have made it back from work in time. When she had picked up the tray of drinks, it had taken her many deep breaths to calm her irritation at the rushed afternoon.

With studied calm, she served her parents and let her eyes sneak back to Noshaba. The young woman was clad in black with a hijab that covered all but her timid eyes. Way more conservative than Shahnaz, who was clad in bright greens and showed sleek dark hair under her loosely draped dupatta. This Noshaba sunk back into the cushions as though trying to disappear.

When all had a drink, Shahnaz took a seat across from the sofa and watched Raja Haider's black beard bob with each breath against the buttons of his kameez. He caressed a scroll of papers and drew it across his lap.

"Too many people are still living rough." His authoritative voice sounded like that of a university lecturer. "Here we are, nearly a year after the earthquake, and my father's office is still in a trailer. Naseer and I work in tents." He raised his scroll and his voice, like a protester at a demonstration. "My excellent blueprints are put aside week after week."

Shahnaz took in the pained expressions on the faces of the Khans, unable to tell if they were embarrassed at their son's vehemence or lost in memories.

Sohail nodded. "Raja Haider spends a great deal of time designing new offices and housing." With a rueful smile, he looked toward his eldest son. "After the quake, he insisted several families pitch their tents in our orchard and use the wood for heat and cooking. It was necessary—and generous—but I missed this year's spring blossoms and summer fruit."

Ammi shook her head sadly. "So much sadness from that day."

Raja Haider nodded agreement. "I was returning from an

early meeting and watched my building slide off its foundation. I pulled a couple of men out, but the concrete slab that was our roof crushed thirty-four colleagues." He stopped, his eyes on the carpet, then slowly raised his head. "Allah was watching over me. He saved me for His work on this earth."

Sohail set his juice on an end table and clasped his hands around one knee, starting a mild rocking of his body. "That day changed us all, I'm afraid. We're so blessed that our children survived."

Maryam added, "I was in the living room and watched cracks run down the walls. To tell the truth, I felt them follow me as I hurried out. I thought the house would be my tomb." After a thoughtful shake of the head, she nodded toward her oldest son. "Insh'allah, Raja Haider will see us through the renovations."

The young man squared his shoulders and raised his voice. "I had our plans drawn six months ago. Four times now I've taken them before the Authority for approval, and each time they've asked for changes, which I've done, and then waited weeks for another appointment." He paused, his brows knit into a streak of tar atop his eyes. "I should have priority, but instead I'm getting the run-around by a never-ending stream of minor government workers puffed up with their authority. I—"

Shahnaz recoiled from the vehemence. So pompous a man. Primed to explode. He probably demanded absolute obedience. Her eyes flickered toward his wife, whose head was bowed, hands clasped in her lap, and she felt a stab of pity. If this rigid man had been her parents' choice for her, Shahnaz would have been adamant in her rejection.

Funny how different he seemed from his brother Naseer. Her potential husband had given off an impression of gentleness and informality, with his shirt open at the neck and his body relaxed. Rather than the forbidding look of his brother, Naseer's face had been inviting.

The mosque down the street sounded its call to prayer: Allah u Akbar, God is Great! Raja Haider moved to the edge of his seat. "I need to pray now. Where shall I go?"

Abu rose and guided his guest into a shadowed corner of the dining room.

Shahnaz stifled her surprise. Generally, people finished their business and then retired, modestly, to a corner to pray. Her parents would, and she imagined the rest of the Khans would as well. It was 2006, for goodness' sake. This Raja Haider seemed to need to display his piety, as if daring others to criticize his righteousness.

When Abu returned, Sohail cleared his throat. Using a roll of his fingers to invite her participation, he commented, "Shahnaz, your father tells us you have a job with Peace. What is it you do?"

"I'm trained as a public health nurse, and I supervise Lady Health Workers. They visit mothers and babies in their homes. We make sure pregnant women stay healthy and children get their shots, things like that. I'm stationed now in Muzaffarabad because of the earthquake, so I'm coming to know your city. My favorite days are ones when I go with my Lady Health Workers on their calls."

"So, what happens in these homes when you arrive? Do people receive you graciously or are some, shall we say, unwelcoming?" He stroked his beard with the sides of his fingers, as if it were the body of a cat he was encouraging to purr.

Shahnaz ran through a number of experiences in her mind. "Well, not everyone is appreciative. I went to one home last month where the new wife is a small woman, not fully grown, and her Lady Health Worker was afraid she'd have trouble delivering. Bibi, the health worker, wanted me to encourage the family to take her to the hospital in Muzaffarabad to have the baby."

She paused as Raja Haider padded to his place and tucked his blueprints against his thigh.

"The father-in-law met us outside their home, arms folded across his chest. When Bibi introduced me, he said he didn't want an outsider interfering in the birth of his grandchild. I said we were so fortunate to have many experienced dais in our communities, and I was so pleased he had a good midwife to call upon. He relaxed a little, and let us examine the girl. I told him later that I was worried about the size of the baby and asked if Bibi could talk with the dai. He agreed, but when I mentioned the doctor serving as back-up, he said no man—other than his son—could touch his daughter-in-law."

Raja Haider growled. "Father, you cannot approve of these women challenging men."

Sohail laid a heavy hand on his son's arm. Raja Haider muttered something, pulled his arm away from his father, and drew his blueprints onto his lap.

With a startled glance at Abu, Shahnaz plunged ahead. "We didn't challenge, not really. We simply found another way to protect the young woman's health."

Sohail smiled. "That was quite a story, Shahnaz. I like it that you're committed to the health of Kashmiri women. We need more people like you."

Shahnaz smiled in return, suppressing her desire to prove Raja Haider wrong.

The hall door opened to show their servant. Ammi moved toward it, then turned and announced that the buffet was ready. As the guests trooped into the dining room, she whispered to Shahnaz to busy herself with ensuring that each man had silverware, a napkin, and a small table for his plate. The men dolloped lamb kabob, keema replete with green chilies, and spicy chicken jalfrezi onto their plates and picked up slices of the thin roti and puffy naan to take back to their seats in the living room. Ammi invited the women to eat in the dining room, allowing Noshaba to remove her hijab. They stood close together at the kitchen end of the table, out of sight of the men. Shahnaz paused for a moment at Noshaba's side, feeling like a gawky giant as she was five or six inches taller than this doll-like figure with dainty features and an upturned nose. Shahnaz asked her if she would like something to drink, and Noshaba whispered "Coke," as though she would be chastised if she asked too loudly. When Shahnaz brought the glass of soda, Noshaba smiled shyly up at her.

While Ammi and Maryam chatted, Shahnaz circulated with the main dishes to encourage seconds for anyone whose plate had empty space. As was often the case during a meal, the men honored the Muslim tradition of concentrating on their food rather than conversation.

When Shahnaz and the family cook had cleared the used dishes and set the table with dessert, Ammi invited the guests to partake, exclaiming that Shahnaz had made the carrot halwa. Both mother and daughter watched as Maryam nibbled her first bites and were gratified when she nodded at Ammi. "It has just the right amount of sugar. I don't like it dripping with sweetness—this is excellent." Then she turned to Shahnaz. "I'm pleased with this young woman."

—•—

The next morning, a Friday, Shahnaz slept late, until it was too hot to be stuck upstairs, and drew a bath. As she washed, she decided Raja Haider was an adequate excuse to refuse this marriage. He was too pushy, at the edge of obnoxious, too certain his opinions were right. Not that she wasn't capable of standing up to him or arguing against his diatribes. But why choose to marry into a household where she'd have to do that regularly? Her judicious side suggested that Raja Haider, too, had some good points—look at how he was helping other people—and, after all, he wasn't in charge of the house. That person was Sohail, and he was a gentle man...who permitted Raja Haider's anger to pervade discussions. By the time she finally threw the ends of her dupatta over her shoulders, she was determined to ask her parents to find another family. Really, she'd say to them, always being on the alert, ready for a fight, was no way to live. She patted the dupatta, relief coursing through her.

As Shahnaz sipped her tea and plucked bites from a chappati, Abu came into the dining room. She watched as he flipped upward the square at the bottom back of his kameez and sat down catty-corner to her. He hated the choking feeling that came with sitting on the tunic and having the collar constrict his throat. She smiled at his automatic movement; his mind was elsewhere. The Raja Haider discussion perhaps? She sat up straight, preparing.

"I just spoke to Sohail," he said. "They want to go ahead with arrangements, but I've stalled things a bit, after last night. Ammi and I were not pleased with Raja Haider, and I needed to clear up a few things." He shifted onto one hip, laying his arm across the back of the chair.

Shahnaz was pleasantly surprised and began the negotiation slowly. "Raja Haider didn't seem an easy man to live with." This mild statement would show she and Abu thought alike.

Abu nodded, shifting his gaze from Shahnaz to the wall. "I asked Sohail quite specifically about that. He said Raja Haider had an extremely difficult day yesterday. He endured insults that rubbed him raw and was escorted out of an office that was supposedly set up to help. Sohail admitted it wasn't excusable, and said the boy isn't always that way. It seems he's won awards for his building designs, as he's incorporated earthquake-resistant requirements into traditional Islamic architecture. Sohail spoke of a mosque Raja Haider conceived that was the focus of a recent conference." He smoothed his moustache and peered again at his daughter.

Shahnaz clung tightly to her emotions, using all the debate

training her father had given her. "I'm glad to hear that, but the ability to design great buildings doesn't make him easy to live with."

"I know, I know. But we must allow for the impossible day."

Shahnaz smiled at the opening he had given her. "Abu, if he can't find any outlet for his anger except other people, and some of them strangers, how very uncomfortable he must be to live with. Many days present difficulties; few reach the level of 'impossibility.'"

Abu grimaced. "You're not being asked to marry *him*, Shahnaz."

"No, only to share a house with him. Abu, you're struggling with his behavior, just as I am." She paused, allowing that thought to sink in. "Have you also talked with Sohail about my working?"

"Yes. We discussed it very openly this morning."

Shahnaz imagined the scenario: Sohail defending his awkward son and Abu his stubborn daughter. She hoped she hadn't come off the worse in the comparison.

"Sohail is very pleased that you are committed to women's health. He said that Maryam agrees this is a great asset and fits well with Naseer's interests in education and moving Kashmir into the twenty-first century." He shifted to face her, eyes intent. "I had not hoped to find a family so positive about this need of yours. You're twenty-three. We've interviewed a dozen families, and it's time to end this search. I know, I know. You're going to say this health work of yours is partially my fault. But how was I to know that letting you get a master's degree was going to make you a zealot?"

Shahnaz's heart froze. It sounded like she had no choice; the deal was done.

Ammi appeared in the doorway, her face pinched, two mugs of tea in her hands. A few drops spilled from the one she set before her husband and, uncharacteristically for the neat woman she was, she failed to mop them up. She sat down hard on her usual chair. "We think Naseer will be an excellent husband for you. He's gentle, smart, concerned about children, and he will allow you to work."

She took several small sips, staring at the mug.

Shahnaz's mind raced. She couldn't let them close all doors and stick her inside the Khan household. She wanted to scream "NO," but with great self-discipline said, "I'd appreciate it if you waited a few days, please, before you make anything final. You haven't heard yet about Naseer's success in his job and his prospects, and we may learn that the family is more conservative than Naseer's appearance suggested."

Ammi looked at Abu, pleading with her eyes. Shahnaz ground her teeth. He'd promised her a part in this decision. He had. Many times.

—••—

Through the rest of the day and night, Shahnaz alternated between fury and self-pity and said nothing aloud. Instead, she rehashed arguments in her head and listened to herself deliver them passionately. Sometimes she envisioned her father being convinced by them and cancelling the marriage. At other times he gave her a thundering scold and ordered her obedience. She didn't want to be a "bad" daughter, a disobedient child, but she objected to this edict. It wasn't fair to teach her to debate and then dismiss her opinion. After all, she was the one who had to live with this new family. Tears didn't seem to ease her anger. Pounding the pillow at three a.m. just woke up Rabia, who growled at her to be quiet. By the time of the call to dawn prayer, she was exhausted. As she placed her prayer rug facing east and bowed in surrender to God, she gritted her teeth, not wanting to surrender to any being. But when she knelt, touched her forehead to the rug, and silently repeated the words of prayer, she felt her body relax and her mind focus on God and the help coming from Him. Along with rolling up her rug, she decided she had to corner her father and argue.

Dressed in one of her more conservative shalwar kameezes, she stepped in a steady rhythm down the stairs. The house was silent, an unusual event since her parents almost always had tea after prayers and talked about the day to come. After she asked the cook for a cup of tea and drank it at the dining room table, she left the empty cup in the sink and went out to the garden. There was her Ammi, alone, staring off at nothing. "Where's Abu?" she asked.

Her mother, startled, stood up and sat back down. "He's...he's gone to his office."

"At this hour?" She paused, knowing why. "So, I'm not going to have the chance to argue with him about this decision, am I?"

"Oh, Shahnaz." Her mother rose and clasped her hands. "It's a good family. Sohail is admired by his colleagues, only in his mid-fifties, one of the men modernizing Kashmir. Imagine—he has an email address. I don't know what that is, really, but Abu says it's important."

"Yes, Ammi." Shahnaz managed a half-smile at her frazzled mother, trying so hard to be a peacemaker. But if Abu thought he could evade this argument, he was wrong.

Her father absented himself until the dinner hour, by which time Shahnaz was wound up and prepared to spring. Ammi flitted in and out of rooms, unnerved by Shahnaz's anger. Rabia and Tahir were "out" when Abu drove in, opened the door quietly, shed his shoes, and slid into his slippers. Shahnaz posted herself in the living room doorway and waited for him to look up.

"I had hoped Ammi would talk you into obedience," he said.

"No. I wish to speak with you." She indicated the living room with her hand.

He shook his head, sighed, and went to his favorite chair.

Shahnaz debated standing and decided it would be more adult to sit and face him, as an equal.

Before she was settled, he cleared his throat. "There is really no point to debate."

She interrupted. "Yes, there is. You set the rules for these marriage arrangements, and you said I could say 'no' to a match if I felt we wouldn't suit. You've changed the rules."

"You don't dislike Naseer. You said so yourself." He crossed his legs.

"But Naseer comes with a family, and as you and Ammi told me, I must live with the whole family."

"And you like Sohail. You've said nothing against Maryam."

"You know they aren't the problem. It's the conservatism, anger, and rigidity of Raja Haider."

"But you won't be married to him."

"I'll be living with him."

"And in a year or two, when you and Naseer have saved some money, you can move out, as your mother and I did."

"Abu, you and I both know that's very complicated, even insulting, unless we move out of Muzaffarabad—and that's where our jobs are."

Abu tapped his fingers against the chair arm. "Every marriage has its advantages and disadvantages. Ammi and I feel the advantages greatly outweigh the disadvantages—especially since you are determined to work. It's a rare family that likes that idea."

"And just who has encouraged me in this idea of working?" Shahnaz swallowed her anger. Abu liked her ambition, her goals. He got her into this mess, and he could get her out.

He rose. "I know, I know. And I am your father. It's ultimately my decision who you marry. I've raised you to stand up for your beliefs, to deal honestly with others, and to obey. I believe you'll manage fine in the Khan family." He turned toward the door.

Shahnaz hurried to block his way, unable to hold onto her fury at being dismissed. "You can't do this. I'm telling you I don't want this marriage."

He put a hand on her shoulder. "Sorry. It's arranged."

She stepped back, forcing his hand to fall. "Then dis-arrange it."

He shook his head. "No."

She slammed the door hard behind him, so filled with rage she couldn't contain it, and screamed. Her Ammi sailed in from the dining room, took her hand, and led her to the couch, murmuring, "It'll be all right. Things have a way of working out. You like Naseer. Your Abu wants the best for you."

When the blast of anger was spent, Shahnaz cried on Ammi's shoulder. She had been sold.

3

The next afternoon, when the Peace truck came to pick her up for the return trip to Muzaffarabad, she eased into the cushioned seat next to Wali, the driver, listened to his quiet prayer for a safe trip, and told herself she had to shelve her roiling emotions. Besides, it would be a relief to focus on the upcoming week of work. As they made their way toward Wah and the Grand Trunk Road, she focused on the details of Peace's first-ever attack on thalassemia. Each time objections to her upcoming marriage intruded, she forced her mind back to how to convince parents to have their marriageable children tested for the gene before finalizing any marriage arrangements. This was a completely anathema process to people who didn't understand genetics and believed the string of children who wasted away from this blood disease were a punishment from God, not something to be questioned or actively fought against by men. She'd had the test. It wasn't a big deal, but then she might as well have grown up in a different country from those in the mountains.

About two hours out of Islamabad, they reached the crowded main street of Abbottabad where Irum's family lived. Wali pulled into their long gravel driveway and tooted his horn to alert a servant to open the gate. The house was tucked behind a row of stores. As Shahnaz walked the few steps from the vehicle to the house, she consciously focused on the well-tended garden, the extravagant white pillars on either side of the doors, and the elegant stained glass in the doors' upper sections. Invited in by the servant, she stepped into the foyer with its dark paneling, large wooden chairs, and the skirt of the sweeping staircase and wrought-iron railing.

It was only a minute from the time Shahnaz asked for Irum to her friend's appearance on the curve of the stairs. As they met, Irum took Shahnaz's arm and guided her into the dining room, past the tea mugs and plate of biscuits arrayed on the table. Nobody was there, and with a glance to check that the servant was out of earshot, Irum asked, "So, how did it go?"

Shahnaz brushed away the hot tears that rolled out of her eyes. "Oh, Irum, they've promised me to Naseer." She fell into her friend's outstretched arms.

Irum patted her back.

With a courageous sniff, Shahnaz reached for the box of tissues on the dining table and plopped down on the nearest chair. After a good blow, she took a deep breath and watched as Irum pulled a chair over to face her. "I'm sorry for behaving badly. I should be getting used to it, but I'm grieving, really grieving, the life I'm going to lose."

"What happened? I thought you were going to say no."

"I did. Abu overruled me."

Irum drew her brows together. "Oh, Shahnaz. I was afraid this would happen." She took Shahnaz's hands between her own. "Any chance you can focus on Naseer's good points?"

"No. Not yet anyway." Shahnaz pulled away and searched for another tissue.

"This has all come in a rush, hasn't it?"

"However gentle Naseer is, I'll still be restricted. You know, having to be home in good time, take care of nephews and nieces, help his sisters with homework. I can only imagine. Not to mention that Naseer comes with this angry brother who thinks it's un-Islamic for women to speak up. His wife is so cowed, it's scary, and it's not hard to guess why."

"The Shahnaz I know is perfectly able to deal with angry men. Yes, this isn't your dream, but insh'allah, Naseer will be on your side. You'll make it work."

"Maybe. Only, right now, I don't even want to try."

They collected Irum's suitcase and purse and walked to the car. Irum took Shahnaz's hand. "I like the name 'Naseer,' a helper and friend. He sounds appropriately named. Insh'allah, Raja Haider also is named well, being a brave lion, unafraid of death, attacking only what needs to be attacked to meet basic needs. Perhaps you just saw him at a 'hungry' time?"

Shahnaz smiled at her friend's attempt to make things better, but the knot in her stomach continued to twist in pain. She had a lot to say to God over the next days, a lot of grief to give to Him and prayers for acceptance of this prescribed future.

—•—

On Monday morning, Shahnaz and Peace's driver picked up Mehnaz, one of Shahnaz's Lady Health Workers, on their way toward Bagh. The young woman was a favorite of the people she served, as her face lit up in smiles at everyone she met and her sympathetic ear drew mothers to confide in her. When Dr. Irshad had lectured them all about thalassemia at their July meeting of Health Workers, Mehnaz had described a family plagued by this disease. With a catch in her voice, she'd described the daughter who had died and the baby who was likely to die as well. Shahnaz was going along to see if there was anything she could do or say to help the family.

As they bounced along the switchbacks approaching the town of Bagh, Shahnaz asked for details.

Mehnaz squinted her eyes for a few moments. "The house holds three generations, like most around here. Several adult children and just the one grandchild, a little boy of eleven months. The baby's father is the eldest of his generation, and the others are not yet married. I've been seeing the family for about a year. When I first visited, they had a little girl, eighteen months old, whose tummy was badly swollen. Her forehead and cheeks bulged—the thalassemia was pretty well advanced—and she'd stopped growing. I talked to them about treatment for her, but ten thousand rupees a month for a blood transfusion was not possible, not with their house so badly damaged and the child's father out of work."

"This is such a sad reality." Shahnaz already had a picture of what she would see: half a dwelling, droopy occupants, and perhaps a small grave out back.

"They were ecstatic when a healthy-looking boy was born last September. I tried to be optimistic about his chances, but it's clear now he has the disease, too."

Shahnaz sighed. "I hate the reality of this, but it's probably a good thing he's a boy. They might scrape up the money for his treatment."

"I'm afraid it's out of the question, unless more of the men find jobs."

It was quiet in the car for a few moments, until Shahnaz had another thought. "Are the elders arranging for another of their children to marry yet?"

"I haven't had the nerve to ask." Mehnaz looked out the window and then back at Shahnaz. "I should have. It's just that they all love that little boy so much, I didn't want to bring them more sadness."

When the truck pulled into the family's compound, a parade of adults emerged from behind the tarp that served as the fourth wall to the remaining room of the house: an older couple, three adult young men, and a young woman holding a little boy.

After introductions, Mehnaz brought out her scales and weighed little Pervez. She charted his height, and Shahnaz could see that his growth was leveling out instead of continuing on the normal path. His face was round, with large chocolate eyes, but pale, anemic.

Pervez's mother picked him up and rocked him in her arms.

Mehnaz rubbed Pervez's back. "We all want you to grow up big and strong."

He snuggled into his mother's chest.

"It's bad, isn't it?" the young mother said.

"Yes, I'm afraid so. He shows the early signs of thalassemia. But, come, let's get out of the sun and talk about what to do." Mehnaz guided the mother and child behind the tarp.

One of the men pulled a corner of the canvas up by an attached rope, which let in light and a tiny breeze, and the others trooped inside as well. The young father took his son as the mother made tea. Shahnaz and Mehnaz took seats at the small table.

Mehnaz led the discussion. "I told you a lot about the disease last month and the treatment. Have you thought about that?"

All eyes turned to the child's grandfather. "We have. This is very hard. Treatment will be needed every month, all his life. We can pay for two or three months. But there is the house. Everyone must eat. Winter is coming." He gestured to the tarp and then the sky.

Shahnaz nodded. "I'm so sorry you face these impossible decisions. I don't mean to add to your misery, but I do want to be sure you understand the situation fully. It is likely that your son's future babies will also have thalassemia, and there is some chance that your other children also carry it."

The man sniffed. "Mehnaz said last month we should have everyone tested, but that costs money, too. It's hard enough to take in this idea that some mystery thing inside us is causing this disease and not Allah in His displeasure. I don't want to hear results that tell me I will have no living grandchildren."

Shahnaz saw the struggle in his face, the sadness, the sense of failure and loss. "You may still have healthy grandchildren. It is a matter of choosing marriage partners for your children who do not carry the bad genes."

The old man ran his hand through his hair. "This is not simple. We are already talking with my brother to wed his daughter to my next son. I cannot ask him for some test, as though his child was not worthy. It is an insult."

Shahnaz and Mehnaz exchanged looks. "I often find that a change in point of view helps in these situations. Perhaps you could tell your brother how much you love your grandchildren and how painful it is to lose them. I'm sure he'll share your views. He must want healthy grandchildren as much as you do." She paused, watching pleasure and sadness cross his face. "Could you offer to pay for both to be tested?"

The young men all stared at the elder.

"I must think." He slapped his thigh and stepped back outside.

Mehnaz turned to Pervez's father. "How's the job search going?"

"My uncle thinks there may be an opening for a driver at the NGO where he works."

Mehnaz grinned. "That sounds good. Insh'allah, you'll get the job."

And then they all looked at Pervez, sucking his thumb against his father's shoulder. Shahnaz knew the Peace drivers earned less than ten thousand rupees a month. That job wouldn't save the little boy.

Back in the truck, the two women stared out the windows and rocked back and forth with the plunging motion of the vehicle avoiding, and inevitably hitting, potholes. As they passed a dirt track off to the left, Mehnaz grasped Shahnaz's arm. "The family that lives down that road won't let me near the tents. There's something going on. Even from ten meters I could smell a mix of blood and feces. Will you try?"

Shahnaz leaned forward. "Wali, turn around. Take that road, over there."

The truck rattled up the track to a couple of sad tents and, several meters beyond them, a lean-to consisting of a tarp tied to what used to be the quarters for animals, now a crumbling stone wall. A gaunt man, around thirty years old, emerged from one of the tents. He swiped his arm across his nose, sniffed, and waved them away. "I told you not to come back. Now, go away!"

Shahnaz and Mehnaz got out of the truck with Wali close behind. It was the driver who called as he waved back to the man. "As-Salaam-Alaikum. Peace be with you." He folded his hands as in prayer and bowed.

The smell Mehnaz had described permeated the air. Shahnaz repeated the greeting. "Someone here is in trouble, and we'd like to help. Please let us."

A girl's face peered out of the gloom of the lean-to. "Over here. Please." She raised a thin hand, imploring.

Shahnaz ran toward her with Mehnaz close behind.

The man yelled to leave the girl be, then came after the women.

The odor overwhelmed whatever cooking smells or animal aromas might have dominated the area. The young woman was in tears as she used her arms to inch herself out of her flimsy shelter. She couldn't have been more than fourteen or fifteen and was so emaciated, it was surprising she could move at all.

Shahnaz knelt in front of her. "I'm Shahnaz, and I'm a nurse. This is Mehnaz. She's a Lady Health Worker—"

The man, now spitting in anger, loomed over the women, his nose stuffed into his elbow. "She's an adulterer, and Allah is punishing her."

The girl stared at the ground, letting mucus from her nose drip to the dirt. "I'm not, I'm not. I've been a faithful wife."

Shahnaz offered her a tissue and put her hand on the girl's head, feeling its greasiness. "Have you had a baby recently?"

The man muttered something angry, something about the girl being fortunate to be allowed to live in her filth. Then he waved a dismissive hand and stalked away.

"Let's start by cleaning you up, shall we?"

The girl shook her head. "It's no use. Since the baby, my body can't hold on. I pee whenever, and the other as well."

Shahnaz turned to Mehnaz. "Get your full kit from the truck. Go with Wali to the main tent, and see if he'll give you a clean sheet."

Mehnaz nodded and trotted off.

"What's your name?"

"Fatima."

Shahnaz crawled into the lean-to and rolled up the soiled sheets and clothing. "Is that man your husband?"

Fatima sniffed. "He was, until I lost the baby and this happened. Now, I don't know..."

"Ah." Shahnaz walked the bundle toward the hose that brought water down the mountain. She dropped the dirty linen on the ground and filled a waiting bucket with water. If there had been a fire going, she would have heated the water, but no cooking fire was evident. Since the day was warm, she hoped cool water would do. When she returned to the lean-to, Fatima hadn't moved. "Do you have clean clothing?"

Fatima nodded and pointed to a pillowcase. "I've been saving it—to be buried in."

Shahnaz closed her eyes, took a deep breath, and retrieved the pillowcase. "You're not going to die, Fatima. Mehnaz and I will see to that."

"I want to die. No one will come near me, the way I am. *I* don't want to be near me."

Mehnaz bustled up to them, triumphant. "That man is full of righteous indignation, but in the end, I got a clean sheet out of him and a couple of towels as well." She set down her suitcase and the linens. "Obstetric fistula?"

"I suspect so."

"What's that?"

Shahnaz squatted before Fatima. "Sometimes, especially with young women, if labor is long, the baby gets stuck. It presses on your bladder—that's what usually holds your pee—and cuts off the blood supply so the bladder doesn't work anymore. The baby may also cut off blood to your rectum. That's what holds your solid waste." She studied the girl to make sure she understood. "Was your labor long?"

Fatima wiped her hand across her eyes. "It was horrible. It went on for three or four days. I lost count. The dai, the same midwife who tended my mother, left—I think it was the second day—saying there was nothing she could do."

Shahnaz handed a wet towel to Mehnaz. "While Fatima is out here, why don't you clean the lean-to? Then we'll move in there and get her cleaned up."

"Right." Mehnaz started on the tarp that covered the ground.

The smell from Fatima intensified, and she hung her head. "It's diarrhea, again." She sniveled and then sobbed. "I can't stop it."

"A surgeon is the only one who can stop it. For now, know that this didn't happen as God's punishment for adultery. It happened because you're young, the baby was too big for you to deliver properly, and you needed an operation, a Caesarian section, for it to come out alive."

Mehnaz dipped the towel in the bucket, wrung it out, and crawled back in the lean-to. It was looking better already. Not exactly sanitary, but livable.

Fatima pointed to the man's tent. "He can't afford surgery. Not that he'd spend any more rupees on me, anyway." She sniffed and scrubbed her nose with her sleeve.

Shahnaz rocked a little in her squat. "How about your parents?"

"He's convinced them I'm an adulterer." Her whisper was just audible.

Mehnaz stopped and caught Shahnaz's eye.

Shahnaz handed Fatima another tissue. "Can you stand?"

Slowly, Fatima shook her head.

"It happens sometimes. All that leaking burns your legs, causes damage to your nerves, and interferes with your ability to walk." She tilted Fatima's head up and smiled into her teary eyes. "C'mon, let's get you under cover and cleaned up."

Together, Shahnaz and Mehnaz helped Fatima wash, offered her diapers to use and salve to put on her burned thighs, and as Mehnaz talked to her about her care, Shahnaz headed for the main tent.

Wali called from next to the truck. "Want me to come?"

Shahnaz waved for him to join her and waited until he caught up. Funny how important drivers were to the success of these visits. Wali pictured himself their security force, and at times like this, Shahnaz reveled in his commitment.

From outside the tent, Shahnaz called, asking permission to enter. The man certainly heard them coming, but he didn't speak. He probably hoped if he stayed quiet, they'd leave.

Finally, a grudging rumble sounded. "All right, come in."

With a subservient hand to her heart and a bow, Shahnaz again introduced herself and Wali. "Your wife is suffering the consequences of a difficult birth. Her condition will not improve without the assistance of a doctor. Will you allow that?"

"What's the use? She's no good to me now. Can't be a wife, can't even stand. It's that neighbor of ours. I've seen him watch her and want her. She must have snuck off with him when I wasn't here."

"She's very young and scared. In my experience, many girls her age have trouble giving birth. When the baby tried to be born, it injured her so she cannot control her body functions as she used to." Her words had to be carefully chosen, as women did not discuss the workings of the body with unrelated men. "Her problems can be fixed, if you'll allow her to see a doctor."

He stood, walked to the opposite end of the hot tent, and pushed open a flap. "What's the use? I can't pay."

Wali stood like a sentinel, betraying no emotion.

Shahnaz rolled on. "Our local doctor may be able to help. He can't do the surgery she needs, but he has many friends who, insh'allah, may be willing to take care of Fatima. I can ask this afternoon."

"I don't take charity."

"We've all suffered from this earthquake, but some good has come from it. There are doctors willing to help people at much reduced cost—or no cost. It is a part of their zakat, giving to those in need."

"Not to me."

Shahnaz took a deep breath. "Sir, I understand your reluctance. I do. But to have any chance of recovery, Fatima must eat and drink lots of water. Could you see she gets what she needs—and plenty of hot water to wash?"

He made a guttural sound, half laugh. "That's a joke. She can't stay clean. No one comes here anymore with her ghastly smell."

"Insh'allah, Dr. Irshad will come, if you let him."

"I doubt it. This place is too much, even for a doctor."

He continued to stare at the world beyond and said nothing more.

Shahnaz allowed Wali to push open the tent flap behind them, and they walked several feet before Wali cleared his throat. "Will Dr. Irshad come?"

"Insh'allah. Insh'allah."

Shahnaz arrived at her parents' home the next weekend exhausted from the emotional toll of her week. Yes, she'd found a new Lady Health Worker for Rawalakot and the plans were solidifying for the thalassemia campaign. But Dr. Irshad didn't know if any of his colleagues were doing free surgery for fistula patients. And baby Pervez was only getting worse. Her prayers earlier that afternoon had been critical for her to feel any sense of accomplishment, any tranquility. How could God approve of her marriage when so many of his people suffered so?

Ammi met her at the door, effusive in her greeting and hug, yet Shahnaz could see anxiety lurking in the depths of her brown eyes.

"No more tantrums, Ammi. I'm—well, not pleased, more like getting reconciled to the marriage."

As Shahnaz changed from outdoor shoes to indoor slippers, her mother picked up her small suitcase to carry upstairs. They shared a companionable silence. When they reached Shahnaz's bedroom, Ammi retrieved hangers, shook out Shahnaz's shalwar kameezes, and told a series of unimportant stories about neighbors and relatives. More and more alert to the fact her mother was avoiding something, Shahnaz stopped her mother's movements by putting firm hands on her upper arms. "What is it you need to tell me—and don't want to?"

Ammi dropped her hands, allowing a new outfit to slip to the floor. "You know Ramazan is coming soon, and we can't have a proper celebration while we're fasting."

Shahnaz's hands froze in place. "I thought the marriage was going to happen in April or May."

Ammi sat down hard on the bed, as though her legs had given way, slipping out of Shahnaz's hold. "The Khans are so happy with the arrangements; they suggested having the Mangni to celebrate your engagement before Ramazan starts in October and the wedding after Eid, in November. Abu agreed." She lifted the kameez off the floor and fiddled to get its shoulders squarely on the hanger.

Shahnaz turned and walked to the window, staring out at nothing. "Too soon. It's too soon." Panic rose in her throat, and she massaged it with her hand. She had too much to do. Fatima would die if Shahnaz didn't find her a surgeon. That new thalassemia campaign was just getting off the ground, and polio had crept back into the country. Oh, God, is this what you want for me? Her voice came out as a whisper. "So, it's all arranged?"

Ammi had tears in her voice. "Yes. Yes, it is."

"Then I'd like to be alone, Ammi, if you wouldn't mind." She pulled the hanger gently from her mother's hands, took it to the closet, and returned to the window.

Ammi's footsteps sounded as she crossed the carpet and tapped on the tile of the hall. The bedroom door clicked shut.

Shahnaz moved slowly to the bed and clasped its solid wooden footboard. This was it, then, the end of her independence, the time that obedience would take over. Yes, she was more fortunate than many girls: her parents had let her see the man she would marry before the wedding, they'd asked what she wanted in a husband, and it seemed like they'd found it in Naseer. She shouldn't feel devastated, yet that was a fine description of the emptiness in her gut, the sag in her shoulders, and her huge sense of loss.

Her eyes strayed to the litchi tree in the backyard. It reached broadly for the sun, stood its ground in a stately manner, and allowed its twigs and leaves to wave their green flags, as flexible as the wind required. She should act that way, stay rooted in her dreams, act dignified, and accept this future God was providing.

The door behind her swung open, and Rabia burst into their bedroom. "Are you going to have another of your tantrums? Ammi's all worried downstairs, pacing the hall. Tahir's made himself scarce. I think Abu's having dinner out."

When Shahnaz turned, she saw her determined sister, fists on hips, staring her down.

Her emotions drained, Shahnaz shook her head. "No."

"Good." Rabia put her hand out to grab the doorknob, pulling the door to her side. "I'll leave you alone. I sure hope you come to terms with this marriage. It's my big chance, which you'd know if you thought about someone besides yourself. The guests will be assessing me as a marriage prospect. With you out of the way, it'll be my turn." With a satisfied smile, she shut the door.

Shahnaz didn't know whether to laugh or cry.

———••——

At the end of September, Shahnaz was in the hostel ironing her turquoise dupatta. She'd made it through last weekend's sumptuous Mangni, and it had been fun to be treated as special, to be the 'fiancée,' the center of so many women's attention. Ammi and Abu had spared no expense with her clothes, the flower displays in the yard, and the food at the barbecue. They'd bowed to the conservative leanings of the Khans and kept the women in the back garden, the men in the front. But they'd allowed music and pretended not to hear when her friends played their favorite popular tunes. She had about six weeks now, six weeks to fill with work, the camaraderie of the women in the hostel, and yes, wedding plans. The iron spit steam, and she wiped the sweat from her brow. The heat was staying with them this fall.

Her mobile rang.

"Shahnaz? This is Naseer. My parents have said we may talk on the phone. Is that all right with you?"

He had a gentle, welcoming voice. Shahnaz felt a blush creep up her cheeks. He did seem a nice man. She shouldn't blame him for the marriage decision. "Yes, yes, I'm so pleased." She sat down on the edge of her bed, crossing one leg over the other.

"I want to thank you for that party and the chance to get to know your father better and your brother a little. The front garden was filled with relatives, and as I told your father, the food was superb and there was so much of it."

Shahnaz smiled and played with the fringe of her dupatta. "That's my Ammi. Worried there won't be enough, so she adds twenty to the estimated number of guests."

"My mother, too. Do you suppose it's a Kashmiri trait?"

"Maybe. I liked your mother so much. As each person came through the back gate, she told me some important detail about them, so I always had something to talk about. So kind, so very kind."

"That's my Ammi."

A few moments of silence intruded, as Shahnaz searched for a comfortable topic. She couldn't very well bring up the topic uppermost in her mind—delaying this wedding. Maybe his work? That should be safe. "Tell me more about your job. Do you like it?"

"Ah, yes. We share an interest in educating people, don't we?" She heard pleasure in his round tones. "I'm glad of that, and Abu related your stories of work to me. We have many things in common." He paused. "I do like my job, most of the time. I'm okay with writing training materials, but mostly I like doing the training, spending time getting to know the teachers, getting them to speak

English and help each other. Your health work involves the same kinds of interactions, doesn't it?"

Shahnaz drew up her legs as she agreed with him about the joys and challenges of persuading people to try out new ideas and new practices. "I'm afraid my job also has another side: consoling women who have lost a child, and dealing with babies who are dying because of a lack of money to pay for treatment."

"You must have great courage to deal with such things."

How nice of him to say that! Such color in his voice, such sincerity, such understanding. And when they had exhausted the job exchange, she gathered up that courage he'd talked about and asked about his brother. If she was going to spend her life with this man, better start it out with honesty, not avoiding difficult subjects. "I found Raja Haider a little intimidating. Is he always so—"

"Arrogant? Preachy? Know-it-all?"

Shahnaz laughed. "Well, yes. I was searching for a more polite adjective, but those work."

"Oh, he blusters a lot and gives more than his share of lectures, most of which we all ignore, but some start major arguments. My sister Nooran—the one training to be a doctor—tells him he's hopelessly behind the times, and my youngest brother Qadir orders him to 'get real.' He harrumphs and calls them all un-Islamic, but I know he loves them. It's just that he went to a madrassa, unlike the rest of us, and he's joined this group called Lashkar-i-Taiba—they helped a lot after the earthquake with food, water, blankets, tents, that kind of thing. They're pretty conservative, as far as I can tell. Fits with his outdated ideas of our religion. Did he go off on one of his lectures when you met him?"

"A little. He was upset about not having his building plans approved and about my arguing with an imam."

Naseer chuckled. "Sounds like you caught the lion on the hunt for prey."

Shahnaz treasured the laughter in his voice. He didn't seem to think of his brother as a threat, just an annoyance. She grabbed onto this new image of Raja Haider. Plumping her bed pillows against the wall, she relaxed into them and stretched out. So far, Naseer was okay, and maybe better than okay. "I had the chance to talk a little with Noshaba at the Mangni. She was awfully quiet. What's she usually like?"

Again, Naseer chuckled. "She's quiet with all of us, and my younger brothers refer to her as the 'mouse' who disappears from a room when others enter and utters short squeaks if someone addresses her. I think she's fine, really. Did she tell you she's pregnant? I know she's not been feeling well, and between that and her shyness, I can see why she wasn't talkative. It'll be a pleasure to have someone who enlivens our conversations—as I'm sure you will."

"I hope so." Shahnaz smiled with pleasure. Two problems cut down to less bothersome sizes.

4

For the first time ever, Shahnaz found the holy month of
Ramazan to be short. Oh, the days sometimes seemed interminable, her tongue thick with paste and her stomach
pinched with hunger. But the wedding date, November
17, loomed so large, like a hovering albatross, she could not escape
its shadow. At each of the five daily prayer times, and often in the
car or as she went to sleep, she prayed for this marriage to turn
out well, for the Khans to let her do her work. At Peace, she assigned herself a string of tasks: calling every surgeon who operated
in Kashmir and every NGO doing health work, organizing a huge
two-day event to publicize thalassemia, getting all patient records
corrected and updated, Finally, Irum protested, telling her she
was wearing herself out and wouldn't even be able to stay awake
through her wedding celebration. Perhaps she was overdoing it,
but Shahnaz was desperate to seize every minute and fill it with
the energy that might soon be syphoned elsewhere.

Every weekend she dutifully traveled to Islamabad. Ammi
filled the days with wedding details: how large should the tents
be to comfortably seat all the guests and cover enough of the lawn
before the Faisal Mosque so that the affair didn't look shabby? Did

Shahnaz like the carpets she'd ordered to make the path from the tent's entry to the raised takht where she and Naseer would sit, or should she only allow ones with red predominating? Should she include all meat dishes on the buffet or one with only vegetables? Were the extra-large invitations, scripted in black and decorated with pink flowers and gold scrolls, over the top? Shahnaz tried hard to care. Ammi was working so hard, and her appraising glances told Shahnaz she was well aware of her daughter's ambivalence. It was not going to be discussed.

It would be untrue to say Shahnaz disliked all the attention, all the shopping. When Ammi took her to their favorite fabric stores to select materials for the twenty-five shalwar kameezes their tailor would craft for her, she lost her regrets in the joy of feeling so much softness, choosing among the vivid colors, and debating neckline and sleeve styles with the staff. When relatives came to discuss the additional outfits that they would be giving to her—twenty-six more—she was overwhelmed at the treasure coming her way. And that first Saturday in November when Ammi took her and Rabia on a buying spree for the couple's bedroom furniture, television and DVD player, linens, and their gifts for members of the groom's family, she broke down in tears and told Ammi it was just too much; she didn't deserve all this bounty.

Nearly every night, during the week and on the weekend, she ended the day with a phone conversation with Naseer and did her best to sound cheery. It wasn't difficult, as Naseer had a storehouse of jokes and puns, told stories of his day that made her laugh, and invited her to share her daily adventures. She did like the man, she truly did. She just couldn't get over the feeling that marriage was bound to interfere with the health work that desperately needed to be done.

On the Saturday afternoon a week before the wedding, Shahnaz found herself nodding off in the lasting heat of the afternoon and the drone of the television. She had an hour before Ammi was taking her to her aunt's house to try on some of the new outfits. Having slept little in the past weeks, her body felt like an emptied spigot. Awaking to a violent shaking, she squinted into the delighted face of her sister.

"I'm up, I'm up, stop it." Shahnaz rubbed her eyes.

Rabia pranced about the room like a winning thoroughbred. "Guess what?"

Shahnaz used both hands to push herself into a full sitting position and flattened the skirt of her kameez. "I haven't a clue what you've been up to. Eaten a canary, perhaps?"

Rabia bounced down onto the couch. "Of course I haven't. What a stupid guess."

"Well, you look like a cat, bounding about." Seeing her sister's perplexed look, she added, "It's one of those English expressions, you know, looking like the cat that swallowed the canary?"

Rabia shrugged her shoulders. "Who cares? I've been to see Auntie, and she's going to find me a husband on your wedding weekend."

"Rabia, you're not supposed to *ask* anyone to do that. It's Ammi's role. I can't believe how pushy you are. What must Auntie think of you?"

"Oh, take your hand away from your face. Just because you don't have the courage to ask doesn't mean I have to forego what I want. This is my *life* I'm talking about!" Rabia leapt to her feet and began pacing the room.

Shahnaz sat on her hand and looked into her sister's serious face. That Rabia: she wanted what she wanted *now* and with all her being. It had been that way with toys as a child, with make-up as a teenager, and now with finding a husband. "I know, I know. Here I am, the center of Ammi's attention, and you've been forgotten." And then another train of thought assailed her. "How did you avoid her inevitable offer of her son?"

Rabia turned and grinned, her oval face round with glee. "I told her I was totally unsuitable as a wife for Hamid, that he's sweet and kind and deserves a quiet girl who would mind him and adore him, whereas I'm strong and brash and would overwhelm him. I was careful not to say that his big stomach and chewing with his mouth open are a turn-off. You'd be surprised at how tactful I was." She raised her eyebrows as if daring Shahnaz to contradict her.

Shahnaz sat mute.

"I even told her I'd likely turn into a shrew like in that Shakespeare play, only I can't be tamed—at least not by a wimp like Hamid. And please note, sister dear, that I just made a literary allusion. Contrary to your opinion, I did learn things in school."

Shahnaz ignored the jab and even squelched her anxiety that Rabia had upset their mother's favorite sister. "So, what happened then?"

Rabia collapsed again on the couch. "Well, she agreed that we were unsuitable and said some unkind things about me, but I ignored all that. Then I told her what I want in a husband: well off, good prospects, maybe going abroad, big house so we have space of our own, maybe a little driven to succeed, that sort of thing." She busied her hands with one of the couch pillows, untangling the gold fringe.

"You're not looking at me, Rabia. What are you not saying?"

"Oh, you know how Auntie is. She had to put down the qualities I value as un-Islamic and immodest, rant against Ammi's raising independent daughters, and exclaim that no family would want me." She picked up the fringed pillow and plumped it against the corner of the sofa. When she turned back to Shahnaz, it was with a defiant giggle. "But I got my way. I agreed to her listing of my bad traits, assured her she needed to be certain Hamid didn't grow attached to me, and told her the best way to do that was to find me a different husband—and she agreed!"

Shahnaz shook her head in disbelief, but as she opened her mouth to point out the errors in lying, greed, and pride, she was assailed by the thought that she wasn't being exactly truthful to people about her upcoming marriage. Only last night, she'd told a group of school friends she was "thrilled" by it. Who was she to criticize? Also, a small voice from deep in her heart chided her with the truth that she wished she knew how to get her way as effectively as Rabia did.

That night, on the phone with Naseer, she reported that relatives would be looking for a suitable match for Rabia at their wedding. In amongst their laughter over how many women loved this custom, Naseer said he would alert his mother, too, as she always had ideas of what boy would match well with each girl.

—•—

The wedding festivities began early in the week with the arrival of Abu's younger brother, his wife, and their five children, who drove down from Rawalakot, and his older brother, his wife, and their three children, who flew in from the States. All would be crowding into Shahnaz's home. Six bedrooms no longer felt like a lot, and the TV room was transformed into a dining area. With the furniture pushed against the walls and a large carpet on which serving dishes could proliferate, it invited raucous conversation and shared laughter.

Shahnaz was especially drawn to her cousin Talaat from Detroit, the twenty-four-year-old daughter of Abu's older brother. It had been ten years since the two had last been together, and had things ever changed! Talaat walked around the house in jeans and a T-shirt, showing off her body as Shahnaz did not dare to do. On Thursday, when they were alone in Shahnaz's bedroom, she couldn't resist an inquiry. "Do you always dress like that?"

Talaat had a grin that spread across her face. "Of course not. Sometimes I wear much more revealing tops that show my cleavage and track my curves." She pulled her T-shirt away from her stomach, suggesting it had far too much material. "But..." She sighed. "...I promised my Abu I would be more circumspect here."

Shahnaz plunked down on the bed, her jaw dropping in awe. "And he permits that?"

"Shahnaz, he exhausted himself over a period of *years* objecting, but since I moved away from home, he's had to back off." She checked herself in the full-length mirror and shifted a few of her long dark hairs back into place.

Shahnaz felt her jaw drop further. "You moved away from home?"

"Yes, though I promised not to tell any of my aunts and uncles." She shook her head, still checking her image in the mirror, then scraping at a small mark above one knee. "I am the bane of my father's existence, or so he says, for this independent streak I have." Dimples appeared on her cheeks as she turned toward her cousin.

"But where do you live?" Shahnaz was confused. "Still in Detroit, near home?"

"Oh, yes. I share a house with three other girls, all Muslim, all working. We're only a couple of miles from my parents." Talaat sat down on the chair next to the bed and relaxed against its pillows.

"You're working? Do lots of Muslim girls work in the States? I thought when a family was rich like Khadim Uncle that women didn't work. And why didn't anyone tell me?" This last part sounded to her like a wail, and she applied a strong brake to her emotions. After all, it was a different world over there.

Talaat leaned forward to pat Shahnaz's leg. "Lots of women work in the States, even Muslim women. I studied fashion in college and got a job as an assistant buyer for a department store. Abu did object, but he's come 'round." She pulled a foot underneath her. "I get to search for clothes appropriate for Muslim women—and elegant to boot. It's great fun. And since he spent hours telling me how worried he was about what I was getting into, with twenty-four seven on my own, I keep pointing out to him that the job keeps me off the streets."

"Wow. I'm fighting to work, too. It takes a lot of courage to keep arguing. Insh'allah, I'll win, too."

Talaat cocked her head. "You should emigrate, kiddo. You've got all the chutzpah needed to succeed in the States."

Shahnaz wasn't sure this was a compliment. "Is chutzpah good?"

"It's excellent."

Shahnaz laughed.

"So..." Talaat lengthened the syllable by several beats. "How are you doing with this marriage? You don't seem all that pleased, from what I can tell, more like resigned."

Shahnaz picked at a loose thread on the hem of her kameez. "I hoped it didn't show." She looked into Talaat's sympathetic eyes. "I like Naseer. It's not that. It's just too soon. I want more time to see what I'm capable of, to do this health work, to make a difference."

"Yeah, I get it. And the push to get pregnant on the honeymoon is going to mess up that desire big time."

Shahnaz nodded.

Interrupted by a knock on the door and the appearance of her mother, Shahnaz urged Talaat to come with her and Rabia to Annie's salon. It was time for her full body wax, and Rabia was likely to be teasing, if not insulting. Talaat rose to the occasion, keeping the sisters and salon staff in stitches at her stories of American men and how Talaat made clear her boundaries—no wandering hands, no kissing until she felt they knew each other well enough, and no alcohol or smoking in her presence. Shahnaz envied Talaat's cool assurance and, as she steeled herself to the pain of her treatment, felt a growing power in her cleansed body and inner spirit—that chutzpah as Talaat labeled it. She would walk into this marriage proudly and give her full self to making it work—for her and the Khans.

Talaat was also integral to the lengthy henna painting of hands and feet on Friday morning. She advised Shahnaz on flattering patterns, chatted with the woman doing the painting as a professional fashion colleague, and made sure the henna was deeply colored so the bride's mother-in-law would love her and she her mother-in-law. When Rabia's volume rose to a strident level, Talaat adeptly steered her into more subdued conversation. Shahnaz admitted to some relief when her cousin appeared for the appointment in a shalwar kameez, though she also shivered at the audacity of the design. The shimmery material traced the smooth curves of Talaat's body from shoulders to hips, and the short sleeves showed off well-defined muscles that were different from the usual rounded Pakistani arms. Having ascertained that Talaat had designed the suit herself, Shahnaz complimented her taste and thought she'd like to try it on herself. Her arms might not be as well toned, but her bust would fill it out to admiration.

The Friday evening celebration of the Mehndi began with the gathering of women relatives and friends in Shahnaz's bedroom. One person after another admired the henna paintings against her deep green raw silk shalwar kameez, her sparkling emerald earrings, and her delicate sandals, dyed to match the silk. In a moment of inspiration, Shahnaz introduced Talaat to her work colleague Irum, hoping to give Irum someone to talk to who might provide a sense of pride about working and not being married. Shahnaz surreptitiously watched the pair and heard snatches of conversation full of colors and styles and the textures of guests' clothes.

At about 9:00 p.m., Shahnaz and her twenty-something cousins descended to the side door where Ammi was waiting to lead them through the flower-covered archway to the tent in the back garden. Shahnaz's curled and shining hair spread across her shoulders and down her back, making her feel elegant and beautiful. The evening was just cool enough to appreciate the dupatta, which she wore draped across her chest with the ends thrown over each shoulder. Her younger cousins threw rose petals on everyone, her aunties placed heavy garlands of red roses and bright marigolds over her head, and Rabia offered her sweets from a large round tray. She chose a toasty brown ball of gulab jamun and then followed her cousins to the dais. Its brightly patterned carpets and overstuffed red chair gave the impression of a sultan's castle. The flapping canopy acted like the old-time servants fanning their lady. Rabia put the sweets on the small table before the chair, and Ammi brought another tray of nuts and dried fruit.

Clusters of women stopped to congratulate her and admire the henna. Her cheeks glowed from the appreciation—and from the fact that Ammi had placed a heater just to the right of the dais. In a free moment (as an aunt was repeating the oft-told story of her parents' wedding), she prayed that Naseer was receiving his share of compliments and enjoying his special position in her family's front garden. He had told her he'd be wearing white, with a red sash flowing around his turban and down his left shoulder. A ruby pin would sparkle in its folds. She imagined him in a form-fitting jacket buttoned to his chin, his body relaxed against the chair like a contented maharaja. A small shiver of excitement caused her aunt to go running to a catering staff member to ask that he move the heater closer to Shahnaz. She smiled her thanks, chiding herself that the penance for lying to her aunt would be the overheating of her body.

After the sumptuous meal brought to Shahnaz by her cousins, which she could only push around the plate, the music changed to support several dances and skits organized by the female cousins. She gaped at the free-flowing sinuousness of Talaat and laughed at the recall of impolitic moments of her youth. Thankfully, much of the dialogue was whispered in her direction, and Ammi appeared not to hear.

Shahnaz chatted with each of Naseer's sisters after the skits and laughed at the tales they told of their brother. Nooran let the two younger girls, eighteen-year-old Sadia and thirteen-year-old Rizwana, do most of the telling and winked at Shahnaz as they turned to leave. But where was Noshaba? When Shahnaz asked, the girls looked around, uncertain.

"Perhaps she's in the house," Rizwana said. "She often finds a hole to hide in." Receiving a poke from Sadia, she giggled and defended her idea. "Well, it's true. She disappears when there're a lot of people around."

In the lull of satisfied appetites, Shahnaz went to find Noshaba, hoping to draw her out and make a friend. She tracked her down inside the house, as Rizwana had guessed, in a bedroom by herself, holding a plate of rice and naan and sipping a Pepsi. "Noshaba, may I join you?" Shahnaz inquired quietly. Happy to see the face of her future sister-in-law, Shahnaz examined it with care. Noshaba had dainty brown eyes with long lashes, high cheekbones that served to draw one's eyes to this widest part of her oval face, and a chin that was too retiring to be called decisive. An attractive face, but not a happy one.

Noshaba started, spilling several drops of soda. Looking up with frightened eyes, she nodded in answer to Shahnaz's question.

"I thought we might get to know each other a little," Shahnaz continued as she pulled up a chair. With a smile, she touched Noshaba's knee. The leg froze in place, and when Shahnaz checked Noshaba's face, she found it closed as well. "What is it? You don't like to be touched?"

"I don't feel good." Noshaba busied herself with sopping up Pepsi with her napkin.

"I'm so sorry. Can I help? We have a lot of medications around the house. Would you like something?"

A shake of the head. "I—I'm pregnant, and nothing stays down very long." She hung her head over her plate, as though she was guilty of some sin.

Shahnaz narrowed her eyes. She understood the unpleasantness of morning sickness, but that didn't explain the cringing upon being touched. Best to tamp down her own energy to match this young woman's. "This is your second child, isn't it?"

Noshaba nodded her head, pulled a small bit of naan off the round, and pushed bits of rice around the plate.

Shahnaz watched the small hand scrape the plate. "I'm afraid I don't know if you have a boy or a girl."

The hand stopped. A few whispered words let her know it was a girl.

"Ah, girls are nice, like us. Right?"

Noshaba's thin face, surrounded by black cloth, turned up to Shahnaz with a look of anguish: her mouth open, brows drawn together, and a dull flush spreading across her cheeks.

"Noshaba, what is it? What's wrong?" Shahnaz searched for the other girl's hand, found her fingers, and squeezed. "We're going to be sisters, and I'm a trained nurse. You can tell me."

"My husband wants a boy, and I'm so afraid I'll have another girl and disappoint him again."

"Oh, dear." Shahnaz remembered her resentment that Tahir was favored in her family. She squeezed Noshaba's hand again and leaned back. Better change the subject. "Where does your family live? I don't know much about your background."

"I'm from the same village as Abu. My family has known his for generations, which is why they thought of me when they were looking for a wife for Raja Haider."

"And when were you married?"

"In May of 2003. Everyone in the village was invited, and I was so happy." Her whole body relaxed into the memory. "My father was proud of me. As his third daughter, he'd worried that—at eighteen—I'd be too old for anyone in the village. My uncles had no sons ready for marriage, so my parents put out feelers and found the Khans. Allah must have been watching over me for such good fortune."

Shahnaz did a quick subtraction in her head and noted that Noshaba was younger than she, Rabia's age—just twenty-one—with a two-year-old child, a second one on the way, and worries about disappointing her husband. She leaned forward to hug Noshaba. "I think you're very brave to leave your village and your family, to have a child, and to keep going even when you feel ill."

Noshaba looked at her with wonder in her eyes. "You do? I think my body's at war with me, and the harder I fight, the worse it gets."

Shahnaz smiled. "Perhaps you might stop the battle for a time—just give in to it. I know when I'm not feeling well, taking off my outer garments and resting on the bed makes things a lot better. Shall I help you out of your abaya and dupatta?"

Tears sparkled in Noshaba's eyes. She nodded, and Shahnaz pulled the coat off the waif's shoulders and then folded the black headscarf. She thought the chocolate brown of Noshaba's shalwar kameez was a color that made her disappear into the night's dimness, but she said nothing about it, just pulled a light bed covering up to her shoulders.

—•—

On Saturday morning, after only three or four hours of sleep,

Shahnaz donned one of her new silk shalwar kameezes for the signing of the marriage contract. Abu had explained to her that at 11:00 a.m. she, along with him, Ammi, and the relatives staying in their house, would be expected in the living room where his older brother would read the contract aloud, she would sign, and her uncles would witness her signature. The men would then take the contract across the hall to the TV room, where the ritual would be repeated with Naseer, his relatives, and the imam who had prepared the contract. When everyone had signed, her relatives would return to tell her that the agreement was accepted by all.

She couldn't face breakfast with all the butterflies flitting about her stomach, but agreed to Ammi watching her apply make-up and brushing her hair until its sheen matched the silk's. Usually Shahnaz liked the effect of eye make-up, as it made her smallish eyes more prominent, but today she thought it exaggerated the circles of exhaustion under them. Ammi turned her daughter's head back and forth, allowing the light to cast shadows from cheekbones and nose, and announced that more concealer had to be applied; the bride could not look haggard.

Shahnaz obediently covered the dark patches, and hoped her mother understood that this acquiescence meant she was going to be as agreeable as she could today.

The signing took less than half an hour, much less time than she had expected. Really, it was an anticlimax. The men congratulated Abu and each other for the successful acceptance of the contract. The women clustered around Shahnaz, most of them quiet while they escorted her back upstairs. Just as well. Shahnaz had stared at the bold letters of her husband's name and seen imaginary doors slamming shut.

That evening, twenty or thirty cars filled the street outside her parents' house, lining up to escort the bride's vehicle to the Faisal Mosque for the Nikah to celebrate their wedding contract. Streams of rose petals were thrown on guests as they entered the center of the three circus-sized tents set up for the celebration, and catering staff offered them sweets. She bowed her head to receive heavy garlands, praying they would not stain her red kameez and its flowered embroidery in crimson and black. It had cost a small fortune, and she wanted it to look perfect—at least for all the pictures.

With her mother, Rabia, and a number of female guests, she admired the huge sweeps of flowers on the large takht at the opposite end of the tent. New white paint glistened on the sides of the platform, and thick carpets covered its top. A thousand chairs, covered in white sheeting, sat at attention on either side of a central aisle, the red-patterned carpets her mother had decided on covered the grass, and the air was scented by the curry cooking in the two side tents. A couple hundred men already occupied seats on the left, and about the same number of women were in chairs on the right and deep in conversation. Lots of people milled about, finding friends and relatives and gossiping. Catering staff strode from the center tent to those on each side, toting juice and sodas.

As the group walked toward the women's tent, Rabia stopped and prodded Shahnaz. "See that man? He's perfect. Who is he?"

Shahnaz leaned in to whisper, "You mean the one with the big nose and turned-up moustache?"

"Yes, of course." Rabia hissed each "s." "Look at his kameez— that embroidery was costly."

"Hmm. But he isn't smiling, and he has deep lines above his nose. Better watch out for the angry ones, Rabia."

"I'll just point him out to Auntie, so she can check."

Rabia sounded like she was shopping, absorbed in making the best choice among many options. She darted off on her mission, replaced in a moment by their cousin Talaat, who took Shahnaz's elbow and maneuvered her toward the women's tent, chatting all the time of the people she'd seen.

Heavy canvas formed a door from the central tent to the women's food tent. A caterer held it open for them. Shahnaz drank in the elegance of the room: tables with starched damask coverings and sprays of red roses and white tuberoses, and fairy lights draped from the center tent pole to the sides. The tables around the perimeter would soon be laden with the barbecued meats, curries, and rice her mother had chosen for the buffet. The three tables in the center were already covered with cakes, puddings, and sweets. Standing heaters and dozens of women had warmed the area, and the mixed spices of the curry and barbecue hung in the air.

The moment she entered the women's tent, a crowd surrounded Shahnaz. One cousin touched her arm. "Are you nervous?" Before she could respond, an auntie caressed her cheek. "Beautiful, my dear; your make-up is perfect." A friend pulled her aside. "What do you think? Are you prepared for tonight?" Shahnaz answered "Yes," "Thank you," and "I guess," and told herself it was just as well there was no time for elaborate responses. She was on public display, like a princess, and scared.

Once in her alcove, Talaat fussed with the wedding dupatta to drape it more gracefully over Shahnaz's shoulders. "That looks better. You're beautiful, you know. That pale face and your blushes are very maiden-like, most appropriate."

Shahnaz smiled, relaxing a trifle, and chided herself. The marriage contract was signed; she might as well get used to it and enjoy the celebration. Several new guests burst into the space, and she chatted avidly. In just a few moments, over the hubbub, she heard Rabia's strident voice. "Shahnaz? Naseer's almost here. The horses are pulling up to the tent. C'mon; we need to go!"

Escorted by her sister and cousins, she walked solemnly up the central aisle to the takht where Naseer was waiting and watching. Her stomach lurched and she felt an overwhelming wish to run away. Reminding herself that she'd promised her American cousin she'd approach her marriage with courage, she took a deep breath and focused on her husband. Her initial impression of him was of self-confidence and gentleness. He looked to be taller than she but not enough to loom over her, a man who cared about his appearance but allowed the natural waves of his hair to have their way, and appropriately religious with a neatly trimmed beard of perhaps a quarter-inch in length and that full moustache. Her whole body relaxed as she looked into his soft appraising eyes and saw his broad grin of approval. Chills ran up her torso and a hot blush crept up her cheeks. When she was about ten feet from the dais, he put his hand over his heart and bowed. Her mouth dropped at this honoring of her, and warmth spread down to her fingertips. She smiled with another blush of pleasure and bowed in return.

When the endless pictures had been taken—several with the families of every relative—Shahnaz realized she had not seen Noshaba. "Naseer, where's Noshaba? Isn't she here? Is anything wrong?" Her hand snuck up to her cheek.

He patted the hand still in her lap. "I heard there was an argument over her coming. Raja Haider didn't want her to be with all these men. But Jamil—you remember, he's the next brother after me—told me she was here. Perhaps Rabia could find her?"

"I'll ask. She might even like the assignment."

For nearly half an hour, Shahnaz continued to greet guests, staying up on her platform. Though she often found her eyes straying into corners for Noshaba, she didn't see anyone fully covered. Few women wore black, and it was the color more than anything else that caught her eye as the figure of her sister-in-law sidled up to the back of the takht.

Detaching herself from well-wishers, Shahnaz went to the rear of the platform and knelt down to touch the shoulder of her short sister-in-law. The young woman looked up with a start, her eyes glancing off Shahnaz's face and checking out the group on the takht. One of these eyes was partially shut, her cheek on that side puffing out against its covering, and she winced as she spoke.

"Oh, Noshaba, what happened?" Shahnaz squatted down and touched the purple cheek.

The black-clad pixie stared at the carpeted platform. "I wanted to come to your wedding. You were kind to me last night. I wanted to show you I appreciated it."

"Yes, yes. And I thank you for coming." Shahnaz lightly ran her finger down the side of Noshaba's face. Was this how that angry man responded to having his decisions questioned? What a brute he was.

Her sister-in-law looked into Shahnaz's eyes for a moment as if to check whether to stop or continue, and then resumed talking to her hands. "My husband forbid it. I argued—for the first time in my marriage—and he hit me. I promised I wouldn't talk to strange men. Finally, he said I could come if I stayed in the women's tent. Only Rabia said you asked for me. So I've come to you." Tears congealed her eyelashes, but she managed a small triumphant smile. "I haven't ever disobeyed him before."

Shahnaz froze; no words came to her lips. This was her nightmare, come alive. Did Sohail and Maryam permit this? Was the beating of women a part of their vision of Islam? Did her new husband believe in it also?

Noshaba looked again at the carpet. "I'm too ashamed to show people my face, so I've been hiding." Slowly, she raised her eyes to meet Shahnaz's. "But I have courage, no?"

The bride leaned over to hug her, conscious of not pressing her cheek into the swollen flesh that was Noshaba's face. Her heart raced. "Yes, you do."

◆•◆

As she rode up the elevator with Naseer to their room in the

Marriott Hotel, Shahnaz shivered with fear. She told herself Naseer was honoring her with this stay in a hotel instead of a family home. She should feel special. Instead, she was stuck in the thought that he, too, believed in beatings. Who was this man beside her? Would she grow to love him or fear him? She threw God a prayer that she might enjoy the sex and be given the courage for this married life. When the door closed behind the porter, she turned nervously to see Naseer offering her an expected envelope with a generous ma-har, more money than the usual bride's tribute. Her fingers curled against her face.

"Our parents chose well in promising you to me and me to you," he said. "Now it's up to us to make our marriage work. I will do all in my power. That I promise."

Shahnaz gathered his hands in hers and squeezed. "I will, too. I'll tell you what's in my heart and do my best to belong in your family."

He reached for her dupatta and pulled it gently, so the silk tickled her neck as it ran toward the carpet. As his hands returned to release the buttons of her tunic, she grasped them again. "Wait, please. I must ask you something, because I'm scared and don't want to be."

Naseer raised his eyebrows. "What is it? Is it the sex? I'll be as gentle as I can."

Shahnaz sank onto the bed and drew him down beside her. "No, it's not that. I'm afraid...It's Noshaba...Did you see her today?"

He shook his head.

"She was beaten, her face swollen, one eye shut...I'm not shy, as she is. I have opinions, and I say them...My Abu says he's taught me too well." She smiled, pulled up her proverbial socks, and brought Naseer's hand to her cheek. "I need to know where you stand on beating your wife."

"I didn't know, Shahnaz." He rose and paced the room, drawing his hands down his face. Then he stopped, facing her. "Raja Haider and I may be brothers, but we don't agree on many things. Beating women is one of them." He reached out, taking hold of her shoulders. "Insh'allah, I will never harm you."

Her gnawing fear dulled as he spoke, and she slipped into the bathroom to get ready for bed. When she returned, he was in bed, his naked chest uncovered. He flipped the sheet back on her side of the bed, and she lay down facing him, determined not to allow herself to shake. When he ran his hand down her arm, she got goose bumps and they laughed. Then he bent down to kiss her, and with patience and gentleness roused every fiber of her being and entered her. She gasped and slowly opened her body to him.

Over their buffet breakfast the next morning, Shahnaz kept still so her painful parts would not complain, and instead she focused on her budding happiness in her husband. "I've never slept in such a sumptuous room. I hated wrinkling the comforter and..." she blushed, "...messing up the sheets. Th—thank you...It must have been hard not to stay at your cousin's."

The ends of Naseer's eyes crinkled with his smile. "A little argument. Nothing physical. I was here a few months ago to hear the Minister of Education give a speech and knew I wanted this for us." He scooped up more of the aloo chole with his chappati, pushing the bite into his mouth with his thumb and groaning with pleasure at the spicy potato and chickpea stew. "It's that feeling of being taken care of, that's what I like here and what I want in our marriage."

Shahnaz felt a rush of warmth in her groin and blushed yet again.

The cousin's house was a hotbed of activity when they arrived. Maryam was a bustle of energy, instructing a team of minions in the preparations for the Walima. No catered food for this event. She was determined to make the food with her own hands—or at least to serve as Master Chef. She fussed over Shahnaz, patting her golden dupatta into place, ranted at a cook that he had not ordered enough sweets, swept into the tent in the back garden and made the men move the buffet tables, and bullied Noshaba to speed up the chopping of the chilies. With only an upturning of her lips, Noshaba returned to her task.

To Shahnaz's surprise, the event had men and women together, sharing a tent in the garden. Separate buffet tables meant that conservative women could eat in the house and remove their hijabs, but otherwise Shahnaz found herself chatting with couples and families, meeting male cousins and friends of the Khans. Maryam was everywhere, taking Shahnaz by her elbow from one group to another and then disappearing to greet a new guest or check on dinner preparations.

In a free moment after the meal, Shahnaz sought out Irum and was pleased to see her, draped in white silk with deep blue embroidery that matched her eyes. She was chatting with their boss Amir. It was hard for single women to mingle, as she knew well. Shahnaz took Irum's hands in her own. "I'm very glad you came. It makes this weekend extra special for me." To Amir, she said, "And I'm so proud my boss is here. Thank you for celebrating with us."

With a nod of his dark head and a short glance at Irum, he answered, "It's my pleasure, Shahnaz. And where are you going for your honeymoon?"

"To the Swat Valley. I've heard so much about it, I can't wait to see it." She absorbed the deepening lines between Amir's eyes. "Don't worry, Amir, I'll be back to work next Monday, insh'allah. Perhaps by then you'll have found a surgeon for Fatima?"

The lines disappeared as he broke into a smile. "You never give up, do you? I promise to try to reach all the surgeons you haven't yet talked to." And then he turned to Irum, his eyes lingering on her face.

Ah, she thought.

And then Shahnaz was bumped from behind. Rabia hissed into her ear, "I need to talk to you." And she pulled Shahnaz toward a quiet corner of the tent. "I want you to ask Naseer about his cousin Javed."

Shahnaz rolled her eyes. "Which one is he, Rabia?" She sighed. "I can't tell them all apart yet."

Rabia turned Shahnaz to face the back of the house. "He's talking now to Naseer, over by the kitchen door." She snuck a quick look over her shoulder and then nodded her head twice in the men's direction.

Shahnaz saw a mocha-skinned young man, in his late twenties, of medium build and dressed in a honey beige shalwar kameez. He gesticulated with both arms as he spoke. "Okay, I see him. Why has he achieved this favored status with you?" She pried Rabia's arm from her shoulder.

"Naseer's Ammi pointed him out to Auntie who asked what I thought. He's dreamy, don't you think?"

Shahnaz looked him up and down, spending serious time on his square face. His brown eyes bordered on beady, and his arched eyebrow announced disdain. He looked intense and proud. Not an inviting face. "I think you'd better define 'dreamy' for me. I don't see it."

Rabia rolled her eyes. "Well, Auntie says he has an MBA degree in finance and is a manager at the Standard Charter bank. He's going somewhere."

Shahnaz threw up her hands. "Okay, Rabia, I'll see what I can find out. But don't push me for an answer tonight."

And then, thankfully, her father-in-law found her and extended his hand to show the way to the buffet. Sohail chatted as they crossed the yard, arriving at a busy Maryam who hustled the bride along the tables of food, loading her plate from each dish as it was "made by my own hands." Shahnaz felt like a newly opened flower: carefully tended and blooming.

A feeling of overwhelming sadness overcame her as the evening was ending. She was not going home. She was going away with strangers. No more Ammi to listen to her problems. No Abu to protect her. A wrenching feeling of pulling up her roots. She hugged her mother fiercely, and it took Naseer rubbing her arm and Abu grasping Ammi's arm for them to separate.

-•-

A short week later, Shahnaz and Naseer rolled up the driveway to the Khan house, having spent much of the day on the pot-holed and winding one-lane roads from Swat to Muzaffarabad. The honeymoon had been a grand success. They had a small cottage of the motel to themselves and were stuffed with excellent food. Each day they'd hiked beside a rushing river or climbed the naked hills, and along with the scenery, they'd explored each other.

Maryam burst from the house and rushed to give Shahnaz a hug. "You must be exhausted. Come in, refresh yourself, and have a nap. You, too, Naseer. Your room's ready." She continued chatting as she turned back to the house, confident she would be followed.

Naseer smiled at the disappearing back of his mother, asked the driver to bring their bags into the house, and with a soft pressure on her back, steered Shahnaz toward the door. "After you. It seems Ammi has our afternoon planned."

Feeling nervous about entering this new household and needing a nap after the long bumpy trip, Shahnaz dutifully followed her mother-in-law. Naseer came last, the caboose on their short train. She waved to Sohail, who stood with Raja Haider and a third man arguing over blueprints taped to the wall. He smiled in return. Maryam kept up a patter of words: the living room served as a storage facility for the dining room furniture as one of that room's walls had crumbled in the earthquake and the others were unsound. Even this room had severe cracks, which meant the built-in china cabinet listed and the glass in its doors was missing, though bits still sparkled in the grooves.

They passed the kitchen, where the cook was busy chopping onions, and entered the courtyard. The house formed three sides of a square with a garden in the middle and a boundary wall as the fourth edge. A few flowers and one yellow bush still bloomed, and a large jacaranda tree formed a bower over a bench near the center. It looked a peaceful place, except that the right end of the bedroom section—along the back of the property—had collapsed. She could make out a double bed and dresser, which kept a section of the roof from dissolving on the floor, and saw that the dusty carpet had a red geometric pattern. Chunks of concrete from the nearest wall lay abandoned in that corner of the yard, as though awaiting the artist who planned to use them in a collage. She felt disconcerted, out of kilter. Would they be safe sleeping here? Should the Khans have spent so much money on a wedding reception when the house was missing walls?

Maryam glanced at Shahnaz and waved her hand toward the destruction. "Not to worry. Raja Haider will fix the problem. You and Naseer are in this room." She opened the door to the third room from the right along the back section, inviting Shahnaz into a retreat now filled with the furnishings from her family. The teak frame of the double bed gleamed, showing off the sweeping scroll-work on the headboard. She and her Ammi had chosen a traditional Kashmiri bed covering of red, orange, and dark blue crewelwork on an off-white heavy cotton. Two matching pillow covers comple-mented the spread. The clothes her Ammi had packed for her were hanging in the attached dressing room, and someone had already laid out fresh towels in their bathroom. A few neatly stacked boxes indicated that new occupants were moving in.

"It looks lovely, Ammi. May I call you that now?"

Maryam framed her face with her hands in a movement of surprise. "Of course you may. In fact, you *must!*" Then she enfolded Shahnaz in a hug and patted her back. "Now, take your shoes off and lie down to rest. I can see you're exhausted. You, too, Naseer."

Maybe two hours later, when dusk had darkened the room, Shahnaz awoke to a knock on the door. "Dinner's ready." It was Maryam.

Shahnaz slid her feet off the edge of the bed, shook her head to rid it of sleep, and found her way to the cool water in the bathroom. She wondered that she hadn't even heard or felt Naseer leave the bed or been awakened by the evening call to prayer. She'd pray later; right now, she needed kohl and lipstick to look good for the family.

When she entered the living room, Maryam put an arm around her waist and guided her to a chair next to an already-seated Naseer, keeping up a constant stream of chattering welcome. A subdued Noshaba and her two-year-old daughter Zainab sat across the table from Naseer, next to Raja Haider. After a surreptitious glance at him, Noshaba raised her head to smile at Shahnaz. The younger children spread out along the table's sides: Nooran, Sadia, and Rizwana next to Shahnaz and Jamil and Qadir next to Raja Haider. The parents took chairs on either end. Here she was now, one of the Khans.

Maryam introduced each dish, encouraging everyone to take large helpings. Sohail, lithe as a pond reed, took small servings of two meat dishes and slowly ate bites of each with chunks of naan. The boys seemed to be following his lead, even Raja Haider ate sparingly. Jamil refused all but one dish, and young Qadir ignored much of what he'd put on his plate. None of the men ate vegetables, though Shahnaz thought the ladyfingers delicious, fried as they were with plenty of green chilies.

When the family finished eating, Maryam yelled "Mageed"

to summon the cook and told him to collect the dinner plates and serve the sweet. In the midst of the movement of plates, Sohail asked about Shahnaz's plans. "In the morning, will you need a ride to your office? My driver could drop you."

"Oh, no, thank you. Peace offers pick-and-drop, and the driver knows to collect me here." This was the first Shahnaz had spoken at the meal, happy to feel her way into the family and not wanting to upset normal routines.

As Raja Haider finished his sweet, he addressed her in a matter-of-fact tone. "Shahnaz, please talk to Noshaba tonight about your household duties."

Before Shahnaz thought of a reply, Naseer scraped his chair back from the table, rose, and lifted the chair back into place. "Of course, Shahnaz will consult with Noshaba, but right now we're going to our room to figure out where everything's going to fit. Work starts early tomorrow, and I have no idea where my briefcase is."

5

Shahnaz was nervous all of the last week in January: her breasts were sore and her period was so late she was sure she was pregnant. A part of her was pleased. Naseer certainly would be, and she liked knowing pregnancy was possible. But most of her didn't want this, not now. It felt like an ending, more freedom taken away. Still, tonight she'd tell her husband he was to be a father.

She waited until late evening, in their bedroom, as he came in from washing in the bathroom and she stood across from the bathroom door, hands folded and shivering in the cold. "Naseer? I want to tell you something." Her teeth chattered, and the heater was on full.

He came to her and took her hands into his. "Why aren't you in bed? You look like you're freezing. Shall I leave the gas fire on a little longer?"

Distracted, she looked down at the heater. "No, no. Turn it off. It's that...I'm pregnant." She shivered again, partly from the cold and partly from the sheer nervousness at the change this would bring into her life.

Naseer pulled her into a hug. "Oh, Shahnaz, this is wonderful."

She spoke into his chest. "I didn't want to say anything until I was sure."

As he pushed her back just enough to see her face, he broke into a grand grin. "Just think. We're going to have a child, maybe a son."

They walked, arms around each other, to the bed. Shahnaz looked up into his glistening eyes. "What do you think he'll be like?"

"Insh'allah, a smart, energetic, healthy boy who'll become a good man, an observant Muslim, and perhaps a scientist or a lawyer or a doctor."

Shahnaz crawled under the covers. "For me, being a kind man is essential." She waited while her husband cut off the gas and settled next to her. "And if the baby is a girl?"

"Then I hope she'll be like you: intelligent, generally obedient, but with a mind of her own, daring to question—where one should."

She was a little unsettled by his teasing. "Is that what you think of me?"

"Pretty much." He ran his finger down the outline of her face and kissed her. "I know this will mean a big change for you, not working any more, but I'm sure you'll be as good a mother as you are a health worker."

She pulled away. "I don't want to stop working."

"I didn't mean now. Of course you can work until the baby comes." His forehead wrinkled.

"Yes, and I'll stay home at first, but then I want to go back." Fear and anger mixed together to add a stridency to her tone.

"But..." Naseer looked honestly puzzled. "Mothers stay home with their children."

Shahnaz sat up straight. "They used to, but that's changing."

"If they *have* to work, like those poor Christian women who sweep the streets. But not women in your position."

Was he purposely not understanding her? "You knew I was

committed to my work when you agreed to marry me."

"Yes, but that was when you were single or, anyway, without children." His tone edged toward belligerent.

"It's not as though I'm abandoning a child. You're acting like my working is anti-God or something—"

His volume rose. "Well, it feels like that. I want to order you to stay home. I want my son properly cared for."

She matched his volume, ignoring the inner voice that told her others would hear this argument. "Remember what you said a few minutes ago, that I was 'generally obedient?' This is one of those times when I'm not. Too many women depend on me now. Babies will die without me. You know there aren't nearly enough qualified health workers."

"Don't you want this baby?"

"Of course, I do. But I don't want it to be my whole life."

"It won't be. You'll have me, the house, the family." Everyone in the neighborhood had certainly heard that.

She spit her words through her teeth. "That's not enough, Naseer."

He threw up his hands. "I don't get this. And I don't want to argue any more tonight." He slid down between the sheets and turned his back toward her.

Shahnaz mimicked his actions. This discussion was not over. It was time to dust off her debating skills. He'd find out what it meant for her to have "a mind of her own."

—•—

Just as February touched the earth and it seemed that warmth would return, Irum and Shahnaz bumped along the road toward Dhirkot, where Shahnaz would spend the morning with Bibi. Irum would continue on to visit one of her Health Workers just beyond the town. Pleased to be with her friend, Shahnaz put aside her incipient nausea and her continuing fight with Naseer and brought up a non-family topic. "Irum, did you read about the high school girls from that madrassa in Islamabad who camped out in the children's library?" She rolled her head to watch Irum's face and tasted a burp of stomach acid. "I'll just watch the road, but know that I'm listening."

"Yes. Dressed in black, fully covered, and brandishing those tall wooden poles. How odd of them."

"I can't imagine doing that and saying I'd stay in the library until the government adopts Sharia law. How dare they?"

"Do you think they'd use those sticks, really hit people?"

"I don't know. They looked fierce in the pictures." Shahnaz sighed and laid her head against the back of the seat. With her eyes closed, she juxtaposed the picture of Irum in her pale blue dupatta and delicate earrings against the girls in the photographs.

"It's so strange to me, this violence from Muslim women."

Shahnaz murmured agreement. "What do you suppose is really going on?"

"Hard to say. I'm afraid they want to turn us into the Afghanistan of Taliban days."

Shahnaz turned her head to see her friend's round and open face. "Here we are working on women's health, and we know our prophet Mohammad—Peace Be Upon Him—wanted women to bear healthy children. They need us out in the community, but those girls want to force us to stay in our homes."

"Yes."

"What can their teachers be telling them? I mean, taking over a library? That's bad." Shahnaz shook her head. Then, as the truck climbed the switchbacks from the river valley into the mountains, the air grew colder and she grew quiet. After a jolt, she grabbed the door handle. "Wali, stop please. Now."

The driver glanced at her in the rearview mirror and pulled the car into the mountainside.

Shahnaz jerked the water bottle from the elastic mesh behind the driver's seat, grabbed a couple of tissues from the box, and slid out the door. She had just enough time to walk three steps and crouch before throwing up. As she rinsed her mouth out and wiped her lips, she shivered and pulled her dupatta close about her shoulders. It was going to be a long few months. As she pushed herself to a standing position, she reeled from dizziness and leaned into the jagged stone in front of her.

Irum reached out to take the water bottle when Shahnaz stepped up into the cabin of the truck. Shahnaz nodded her head to reassure her friend, and then told the driver to proceed—pleading for no jagged turns or sharp stops.

She leaned back against the seat, willing her nausea to fade away. It probably wasn't such a good idea for her to do this traveling right now, perhaps Raja Haider was right about that—though for the wrong reason. He'd objected to her frequent day-time journeys and this morning, he'd spoken forcefully against the trip she would make at the end of the day to Islamabad for a ceremony at Kashmiri House to honor her father. He'd argued that women should stay close to home when they were pregnant and not make a spectacle of themselves. Sohail had told him one shouldn't coddle pregnant women. Naseer argued that Shahnaz never made a spectacle of herself, and Maryam had chipped in with the notion that she had earned some time with her parents. Shahnaz had been comforted by this defense of her traveling, especially from Naseer, whose support of her work had definitely waned, but truly, she'd not anticipated this frightful stomach churning.

Wali accelerated slowly and put a tape of traditional music into the car's player.

Shahnaz dozed, coming in and out of consciousness as the

road dictated. When the truck pulled to a stop at Bibi's "health house," she awoke and stretched, noting that her stomach was finally calm. Looking over at Irum, she smiled and slid close enough to prohibit the driver from hearing. "I don't want everyone to know yet, Irum, but I'm pregnant."

Irum's face broke into a radiant smile, and she threw her arm over Shahnaz's shoulders. "I'm so happy for you."

"Hmm. So is Naseer. I'm going to tell my parents tonight. They've been wondering, especially my Ammi."

"Insh'allah, they'll be pleased."

As Wali climbed out of his seat and went around the car to fetch her materials, Shahnaz put her hand on Irum's arm. "We have so little time alone to talk. Forgive me for being pushy, but I've been watching you with Amir. You like him a lot, don't you?"

Irum blushed, her neck blotched with red that crept up into her cheeks. She pulled a tissue from the box on the seat and began to shred it. "He is nice, isn't he? I know—well—I know it's forbidden to choose one's husband and my parents would be appalled, but he's such a good man, a gentle man like Naseer, and I can't help but wish…"

"Oh, Irum, me too."

After they squeezed hands, Shahnaz took her bag from the driver and headed toward the dark green tent that constituted the clinic section of Bibi's house. The mayor of the town had donated mats for the floor, and someone had found a dilapidated desk and a couple of mismatched folding chairs for Bibi and her patients. She really needed some decent storage space, not the cardboard boxes sitting along the back of the tent, but there was little money available for such things. And a health house really needed clean water, a reliable source of light, and a bed.

As Shahnaz and Bibi walked to a nearby village, Shahnaz pushed again for a prosthesis for Bibi's daughter Kameela. "I was thinking, Bibi, that I often visit my family in Islamabad. You know, my parents are looking for a husband for my sister, and we'll be having a wedding sometime this year."

"That'll be nice, time to see your family again."

"Yes." They climbed for a few minutes, and Shahnaz was too breathless to talk. Would she be able to do this in a few months? These supervisory visits were a required part of the job. Well, she'd put that away for now. At the top of the rise, she waited for Bibi, and they stopped to catch their breath. "I was thinking that I could take Kameela. She'd stay with me and my parents. My Ammi loves children. If you came with us the first time, we could visit the clinic and get her fitted for a prosthesis. I could take her to follow-up visits. What do you think?" Shahnaz saw hope and then lines of worry overtake Bibi's face.

"I...I don't know." She stared off in the distance toward the epicenter of the earthquake, where the whole hillside had slid into the river. "I'll talk to my husband. He's so...You know. I'll try. Thank you for offering."

Their second stop in this village was the family with the fourteen-year-old bride, the one who had no business falling pregnant, who was just too undersized and immature. Bibi sat down next to her. "So, tell me how it's going. How are you feeling?"

Shahnaz took a seat nearby, noting the tenderness in Bibi's voice and the tears in the girl's eyes.

"I feel sick all the time. I can't keep food down, and the waste of it angers my mother-in-law."

Her cheeks were hollow and her deep brown eyes prominent in her face. Only the enlarged breasts and the bump in her abdomen spoke of pregnancy. The thin neck, arms, and ankles suggested starvation.

Bibi took the young woman's hand and patted it. "We've brought some hot cereal for you that has extra nutrients in it. A little of that several times a day is easier to keep down than spicy meals."

The girl glanced up at her mother-in-law and quickly back to her hands.

Bibi patted the hands again. "Rice and milk are good, too. Tea, if you can manage it." Then Bibi stood and addressed the mother-in-law and husband. "As you know, morning sickness usually goes away by the second trimester, but some women feel unwell all the way through. You must see that she needs to gain weight, if she's to have a healthy baby."

The woman answered with a dismissive wave of her hand. "Allah will decide. I don't pay attention to the girl's whining. She has duties in this house, and I won't tolerate her shirking."

Bibi walked up close to this woman, locking eyes. "If you want a healthy grandchild and more of them after this one, I'd suggest you change your mind about special diets and working this girl to the bone. She needs this cereal and a diet she can tolerate." She swiveled to confront the young husband. "Perhaps you could help her with chores?"

He took a step back and looked at his wife with a gentle smile. "Yes, sahiba."

"Good. I'll take your wife into the bedroom now and examine her to make sure the baby is growing well."

He nodded.

—•◦•—

On the way to her parents' Islamabad home, the truck dropped Irum in Abbottabad, and an exhausted Shahnaz closed her eyes and reflected on the day. People in these mountains needed a functioning clinic so badly. Bibi did what she could to help pregnant women, but rarely was there a doctor to back her up, and the supply of medications was erratic. Today, God showed his mercy: Bibi would have another conversation with her husband about Kameela, Shahnaz was going to badger Amir to call about the late shipment of medications, and that young pregnant girl had a better chance for a healthy delivery. It was God's work they did, God who had called her to these mountains. Tonight she would call Naseer to tell him about the day, show him why she had to keep doing this job.

When the Peace driver dropped her off, she melted into her mother's embrace. "Oh, Ammi, I'm so tired. Would you mind if I lay down for a half hour before dinner? I'm exhausted, and I want to be alert for the ceremony tonight."

"Well, of course." A smile lit her face. They walked arm-in-arm up the steps to Shahnaz's old room and Ammi tucked her in under the comforter of her childhood. Instead of leaving, as Shahnaz thought she would, Ammi sat down on the edge of the bed and ran her hand over Shahnaz's forehead. "No fever, no special aches to complain of. Could it be you're pregnant?"

Shahnaz offered her a tired grin. "Yes, Ammi. I was going to tell you at dinner, but I should've known you'd figure it out."

Beaming in response, Ammi pulled the comforter over Shahnaz's shoulders and patted her side. "Then you must sleep. And I'll go tell Abu he's about to become a grandfather."

Over dinner, Abu congratulated her. Tahir grumbled that he was sick of conversations about weddings, and babies would be worse. Rabia allowed as how it would be fun to be an aunt and pick out lots of baby clothes—but she would rather be a mother. Then, with hardly time for a breath, she switched the subject. "I have news, too. Remember Naseer's cousin Javed? You know, the one at the Walima?"

"Oh, yes." Shahnaz put her hand to her cheek. "I'm sorry, but in all the flutter of that time, I forgot to ask Naseer about him. Shall I ask tonight?"

"Not to worry," her sister commented with a dismissive wave

of her hand. "Auntie asked Naseer's mother about him, and she thought he'd be a great match for me." She looked at Ammi and Abu, as though daring them to stop her from going on.

Shahnaz looked at each of them, too, curious about the silence. "And...?"

Rabia burst out, "His parents are coming to meet us next week." She sounded gleeful, from her bouncing head and shoulders to her hands clapping. "Isn't it great?"

Shahnaz saw Ammi push food about her plate and Abu stare at his younger daughter as though at an alien creature. My, my. "It seems you think so, Rabia, but are there issues?" She looked again at each of her parents, eyebrows raised.

Abu took up the gauntlet. "I, for one, do not like the young man. He's far too full of himself, and he doesn't respect his elders."

"What did he do, Abu? You are not usually so harsh about people." A sharp kick hit her ankles, coming from Rabia's direction.

Abu harrumphed. "As is my right, I asked him about his job and his prospects, right after Auntie introduced us at your Walima. He looked at me as though I was a peon employed on his estate. He even managed to look down his nose at me, and I'm taller than he is. And then he said, 'I am the bank *manager*. I am in charge of the branch,' as though he was the President, the ruler, the king." He harrumphed again, lips pursed. "Far too full of himself."

Thinking to gather grist for a later milling with her sister, Shahnaz pursued her mother. "Ammi, what did you think of Javed?" She hoped this sounded like an innocent question, though really she was delighted with the prospect of a family debate—one not about her, for a change.

Gazing at the opposite wall, Ammi said, "You know, his second name is Iqbal, and I was hoping he had some of the poet in him. But I'm afraid all I saw was a man of ambition."

"I like ambition," Rabia said.

Ammi tut-tutted. "I know, and some is good. But it must be tempered with care for others, with courtesy to all. Our prophet— Peace Be Upon Him—was ever polite..."

"Ammi, please, not another lecture..." Rabia stopped, her mouth still partially open.

Shahnaz watched the mind wheels turning in the shifting expression on her sister's face and the stillness of her body. Just maybe, Rabia was growing up. Or perhaps, using her wiles to get her way.

Picking up her fork, Rabia adopted a more conciliatory tone and hung her head. "I'm sorry, Ammi. I'm thankful that you and Abu have agreed to meet his parents. I'll wait to see how the evening goes. Insh'allah, you'll see a different side to Javed."

Abu looked as though he was prepared to launch into an emotional diatribe against pert children or arrogant men, but a slow headshake from Ammi stopped him. He turned to Tahir, who had been quiet throughout the exchange, jamming his mouth with bite after bite. "Sit up straight, son. You're going to get a hunchback from the way you hover over that food."

Shahnaz sent an encouraging smile to her startled brother. This plot was a little complicated for an eleven-year-old.

—•—

Only Maryam was moving about when Shahnaz arrived in Muzaffarabad on the Sunday afternoon. The men were at prayer, and Maryam reported that Noshaba had gone to take a nap. "She's due to deliver very soon now, and she needs her rest." Maryam squinted as she scanned Shahnaz's face. "And you don't look so good yourself. What is it?"

"I have some pain in my stomach, Ammi. I'm sure it's nothing but carsickness. Perhaps if I lay down, it'll pass."

Maryam guided Shahnaz back to her bedroom. She turned

on the gas fire, fussed over the lack of space for Shahnaz's shoes in the closet, and then folded the abandoned dupatta, smoothing out all wrinkles. "Now, you just relax and rest. I'll fix you some tea and a hot water bottle."

As she bustled out of the room, Shahnaz imagined her squat figure sprout the feathers of a mother hen tending a chick. And then she tensed as her stomach cramped. This could not be good. She rode the pain, and it passed.

When Maryam woke her for dinner, Shahnaz thought that the worst had passed. Her stomach wasn't happy, but it wasn't doing cartwheels anymore. So, she answered Maryam's query with an assurance that she was feeling much better. As she changed clothes, she noticed a bit of blood on her undergarments. Well, some women did spot and still had healthy babies. But others didn't. She vowed to move very carefully.

That night, Sohail had much to say over dinner. "We spent the whole day meeting about the timber mafia. Do you know that all our roadblocks to check that the logs on trucks have been lawfully cut are yielding next to nothing? The mafia is either paying off the men at the roadblocks—and maybe more senior officials—or they've found other minor roads to use to avoid the blockades. I'm so tired of this ravaging of our mountains...and of this corruption. Don't these people know they may lose everything—houses, farms, children—if they cut down all the trees? Imbeciles." He pressed his naan so hard against a chunk of lamb that most of the meat shot onto the table.

All the family watched as Sohail recovered the escaped meat and sopped up gravy for his next bite.

Naseer broke the silence. "Abu?"

Sohail looked up, his brows knitting and then releasing. "What?"

"I wonder if the education ministry might help you out."

"What did you have in mind?"

Shahnaz glanced at her husband. The food was not sitting well in her stomach, even though she was eating only rice and naan. She rested a bit of her bread on the plate and prayed the conversation would not upset the men—and her.

Naseer rested his forearms on the edge of the table. "We're forever preparing teacher training materials of one sort or another. We've already done three days of training on emergency preparedness, unfortunately *after* the earthquake, but if we thought ahead, we could train teachers about environmental threats and ask them to teach their students and community members. Maybe use some of Shahnaz's Lady Health Workers, too."

Shahnaz looked from her husband's encouraging face to her father-in-law's pensive one. Sohail drummed his fingers on the table.

"What utter nonsense." Raja Haider spit out the words, startling Shahnaz and causing Noshaba to shrink away from him. "We need the Army. These people paid a few rupees an hour to monitor logging trucks can't be trusted. Call in the Federal Constabulary, have them track down the poachers and cut off their hands, as the Qur'an tells us to do with thieves. I have no patience with training and education that'll take years, if it works at all, by which time there'll be no forests left."

Shahnaz felt her husband lean forward and caught his subtle headshake. "How is it you believe in such harsh retribution? Our imam was saying just a few weeks ago that Sura Five talks about 'marking' thieves' hands with a knife, not cutting them off. He went so far as to say it's 'satanic' to cut them off."

"Bah, Naseer. You know that imam's an old woman."

Sohail objected. "Not true. I've known him for nearly fifty years. We were school fellows. He's careful in his study of the Qur'an and in his teaching."

"I'm curious as to just how far you go in supporting violence," Naseer said. "Do you, for instance, support the girls from the Jamia Hafsa madrassa who are carrying weapons and threatening to beat whoever opposes the imposition of Sharia law?"

Raja Haider opened his mouth in what seemed a knee-jerk reaction of arguing against whatever Naseer proposed, and then closed his teeth against his bottom lip. "Actually, I support the idea of Sharia law, as it would bring quicker justice for all of us, instead of the current practice of waiting years for a case to come to court. But I don't support the idea of girls taking up arms, making a public spectacle of themselves, and being the puppets of timid men who aren't willing to put themselves on the line for their beliefs."

Naseer settled against the back of his chair. "I'm oddly comforted you don't see violence as a universal solution."

Maryam cleaned her fingers with a tissue. "And we certainly have many problems that are closer to home than the demand for Sharia law: people are having trouble finding the money to rebuild their homes. They watch their children shiver under tents and don't know where heating fuel is going to come from. Cutting down trees may seem the only option." She chewed slowly, as though anger were far from her person instead of seething in her eldest son, seated close by. "Sohail, how's the work going with other ministries to see to some of these needs?"

"It's slow." Sohail waved a fresh piece of naan toward his eldest son. "We seem to be relying on individuals helping each other, as Raja Haider is doing with Roman's family."

"I'm simply providing charity where it's needed."

Maryam smiled, her eyes catching Sohail's. "It's a great kindness on your part to find them bricks and teach them masonry."

Raja Haider grunted.

As soon as she could politely do so, Shahnaz excused herself. Unexpectedly, Noshaba followed, holding Zainab by the hand. Usually her sister-in-law disappeared into her child's room after supper, but tonight she shadowed Shahnaz into her bedroom.

Shahnaz unwrapped her dupatta and sank down on the bed. "Thank you for coming, Noshaba, but I don't think I can talk tonight. I don't feel well and I want to fall into bed."

Noshaba straightened the bed covers and folded them back. "Tonight I'll help you, and I'll tell Raja Haider we discussed how you'll help me with our new baby."

"Yes, well, I'll just go change." As she disappeared into the bathroom, Shahnaz pondered this unusual behavior. While Noshaba was never demanding and often embarrassed to ask for small favors, she'd never before acted as Shahnaz's helpmate. The best guess was that she'd been told by her husband to have a conversation. Shahnaz smiled at the compromise Noshaba had managed. It looked as though she was trying new ways to deal with that difficult man.

Then she looked at her underwear. More spotting. She sat down on the toilet. The stain was large enough to suggest a steady dribble, not just a random drop from time to time. Maybe she was losing the baby. This was not good: that tiny being inside her should have every possible chance to survive. Wasn't her profession making healthy babies? She'd fight its loss. Rising, she tied the knot to hold her robe together and re-entered the chilly bedroom.

Noshaba patted the bed. "Come. I know what it's like to be tired and sad when you're pregnant."

Confronted by sympathy, Shahnaz's eyes prickled with unshed tears. "Oh, Noshaba, it's more than that. I think I'm losing the baby."

Noshaba ran to Shahnaz and led her to the bed. "Rest, please. I'll get Ammi." She ran awkwardly to the door, her child in her arms, looking like a bat exiting its sleeping cave.

Maryam spent the next few hours flitting about the house, brainstorming with Shahnaz one remedy and then another. First it was the hot water bottle, then hot milk with turmeric, then a massage to relax her shoulders, and finally a suggestion that they try the makeshift hospital. What would Shahnaz think of that?

"I don't want to move, Ammi, please. I'll just stay here and hope for this to pass." Shahnaz had curled herself into the fetal position, with a pillow clutched in her arms. Even opening her eyes seemed difficult as she concentrated on riding the near-constant pains. Until she had to run for the bathroom and felt a spill of liquid leave her body.

In bed once more, Maryam washed Shahnaz's sweating forehead with a damp cloth. "Poor dear." She ran her hand down Shahnaz's face. "We'd all do better with babies if we had a proper hospital or a doctor who'd come to the house. When he was little, I so wanted Raja Haider to study medicine, but as he grew, Sohail and I knew that was not the right path for him. And Naseer was so devoted to education, I couldn't take away his dream. Our Nooran will make a fine doctor one day, but here we are, needing a doctor now, and there's no one who does house calls."

"It's all right, Ammi." And then another cramp sent her running for the toilet, and this time she stayed. The pains came in miserable waves until her body released the fetus. She stared down at the tiny form floating in the toilet bowl. Her baby, dead before it was born. She crumpled to the floor, sobbing, until Maryam came in, giving her warm washcloths to clean herself and a fresh nightgown, talking through Shahnaz's tears about this sadness and how things would get better.

Defeated and unable to stop her tears, Shahnaz staggered back to bed. When she heard the toilet flush, she whimpered. How ironic if it turned out she—who helped others have healthy babies—couldn't bear one of her own. Why did God bring this suffering to her?

Maryam tucked the blankets around her and instructed her,

over and over, to sleep, that sleep would repair her ills. Then she settled on the edge of the bed. "I lost a baby before Raja Haider was born—my first pregnancy, too. I know the sadness you feel."

Shahnaz saw the answering tears in Maryam's eyes, and then watched them roll down her cheeks. She knew she should empathize, but she couldn't muster the energy.

Maryam smiled and squeezed her hand. "Sohail was so kind. He never bothered me about that, and Naseer is like his father. You're not to worry, just go to sleep and I'll tell the family." With a patting of her dupatta into each eye, Maryam stood, let the cloth float downward, and then smoothed away the folds as she left to deliver the news.

Only a few minutes later, Shahnaz awoke to angry voices outside her door. As the knob turned, she saw a heavy evening's darkness and heard Raja Haider, like a small explosion. "This is what happens when women work, Naseer. Shahnaz must quit her job." The sound of a slap echoed, and she wondered if her brother-in-law had hit her husband or his own hand. She struggled to rise, to tell him it wasn't the working, but she stopped at the sound of Naseer's voice.

"She's my wife, not yours. We can continue this discussion later, but now I'm going to her—and I don't want you upsetting her further." He sounded thoroughly annoyed with his brother, certain he was in charge of her and in favor of her working. She lay back against the pillow and thanked God for this husband.

Raja Haider burst again. "You'd better understand that I expect her to care for Noshaba and our baby. No excuses that work comes before family."

"Yes, brother. Good night." She imagined him dismissing Raja Haider with a flick of his hand or maybe a shove.

Closing the door quietly behind him, Naseer crossed the room and sat on the edge of the bed. "Are you awake?" Then he took her hand and rubbed it between his own. "What a stupid question. Who could sleep through that shouting? Let me try again. How're you feeling? Ammi says it wasn't easy."

Shahnaz tried for a smile. "I'll be all right. And thank you for standing up for me. I know how much you wanted this baby—and I did, too. I tried to hold on to it. I..."

Naseer ran his hand along her arm. "Insh'allah, there'll be others. Don't blame yourself. God will bring us children in His own time."

Shahnaz wondered if this were true, hoped it was true, and wanted him to be as positive about her working when—if—she fell pregnant again. But then the picture of her tiny fetus floated into her mind, and she fell into a pit of grief.

6

oshaba took to her bed in the late afternoon of a cold February 15. Shahnaz, who had just arrived home from work, followed her into the bedroom, hoping to be helpful but overcome, yet again, by a wave of grief. Only two weeks ago she, too, had been expecting a child. The strength of her emotions was something of a surprise: her hormones must be going wild. There were flashes of relief that she would be able to continue working, guilt that she might have overdone the work and somehow caused the miscarriage, and sadness from the loss. Each time she saw a pregnant mother, tears came to her eyes. Could she be a professional through these next few hours with Noshaba or was she going to fall apart?

As was the family tradition, Maryam had made arrangements for a dai, a local woman who had attended Noshaba's first birthing. Shahnaz was to serve as her back-up. She hadn't objected, though she wondered at Maryam's intentions. Did her mother-in-law think Shahnaz unreliable these days, or did she not want to subject her to a birth so soon after losing a child? It was like Maryam to be protective.

Before the midwife arrived, Shahnaz prepared the bed, made

Noshaba comfortable, and checked her degree of dilation. It was good to be needed. She disciplined herself to be cheerful and encouraging, and only in a private moment did she shut her eyes and pray to keep control over her jumble of emotions. A moan from Noshaba alerted her to focus on her patient.

When an old woman hobbled into the bedroom, wrapped in a fraying blanket, Shahnaz shot a look of surprise at her mother-in-law. Did this dai have any training? The midwife's smile of greeting showed only four teeth, and those were streaked with brown. Her hair was pulled back into a ponytail, but as she shook the dupatta off her head, Shahnaz could see white roots that had not received henna in a long time. Was this woman clean? Would she pay sufficient attention to the details of birth to ensure a safe delivery?

Maryam smiled at Shahnaz and patted Noshaba's shoulder. "Here's Nusrat to deliver your child. Remember her? She helped you through Zainab's birth."

Noshaba opened her eyes for a moment, nodded, and then closed them again with a moan.

Shahnaz rose as the midwife approached, leaving her clear access to the bed. If this woman were the choice of her mother-in-law, she would honor that...but watch closely. Nusrat threw back the covers, pressed Noshaba's large belly here and there as though tracing the outline of the baby, and then asked when the contractions had started, the time between them now, and how intense they felt.

Noshaba answered in a whisper. "The pains started this morning, but I didn't want to bother anyone until I was sure this was the time." Again, she closed her eyes.

Shahnaz said, "They're four minutes apart, and she's one centimeter dilated." Why hadn't the woman washed her hands? Perhaps she believed touching skin didn't require it?

The midwife grinned and collapsed on Shahnaz's chair.

"You're one of those new lady health workers, aren't you?"

"I'm a Lady Health Supervisor."

"Thought I heard something about that. I suppose you think you know all about delivering babies, what with that training they give you down in Islamabad."

Shahnaz pressed a hand to her chest. "I don't think that. I just want to help."

Nusrat hoisted herself out of the chair and pushed past Shahnaz. "Then stay out of my way. I've delivered hundreds of babies, and I don't need your interference."

Shocked into silence, Shahnaz sank back toward the wall.

Nusrat spoke next to Noshaba. "How long was your last labor, dear?"

Maryam answered this time. "Nearly twenty-four hours. Insh'allah, it'll be shorter this time."

Shahnaz shook her head. Noshaba should have said something earlier, not suffered in pains for hours without talking to anyone. She could have called. Shahnaz would have come home. Of course, this sister-in-law was still a shadow, gliding in and out of rooms with next to no noise. The men—and Shahnaz—had been at work, but surely Maryam had been home. Well, actually, Shahnaz didn't know what Maryam did all day. She assumed she was busy about the business of running a house. Had she not checked on Noshaba?

Suddenly, Noshaba groaned a deep yowl of pain.

Shahnaz stepped up to the bed. Someone should check her progress again.

Nusrat patted Noshaba's hand. "That's okay, my girl. You mind your breathing. It'll ease the pain." Then she pulled back the covers to examine her patient more thoroughly.

As she reached a dirty hand toward Noshaba's vagina, Shahnaz recoiled. "Aren't you going to wash your hands first?"

Nusrat checked her open palms and turned them over.

"They're fine."

"No, no, they're not." She turned to Maryam. "Ammi, it's critical to the health of Noshaba and the baby that her hands be carefully washed." When she looked back at Nusrat, the woman was touching Noshaba. Shahnaz yanked back her hands. "You may not touch her with unclean hands."

Nusrat pulled herself upright. "Maryam, it's her or me. You gotta choose."

It took Maryam only a second. "I'm sorry, Nusrat. It must be Shahnaz. Surely, you can understand that."

Nusrat grabbed her dupatta, threw it over her head and shoulders, and stomped to the door. As she pulled the doorknob, she turned back. "When this girl gets in trouble, don't you come to me to get her out. We're done, Maryam."

Maryam watched the woman leave and sighed. "I think I'll gather the cloths we'll need."

"Ammi, thank you for supporting me. I haven't delivered hundreds of babies, but I do know what to do."

"We're all depending on you." Maryam left the room and returned in a few minutes with a stack of towels. Then she unearthed the baby blankets from the closet and placed them next to the bed.

The gas heater continued to spit at them as it worked to keep the room warm. It hissed to Shahnaz like a warning message: you threw out the midwife. You'd better be successful.

By midnight, Shahnaz was exhausted, and Maryam insisted she find herself some tea and rest for a few minutes. She was surprised to find Sohail, Raja Haider, and Naseer sitting around the dining table, wrapped in thick shawls and discussing the day's news. Somehow she'd expected Sohail and Naseer to be in bed—but, then, the bedrooms were all close together, and one would need earplugs tonight to sleep. Of course, it might be their concern for Noshaba that kept them up, or excitement about a new baby. Shahnaz did need to allow for those feelings on their part.

"Ah, Shahnaz," Sohail said. "How are things going?"

The other men turned to watch her enter the room.

"Things are progressing normally. It shouldn't be long now." She approached the table and leaned on the back of a chair. "Noshaba is very brave."

Raja Haider dismissed her comment with a wave of his hand. "It's her duty. Insh'allah, she will be delivered of a son this time."

Naseer smiled. "And perhaps she'll present you with another daughter."

"Do not joke about this, brother. A son will bring honor to the family, ensure its continuity, and care for me when I am older. A girl must be given to a husband and provided a dowry. She's of little use and much cost to me."

"Frankly, I'd value any child, boy or girl. To my mind, girls also bring honor—and love. They often excel in school, especially those in this family, and they can become teachers or doctors..."

"You know I don't approve of women working."

Naseer groaned. "Yes, and I've never understood that. You expect your daughter to be taught by female teachers; you won't allow Noshaba to see a male doctor or dentist. How do you expect female professionals to be available if parents forbid their daughters to work?"

Raja Haider straightened his spine. "What other parents allow is not my business. My wife and daughter are, and I won't be told how to deal with them."

Sohail pulled at his beard, looking first at one son and then the other.

For a moment, the opponents were quiet: Raja Haider held his stare while Naseer looked thoughtful and, to Shahnaz, a little sad.

She asked, quietly, if anyone would like tea.

Sohail smiled. "Thank you, my dear. That would be excellent."

He swiped his hand across the gathering to indicate that all of them should be served, then clasped the end of the unwrapped shawl and threw it back over his shoulder.

Shahnaz moved to the kitchen, feeling disconcerted at having left a scene of real physical pain to encounter such an emotional exchange. Where did Raja Haider get his ideas? That madrassa might have started it all, but there must be more. A son of Sohail's would have heard liberal views on every school vacation and for years after secondary school.

She filled the kettle, leaned against the sink, and wondered how it was that her husband didn't seem to mind bringing up subjects that were bound to anger Raja Haider. She'd schooled herself to let the less egregious of her brother-in-law's opinions pass without argument, not wanting to be the cause of family dissention. Didn't Naseer feel the violent undertones? Didn't he mind? Or was this just a part of their banter as brothers?

Naseer cleared his throat, and Shahnaz edged toward the door to watch the exchange. "I'm sure you know as well as I do that the Qur'an tells us to value female as well as male children, to teach them to know God and respect their parents. I think its Sura Forty-two that says 'To God belongs the sovereignty of the heavens and the earth. He creates whatever He wills, granting daughters to whomever He wills, and granting sons to whomever He wills.' Are you questioning God's decision?" He paused, staring at his brother. "I'd say it's better to ask *why* He has given you a daughter. Maybe He wants you to learn more about girls."

"More likely, He wants you to obey the Qur'an as He gave it to Our Prophet—Peace Be Upon Him." Using his index finger, he pointed at Naseer. "You need to come with me to Lashkar-i-Taiba, hear Allah's true message."

Sohail interrupted. "How involved are you with that group?"

Shahnaz heard alarm in his voice and told herself to ask Naseer who they were.

Raja Haider answered, full of arrogance, "I respect their commitment to Islam and helping our people. I admire their dedication to act and not just complain about injustice."

"And do you join in their actions?"

"Abu, you know I was with them after the earthquake."

"Yes, you worked day and night to bring water and blankets, to get people to doctors. But now? What about now?"

When Shahnaz returned to the dining table carrying a tray with four mugs of white tea, she could feel the tension between father and son. Sohail bent forward, his eyes narrowed. But before Raja Haider answered, Maryam swirled from the passageway into the room. "She wants to push, Shahnaz. Better come back."

And in little more than an hour, Noshaba's second daughter was born into Shahnaz's clean hands. She wrapped her in a blanket and gave the squalling infant to Maryam to wash and swaddle. As she chatted with a silent Noshaba through the delivery of the afterbirth, she fought her envy at her sister-in-law having a healthy baby, knowing that Noshaba was disappointed at the birth of another girl. Probably also scared of her husband's reaction. Shahnaz allowed her anger with Raja Haider and his antiquated ideas to fill her mind. She'd have a word or two with him—before he saw the baby.

When baby and mother were comfortably nestled together, Maryam and Shahnaz returned to the men. Maryam clasped her hands and allowed them to drop onto her kameez. "Raja Haider, you have a lovely daughter whom I believe I'll name Riffat. Naseer, your wife was extraordinary—such a blessing it is to have a trained nurse in the family."

Shahnaz watched Raja Haider murmur "Riffat" and shake his head.

Ignoring her son, Maryam beckoned to Sohail. "Come, grandfather, you must whisper azaan in her ear, calling her to her first prayer."

Shahnaz stared at her brother-in-law, wanting to shake him and yell that he should be thankful to have a healthy child. Her hands formed fists.

To no one in particular, Raja Haider grumbled, "Useless, just useless."

Shahnaz recoiled. "They are not useless—neither your wife nor your daughter. Noshaba has endured hours of pain for you, and she's in your room terrified you'll be angry at this perfect child she's borne. I expect you to go in that room and thank her." She shot her arm out to point toward the bedroom.

Naseer threw an arm around Shahnaz's shoulders and pulled her to him. "Perhaps my brother needs a few moments to compose himself before he goes to greet his new daughter. Shall we leave him?"

"No!" Raja Haider shoved back his chair, rose to full height, and glared at Shahnaz. "How dare you speak to me like that. Naseer, you will discipline your wife for this outrage—or I'll do it for you." His eyes blazed. He hit the table with the palm of his hand and stalked out of the room.

Shahnaz was shaking with rage. "He can't speak to me that way and leave." She took a step to follow, but Naseer held on, pulling her back.

"I don't think that's a good idea."

"You're going to let him get away with this?"

"He really wanted a boy, you know that. Give him time to get adjusted, that's all." He tried to pull Shahnaz into a hug.

She resisted. "Whose side are you on? Do you value women as little as he does?"

"You know the answer to that. I value you a great deal, too much to let you get into a fight you can't win."

From the first day after Riffat's birth, Shahnaz had charge of her for a few hours from the time she got home from work until their late dinner. One or another of the Khan sisters spent this time caring for two-year-old Zainab, giving Noshaba the chance for a worry-free nap. After dinner, Noshaba generally nursed the baby, returned Riffat to Shahnaz, and put Zainab to bed. Because of Raja Haider's lack of patience with his daughters, the women kept them out of the main living areas.

Every evening, Shahnaz retreated to her bedroom with the tiny girl, walked the baby back and forth across the room, and cried. About a week into Riffat's life, Naseer entered their room as she was pacing, whispering, and patting the baby. Tears were running down her cheeks. "I'm so sorry I lost our baby. I can't stop crying."

He took her and the baby into his arms. "I'm sorry, too, but it wasn't your fault. Please don't grieve for that reason."

Safe in his embrace, she cried herself out, pulling away when the baby started to fuss. Sniffing back her tears, she glanced at the concerned face of her husband and sighed. "How can Raja Haider be disappointed in this baby—this blameless being that he created?" Shahnaz bent to kiss the baby's head and swept a small black curl off her forehead.

Naseer looked into the face of his niece and ran two fingers down the side of the child's face. She turned toward his hand.

Shahnaz dropped her head against Naseer's chest, fresh tears flowing. "Look at that. She's ready to love anyone who's kind to her."

Naseer smiled, kissed Shahnaz's head, and settled into their overstuffed chair, legs outstretched, head resting on the back of the chair. "I remember, when I was little, idolizing my brother. After all, he was bigger; he could whack a cricket ball and run much faster than I could. Abu praised him more often than me, and I wanted to hear those words, too."

Shahnaz rocked from one leg to the other as the baby drifted into sleep. Quietly, she asked, "Do you still admire him?"

"Sometimes. When he's generous, as he is with the neighbors. I dislike him when he's so ungenerous with us." Naseer stared at the window, which framed the night. "Did you know he went away to school—a madrassa?"

She nodded and then, realizing he wasn't looking at her, said, "Yes."

"Things changed for us. He'd come home and order me around. He wouldn't play cricket with me, or any game. He was angry, and sometimes he beat me up. It didn't take long for me to make myself scarce. I'd go over to my cousin's house most after-noons, which Ammi allowed because Ashraf and I were in the same class. When Raja Haider took to coming over, too, things got more difficult. He'd act the bully, but it didn't work because the two of us would fight him and, though we got bloodied in the process, we usually won."

Shahnaz set the sleeping baby down on their bed, wedged between two pillows, and sat down on the mattress across from her husband. She liked his storytelling, his voice modulating to provide color; his words mimicking the language style of each character; and his speech intensifying and then easing off as emotions changed.

"I think I learned in those months just how far I could push him and how I could outwit him. Words, finesse, a little diplomacy." He stirred and stuck a small pillow behind his lower back. "Now, I find I'm not afraid of him; I don't need to agree with him, but I do try to live together honestly—to speak up when it's right for me to disagree."

He grinned, a little crookedly. "I know it isn't always comfort-able for you, and I'm sorry about that."

"You're kind to think of me. But...umm...why isn't it right for you to object to his beating Noshaba?"

Naseer scrunched his face into a look of pain. "I have objected. But my words didn't make any difference."

"I'm glad you've said something. See, I'm worried that I'll be the cause of his beating her, and I let things go by that I feel I shouldn't. And then he makes me so angry I can't stay quiet—like when Riffat was born. Now I'm afraid he's going to insist I stay home and care for her. I love the baby. But..."

"So far, we're winning this particular battle."

Shahnaz turned to her husband, surprised. She hadn't heard of this battle.

He was smiling. "You're so good with the baby that Abu and I have persuaded Raja Haider to give up his campaign for you to stop work. Also, Noshaba's been insistent that she doesn't need you during the day." He paused, tapping his fingers on the chair arm. "I haven't seen her so adamant with Raja Haider before—you have a good effect on that mouse, Shahnaz."

"I? How could I? I never asked her to give me less work or to defend me."

Naseer slowly opened his lips into a broad smile and raised his eyebrows. "And yet you have great persuasive power. I think Noshaba looks up to you; we're seeing the mouse emerge from hiding to face the cat."

"But I don't want her to defy her husband." Shahnaz pushed off the mattress and began pacing, her fingers curled against her cheek. "I don't want her beaten because of me."

Naseer rose and held Shahnaz's arms, stopping her in front of him. "Shahnaz, look at me."

She turned her face upward.

"You're not asking Noshaba to change her behavior or encouraging her. She's *choosing* to do so, on her own, and doesn't she have the freedom to be her own person and define, with her husband, the role she'll take as his wife?"

"Yes, certainly." Shahnaz laid her forehead against Naseer's chest. "I just don't want her hurt."

—•—

A few days later, when Shahnaz returned from a supervisory visit to the rambling house that served as the Peace office, she was elated. The rest of the staff were just dispersing from their lunch in the big dining room, so she took her plate of chicken biryani to her desk, the rice spicy and steaming. Irum was back as well, and in this large bedroom that was now the office for the six female social organizers, they had desks next to each other.

"Such a good morning, Irum. I watched about twenty people up at Dharian Bambian build most of a temporary clinic. They got the walls and roof up and were fitting the door when I left. Madame Salima, the Lady Health Worker, has such fire in her. Her husband, who's a carpenter, was there with his tools, acting as foreman. She cheered everyone on, made sure there was plenty of tea, and even managed to immunize a couple of children. It's her energy that convinced people to donate money, materials, and labor to make this happen."

Irum had a thoughtful expression on her face, her earrings sparkling from the overhead lights. "When they move in, you should write them up for Peace's brochure. Take some good pictures. You have just the right touch, Shahnaz—getting people to help themselves."

Shahnaz leaned back against her chair, reflecting on how self-assured she could be in her health work and how unsure she was feeling at home. "Irum, do you think what we're doing is going to cause women problems?"

Irum turned sideways in her chair to face Shahnaz, sliding

her arm over its back and hugging it. "I don't understand."

Shahnaz looked at her hands as she spoke. "Well, here we are asking Lady Health Workers to encourage couples to use contraception, and men may not like that. I mean, well, I've seen what happened to Noshaba when she tried to express an opinion, and..." She crossed her arms over her chest, glancing at her friend. "I don't want to be the reason more women are beaten."

Irum reached over to touch Shahnaz's hands. "You're right that Peace is encouraging them to change the patterns of decades. It might be threatening to men."

Shahnaz nodded her head, now more worried by Irum's agreement.

"But, I think you're not giving enough credit to the women."

"What do you mean? I admire them so much."

"Yes, I know. But you're forgetting that most of them have spent years figuring out how to deal with men. They know better than to declare the world is changing or announce they're taking over family decision-making. Imagine trying that—none of us would, right?"

Shahnaz laughed at the picture Irum was drawing. "Yeah. I should give them more credit. I just want so much for women to blossom, to use their God-given talents." She let the sentence drift off. "Irum, how are you dealing with your parents about Amir?"

Irum blushed. "Oh, my. You caught me." She dropped her head onto her arm. "I haven't told them. Oh, I've mentioned him, though only to say he's my boss. Nothing more."

"Is it weighing on you, this not telling?"

"Yes. This is the first time I haven't spoken to them about something important to me. I've been telling myself it's because I'm still getting to know him, I'm not sure what he's feeling or what I want." She turned to her desk, rested her elbows on its edge and her chin on her hands, and stared at the blank computer screen.

"But that's a lie. The truth is I don't want to be told 'no.'"

Shahnaz laid her arm over Irum's shoulder and gave her a squeeze. "You're good for each other, you and Amir. You'll find the courage to talk with your parents when the time is right. I know it."

—••—

Just before the first pick-and-drop car was scheduled to leave the office in Muzaffarabad's well-to-do Upper Chattar district, Shahnaz's mobile rang. It was her mother, and Shahnaz felt a wash of relief that she could talk to a wiser, older woman about how she was feeling. "Ammi, how kind of you to call."

She sat back down in her chair, mouthed to Irum to tell the driver to go on without her. She wanted private time with her mother. At first she listened to the saga of the previous night's visit to the home of Javed, the Khan cousin that Rabia seemed to be set on marrying. "His parents were condescending, Shahnaz, as though we're not worth their time, and yet they're continuing this negotiation. It's odd. They waited a whole month after coming to our house before issuing the invitation to theirs, which doesn't sound promising, but they've checked with Abu's employer, and I think they had a long talk with Sohail and Maryam. At least, the mother made some reference to Sohail which must have meant she'd asked them about you and us. I can't figure them out. Are they courting us? Are we in competition with families of higher social status—I just don't know."

Shahnaz saw the hall lights go out, signaling that the other staff on the first floor were leaving. Amir stuck his head in the door. She waved to him. "Good night. I'll take the next car." Then she leaned back and her chair gave its signature squeak. "Sorry, Ammi. I heard your worries, but not why you haven't said 'no' to the family. What did *you* think of them?"

"Oh, dear." Her mother sighed. "I don't like them much. They're keeping an uncomfortable distance, and it doesn't feel as though their home is a happy one. I own that it's elegant. The carpets have come down through generations; the windows had thick drapes in deep colors. The living room was warm, in every corner, and we drank from crystal."

"But you didn't enjoy it."

"No." A long silence. "If this were a husband for you, the answer would be 'no.' You're so sensible, so attuned to how others are feeling. But it's Rabia. Maybe he's right for her. She's certainly made up her mind he's the one."

"Yes, he's all she can talk about." It was classic Rabia determination. Like when she was ten and wanted to wear make up. Ammi had forbidden it, but Rabia convinced a friend to buy some make-up and keep it for her. She'd walk to the friend's house before school, put it on, and then wash it off before coming home. Until her teacher called Ammi.

"Shahnaz, would you talk to her?"

Shahnaz couldn't imagine that she could sway any decision her sister had made. She'd had no effect on her steam rolling sister even last summer when Rabia had snuck out to meet a group of friends whom Abu had forbidden her to see. Yet, she agreed with Ammi that this choice of husband didn't seem destined to provide happiness for Rabia. "I'll try, Ammi."

"Let me get her."

This was not the conversation Shahnaz had hoped to have, and she felt a sudden panic that another burden was settling on her shoulders. What to say?

"Shahnaz," Rabia said with a rush, "I'm so glad you called as I have to tell you what Ammi said about Javed's house. Do you know it has ten or eleven bedrooms? Ammi wasn't sure how many. And she saw one bathroom that had the cutest pink tiles with delicate bouquets of pink and white flowers painted on them. I think that's enchanting. A house for a princess! Oh, and the carpets. So thick that they left bits of lint on the tops of her shoes. Oh, and when they were over here, you wouldn't believe the incredible shalwar kameez that his mother was wearing. Ammi told me all about it. To die for. It had..."

Shahnaz couldn't bear to hear more of wealth and privilege. "Tell me about what Ammi and Abu say about Javed."

"Well, you know them. Always putting down what I want."

Shahnaz smiled at this exaggeration, pleased that she could not be seen. "Tell me more about what he's like. I don't have a complete picture."

"Abu says he's likely to get a promotion and maybe move to a larger branch of the bank, in Lahore or Karachi. I mean, Islamabad is okay but it's a backwater compared to the bigger cities. And maybe he'll think about moving to Dubai or the Emirates or even London. Wouldn't that be just unbelievable?"

Shahnaz laughed. "You sound sure that it would be great." She paused for a moment, bringing her negotiation skills to the forefront of her mind. "Rabia, one thing I've found in my marriage is how important it is to think about the family you're moving into. It's not just the husband—though he's important—it's also all the other members of the household who..."

"Oh, Shahnaz, don't worry so much. Javed is most likely going to be transferred away from the family, and we'll have our own house and lots of servants. I won't have parents and older brothers around like you do."

It sounded as though Rabia had figured it all out, that there was no crack of the door through which Shahnaz could maneuver the conversation. "Rabia, I'd like you to promise me something."

The voice came back full of suspicion. "What?"

Shahnaz rubbed her forehead. "Promise me that the next time

we talk you'll tell me lots more about Javed, whether he's kind to his sisters, what he wants from marriage, what he likes about his job. That kind of thing."

"How am I supposed to find out stuff like that?" She sounded annoyed.

"Ask Ammi lots of questions about him. She or Abu or Auntie will find out."

Rabia hesitated. "Oh, all right. I guess I could do that."

—•—

As Shahnaz opened the door to the Khan house that night, she could hear Raja Haider yelling. Her first sight was of Noshaba's face, squeezed taut in fear, as she stood before her husband and clung to her squalling baby. Her next sight was Raja Haider's open maw and raised arm brandishing his roll of blueprints.

"Put that baby down. Make her stop crying. You have no idea how to deal with children. Where's Shahnaz? She's supposed to be in charge now. That girl is never where you want her to be."

Quietly, Shahnaz stashed her canvas tote behind the end table, her body awash in determination, adrenalin pumping through every artery. She was not going to be the cause of Noshaba being beaten. She was going to stand up to this man. Her mind flashed back to a string of evenings when she was preparing for a school debate. Abu had thrown a series of retorts at her and given her one minute to counter each. He'd taught her to make perfect arguments, use different approaches, and suppress personal feelings until she was convincing. With his voice coaching her now, she inhaled deeply. This gruff man would learn that the women in his house had valid reasons for their actions.

Walking toward the couple, she extended her arms. "May I take the baby, Noshaba? I'm so sorry to be late. I know how you count on me." She scooped Riffat from her mother's arms and felt a tug on her trousers. She looked down to see Zainab, thumb glued to her tongue, leaning into her mother's legs. "Ah, sweetie, are you here, too? Come, let's find ourselves a quieter place to play." She took the child's hand and started toward the bedrooms.

As though having a sudden thought, she stopped and turned back to her brother-in-law. "I'm so sorry, Raja Haider, that I wasn't here earlier. I realize there's no adequate excuse, so allow me to beg your pardon and take both children with me. I'm sure you and Noshaba would like some time on your own—perhaps to review those blueprints?"

She wondered if she'd gone too far. Her brother-in-law's face had drained its red anger, which she hoped would erase an impending beating of Noshaba, but in its place was a sort of astonishment that might earn her retribution. Ah, well, she thought with an inward "hoorah," she would be polite—even solicitous—over dinner. Her Abu had also taught her that a debate should end with a handshake and congratulations to the opponent for a good effort. She would find something on which to compliment him at the meal.

Sohail took charge of the conversation around the supper table. He had spent much of the day with a joint task force of the forestry and justice ministries. Instead of eating, he pushed the pieces of meat around his plate. "The timber mafia are taking over. There's no will in this government to stop them. The justice people say their hands are tied. By whom, I asked. And how can we let that happen?" His hands flew up to enforce the question. "My people say they can't move against the mafia without the clear knowledge that the courts will prosecute those arrested." He dropped his head onto his open hands, shaking it back and forth. "I'm too old for this. Someone younger, with more energy, needs to take up this struggle."

Maryam replied, "You know you're the best man in Kashmir for this post: such experience, such dedication. Today is just one of those bad days when things look impossible."

Sohail looked up at her, his face sagging, and pushed his chair back from the table. "I think, my dear, that I will go rest." Using his arms to hike his body upward, he rose and shuffled toward the door, massaging his left arm.

When he had closed it behind him, there was silence as the adults looked at each other. This depression was unlike Sohail, usually so thoughtful and optimistic.

Turning her gaze back to her children, Maryam broke the mood. "I believe I'll give him a few minutes to get comfortable and then take in some tea." She called to the cook and gave him the order, and then brightly asked her children a question that was destined to encourage them to chatter.

Raja Haider, who had seemed to be off in his own cloudy sky, cleared his throat and glared at Shahnaz. "Why were you late today?" He shifted his gaze to Naseer and then back to Shahnaz. "It's your duty to help Noshaba in the afternoons. She's been lenient with you, and I've spoken to her on that point more than once."

As she listened to Raja Haider, Shahnaz could see Noshaba's pinched face. She sent her what she hoped was a reassuring smile, and answered her brother-in-law calmly. "I am sorry. I had a phone call from my mother and I didn't feel I could either talk to her in the car where others could hear or call later. She was upset." This felt good, this exchange. Raja Haider was listening; maybe her earlier challenge to him had had the effect of opening discussion.

Raja Haider addressed Naseer. "Shahnaz is now a part of *this* family, brother, and I expect you to make sure she honors her commitments here."

Naseer served himself more cauliflower with chilies, took a bite, and asked his mother to compliment the cook.

Shahnaz was surprised, even awed, by her husband's delay in answering. She watched the color rise again on Raja Haider's throat and face. She looked down at her lap, hoping she looked penitent and praying she could stifle her smile. Naseer was even more daring than she.

As Naseer took another bite of vegetables, she stole a look around the table. The younger children were looking jerkily from one brother to the other, Noshaba huddled into her chair like a kitten into its mother, and Raja Haider looked like his high blood pressure would burst out his orifices. Only Maryam was eating, and her chewing was out of tempo.

Naseer leaned back in his chair. "It's interesting that you find her disobedient. I don't have that experience, but then I ask her politely to help. Perhaps that makes the difference?"

Shahnaz transferred her gaze from her husband to Raja Haider. In her head, she was cheering on her husband. In her heart, she feared a violent response.

A sharp scraping noise signaled that Maryam had pushed back her chair. "Excuse me, but I need to check on Sohail. Please, finish your dinner." And she walked in a sedate manner toward the bedrooms. Her children watched her retreat, the mood somber, the argument on hold.

Shahnaz excused herself to tend to the baby and spent most of the next few minutes wondering how she had dared to stand up to Raja Haider, whether retribution would follow, and how it was Naseer dared to challenge his brother.

Thankfully, Riffat drifted into sleep, and as Shahnaz settled her on the bed, Naseer opened the door.

"Ah, good," he said in a clipped tone. "Abu needs us, Shahnaz. He's too weak to walk. We've got to get him to the hospital."

"What's wrong? What happened?"

"He tried to get out of bed and fell. His color's ashen, his breathing's ragged...He needs a doctor."

Frightened at what such symptoms suggested, Shahnaz

gathered up the baby and hurried with her husband to Raja Haider's room.

Naseer did the talking. "Brother, we must get Abu to the hospital. Help me carry him to the car. Shahnaz will come with us."

Raja Haider had thunderclouds on his forehead as he stood to his full height. "What is this? She cannot go. I'll go."

Naseer changed his tone to a plea. "Please, let's not argue. Ammi wants her. She's a nurse. Help me get Abu to the car. He can't walk and he's muttering gibberish. He may be dying." Then Naseer took his brother by the arm and pulled him toward the door.

Shahnaz handed the baby to Noshaba. "I'll come back when I can. Will you be all right?"

Noshaba nodded.

When the men had carried Sohail to the car, Maryam insisted he be strapped into the front seat, beside the driver. Then she turned to her eldest son and waved him toward the house. "I have no patience with you, Raja Haider. I want you to stay here and take care of the younger ones, and I expect you to obey. Shahnaz, Naseer, get in the back. We're leaving *now*."

Shahnaz looked back at an astonished Raja Haider while Maryam gave orders for the driver to hurry.

The hospital comprised two truck shipping containers, like those on the backs of semi's or railroad cars, though these containers sat on the flat dirt lot that had held the proper hospital before the earthquake. Shahnaz and Naseer climbed the cement block step into the metal container on the left to find a reception area, an examining room, and a small adjoining storeroom that looked like it held supplies and pharmaceuticals. They reported in to the nurse and asked the chowkidar to help them carry Sohail. The nurse directed them to take him to the other container, where they could lay him on a bed. She followed as the men settled Sohail in the double room to the left of the doorway and took up the phone in the small nurse's station to call the doctor. While they waited for his arrival, she charted temperature, blood pressure, and rate of respiration.

Maryam fluttered about the sparsely furnished room. "It's too cold in here, Naseer. We need to bring a heater from home." As Sohail rolled his head back and forth, she felt the pillow and declared that he must bring two of those from home as well. When she settled into the chair the nurse brought, she found her husband's hand, folded into a claw under the blanket. "He's far too cold. Bring the heavy quilt from our bed, too."

"Ammi?" Naseer said, laying his hand on her shoulder. "I'd like to stay here and be with you when the doctor comes. Would it be all right if Shahnaz collects what you need?"

Maryam rubbed Sohail's hand between hers. "Yes, yes, the nurse is here. Shahnaz can go."

Following a quick conversation with her husband, Shahnaz took her list out to their driver and accompanied him home. She wondered if the family had a thermos that she could fill with hot tea—it did look as though this would be a long night—and perhaps an extra sweater for each of them and Maryam's warm socks. Energized by her responsibility, she strategized: she'd give the list to Raja Haider, let him find things and assign her tasks. She'd avoid arguments and insist on speed. Sohail did not look good.

Her brother-in-law met her at the door. "How is he?"

"There's no change. When I left, Dr. Irshad hadn't seen him yet. Ammi gave me this list of things to bring." She handed him the hastily scrawled note.

He eyed her with suspicion, then scanned the list. "You take care of the bedding and clothes. I'll get the heater and extra gas."

It took her only a few minutes to ask the cook to fill a thermos, send Nooran to find sweaters and wool socks, and tell the younger girls to tie up the blanket and pillows. Shahnaz then ran to her bedroom to collect warm shawls for Naseer and herself and stopped to let Noshaba know what was happening. When she returned to the living room, all five of Sohail's younger children were lined up with the packages before them. "Where's Raja Haider?"

Jamil answered. "We didn't have an extra gas canister. He's gone to my uncle's in the car."

"Oh." She looked at the line-up of anxious faces. "Thank you all for your help. Why don't we sit down while we wait?"

Fifteen-year-old Qadir stationed himself near the front door. "I'll watch for him."

"Good."

Nooran asked, "Is it a stroke?"

"I suspect so."

Thirteen-year-old Rizwana's voice whispered, "Is he going to be all right?"

"I don't know. One of us will call or come tell you as soon as he's been seen by the doctor."

After twenty minutes of waiting and exchanging worried remarks, Qadir opened the door and Raja Haider breezed in, a gas canister under his arm. "That took longer than I'd hoped."

Shahnaz jumped up. "I'm glad you found one. It's exactly what they need."

He looked her up and down. "Do you know how to attach this?"

How very helpful of him—what a different man he was tonight. "I'm afraid I don't, but Naseer will. Now, can I leave your anxious brothers and sisters in your care? I promise to call with any news."

"Yes, yes, of course." He picked up the heater and told his brothers to bring the rest of the bundles to the car. When the car was packed, he held Shahnaz's door open. "Take...take good care of him."

"We will, I promise."

At the hospital, Dr. Irshad was seated by the bed, folding his stethoscope. Shahnaz admired this man with the magic hands. He was well over six feet tall, but it was his long fingers that captured her eye. They were at least an inch longer than hers, she was sure, yet delicate in their movements. He offered Shahnaz a grave smile and then carried on the argument he had been directing to the family, drawing pictures with his hands.

"He should be in PIMS—the Pakistan Institute of Medical Sciences in Islamabad. He's had a stroke and his left side is paralyzed. He needs some tests that I just can't do here. Well, you can see for yourselves we don't have the equipment." He pointed to the corners of the nearly empty room. "We only got the beds a month ago. There's no heat, only a bare light bulb which only works a few hours a day. How they think we can treat people here is beyond me." He shook his head several times, then leveled an index finger at them all. "He's going to need rehabilitation. Insh'allah, they will be able to offer him that. But—and this is a large but—I don't think it's safe to move him now. His blood pressure keeps dropping dangerously low, and I'm afraid he wouldn't survive the ride. Let's wait until tomorrow and see if he's stabilized." He unfolded his lanky frame, bag in hand, shook Naseer's hand, nodded at the women, and left the room.

7

In the week after his stroke, Sohail's blood pressure continued to fluctuate, and the doctor would not permit him to leave for the superior facilities in Islamabad. The family reorganized its activities so someone stayed with him at all times. It was generally agreed that women were better at tending the sick, and most of the time Maryam insisted on being with him. But with no food, no heat, and only a toilet and tiny sink for washing up, Maryam needed breaks at home. Shahnaz was an obvious choice and repeatedly offered her services. After skipping dinner for the second night in a row when the nurse called to say Sohail was restless and moaning, Maryam allowed Shahnaz to relieve her. Sohail was relaxed in Shahnaz's company, as though he felt safe, so, after work, Shahnaz had the Peace driver drop her at the hospital. She and Maryam discussed Sohail's progress, out of his hearing, and then the family driver took Maryam home for a much-needed nap, shower, and dinner. Naseer brought dinner to the hospital about eight o'clock, fed his father, and tended to his personal needs. Shahnaz returned home after their dinners-for-three and cared for the baby for a couple of hours before falling into her own bed.

Sohail had diminished to a frail old man in just a few days.

With his left side paralyzed, he could not even shuffle to the bathroom. His left arm was frozen in a crooked position and his hand locked into a claw that could scratch at what he wanted but not reach for it or hold on. Though he seemed to understand what was said to him or asked of him, his speech was unintelligible and he found his inability to communicate as frustrating as did his listeners. Maryam, Naseer, and Shahnaz had all taken to asking questions that could be answered by a nod or shake of the head. They found themselves doing a good deal of head shaking as well in their processing of what had happened to this smart, dedicated, articulate man.

Once, when Naseer had to leave for a training program in Peshawar, Raja Haider came for the evening. But that only happened the one time. Maryam told Shahnaz, in a whispered conversation outside the container, that he had so upset his father that Sohail hadn't slept much of the night. Rather, he had bubbled rage from lips that could not pronounce the reasons. Maryam had called her oldest son just this morning to ask what had happened, and she'd been astonished—and appalled—at what he'd said to his father. Did Shahnaz know that Raja Haider had the audacity to say that he had been praying about the stroke and believed that God sent it to teach Sohail to live a stricter Islamic life?

Shahnaz's hand flew to her face. "How could he say such a thing?"

Maryam shook her head slowly, and took Shahnaz's arm and led her further from the trailer, well out of earshot of those inside the open door.

When they stopped, Shahnaz hugged her mother-in-law. "I don't understand him. I've never known Abu to miss his prayers. I know he fasted during Ramazan, even though the doctor had cautioned him. And that story you told me about your Hajj journey and how he gave you that gold bracelet at the Ka'aba, one he made himself? It just shows his strong faith. He gives from his heart as well as his wallet. What did Raja Haider mean?"

Maryam's hands shook as she wiped tears from her eyes. "He says Sohail doesn't always rise for morning prayer, he looks the other way when the younger boys skip prayers, he lets meetings run through prayer time, and he's given his wife and daughters too much freedom. My eldest son thinks it's against God's command to let Nooran become a doctor or allow the other girls to go to college." She swiped her eyes with the back of her hand. "It's that madrassa. They fed him these ideas, and now he's turned against us."

"What did you say back to him?"

"I got angry. I told him he was using religion to bully others and he'd never be the equal of Sohail." She looked down at the backs of her hands and inhaled a noisy breath. "I shouldn't have done that. I don't wish to have a war with my son. But he shouldn't have spoken to Sohail as he did."

"I'm so sorry. Please, please, go home and sleep. Raja Haider is wrong. We know he is."

Maryam dried her face and then straightened her dupatta over her hair. "We should never have sent him to that school, but we were young and the imam—Sohail's school friend—said it would be perfect for him. He'd know the Qur'an and grow up a good Muslim." She paused and looked off into the fading sky. Then she sighed and trudged the short distance to the car. "Well, we did learn from our mistake. The younger children went to school near home."

Shahnaz smiled as she closed the car door behind Maryam. Her mother-in-law had a fine sense of herself: you could count on her to speak her mind—and to recover from this trauma. She'd figure out a way to deal with her son. And meanwhile, Shahnaz treasured the stories she had told the past few nights, when Sohail slept. They were often tales of Naseer's childhood, about his love of stories, his favorite books, his kindness to his younger siblings, and his talent for languages. Some had been about Sohail and their marriage. As she ambled back to the trailer, Shahnaz replayed Maryam's description of her and Sohail's struggle to learn English in their middle and high school years. Both had spoken Kashmiri at home and Urdu in primary school. Naseer, on the other hand, inhaled these three languages plus Arabic and had even studied some French along the way. Maryam often patted Shahnaz's arm, assuring her that "He's a good man." Shahnaz could only nod in agreement as her throat tightened with tears.

—•—

Without Sohail and Maryam's steadying presence, the household changed: Raja Haider took the reins with a vengeance. For the first few days, Shahnaz felt an increase in tension which she could attribute to nervousness over the condition of Sohail. But on a Monday in March she traveled far up the Neelum Valley and arrived home late. She had warned Maryam, who had stayed with Sohail, and Naseer, who would take dinner over as usual, but she had not thought to tell Raja Haider, as she expected to return in plenty of time to care for the baby. Her brother-in-law met her at the door, his face suffused with anger and raging high blood pressure. He ordered Noshaba to stand next to Shahnaz, to face him, and to explain why she had allowed Shahnaz to shirk her responsibilities. The women looked at each other, and Shahnaz could see that Noshaba was petrified into silence. Her eyes bugged out in panic, and the baby was screaming in her arms.

Shahnaz looked back at Raja Haider, wondering what words to use to justify herself and protect Noshaba. She felt a shiver of fear, of inadequacy, but conjured up the image of her father and looked her brother-in-law straight in the eye. "I'm sorry I'm late. I couldn't avoid it. A baby had inhaled amniotic fluid and was dying.

It took time to deal with the family's grief."

"She's responsible for you, and she didn't do her duty." And with a glance in her direction, he slapped Noshaba hard on the side of her head.

Shahnaz's jaw dropped in astonishment. Noshaba melted to the floor, and Shahnaz dived to make sure the baby didn't hit her head.

Raja Haider roared at Shahnaz to stand before him.

With the terrified baby in her arms, she scrambled toward the sofa. "Your daughter..." With rage growing in her chest, she tucked Riffat into the crease where the back of the sofa met the seat, willing the child to stop wailing. Seeing a small movement from the corner of her eye, she looked to the arm of the couch where she could just see the face of two-year-old Zainab, eyes widened and cheeks indented from sucking her thumb into her mouth. With angry determination, she turned to face Raja Haider. "How can you beat the ones you love? Do you care so little for them?" She curbed her own desperate desire to hit him, and bent to pull Noshaba up from the floor. Her sister-in-law's face held terror and she shook off Shahnaz's hands. So Shahnaz stood alone, her mind picking at the lessons her husband had told her about dealing with Raja Haider.

"You must learn obedience." He pointed at Shahnaz with one hand and slapped her cheek with the other.

She groaned with the intense throb of pain along her jaw and staggered into the sideboard, just catching herself from falling. Tears sprang into her eyes, but she fought them with internal rage. Slowing, she rotated her head to face him again.

He closed the distance between them and punched her shoulders with the heel of first one hand and then the other. "I set the rules in this house, and you *will* obey." His jabs punctuated the sentences.

If she were a man, she knew she'd hit back, but the force of his blows made her stumble and fight for balance. Taking a conscious breath, she looked him in the eye, her peripheral vision checking on the fists at his sides. "Your father is still alive. I obey him and my husband."

"I'm in charge of this house." His hands unclenched and clenched again.

"That doesn't give you the right to beat all of us." She felt a tear coursing down her cheek and refused to break her intense concentration by brushing it away.

"Our imams teach that men must take charge. This is a scourge of the modern age: women like you thinking they can do the jobs of men."

Noshaba, still cowering on the floor, reached for Shahnaz's sleeve.

Shahnaz shook off the probing hand, her mind racing over Qur'anic verses. "I can't believe that gentle man who Sohail brought home to dinner, his imam, would say that violence is the way to take charge. His Islam is a religion of peace. He told us how he welcomed foreigners—men and women—after the earthquake, struggling to speak English to thank them for tents and supplies." She realized, with a flash of fright, that she didn't honestly know how this imam felt about men beating women or women's rights, but she wanted to keep Raja Haider talking. She watched his chest rise and fall as though he was engaged in exhausting physical labor, his fists still tight.

"I'm not talking about that weakling. My school had *educated* imams who understood that beating is the way to obedience."

Shahnaz's jaw dropped at this distorted idea. "And you think the beatings made you a better Muslim and a better man?"

The baby screeched, deflecting Shahnaz's attention with her thrashing fists.

Then Raja Haider came at her, palms raised. "How dare you

question my teachers. What do you, a woman, know of sacred teachings?" He swung first his right arm and then his left, hitting her face with the back of each hand and shoving her into an end table. Its lamp crashed to the floor, and Shahnaz followed, landing hard on her hip. Her face flamed with pain, and she tasted blood from her split lip. He might well have broken her jaw. Pushing on the hand that had stopped her fall, she shifted her weight and gasped at the streak of pain from her hip down her leg. With eyes closed, she tried to breathe deeply to control the screaming of her outraged muscles. He was a mad man, out of control, and she was making him madder.

She groaned and let her body slip to the floor. Pain coursed down her side, her face throbbed, and her anger boiled. She wouldn't let him win, but she couldn't get up, not yet.

Riffat raged on, giving voice to Shahnaz's feelings.

Raja Haider loomed over his sister-in-law, his arm swinging across the wreckage. "Now clean up this mess and get it through your head that, in this house, you *will* do as I say."

Noshaba crawled to her side and laid her hand on Shahnaz's arm. "Stay still. Please."

Shahnaz nodded, eyes closed, nursing her pain.

Raja Haider yelled, "Noshaba, clean this up. Now!" He pointed to the bits of lamp and light bulb decorating the carpet.

After another gentle rub of Shahnaz's arm, Noshaba rose and stumbled toward the kitchen.

"Where are you going? I told you to clean up."

She squeezed her arms across her body and bowed her head. "To get the broom. In the kitchen."

"Then move."

With a glance back at Shahnaz, Noshaba jogged into the hall.

Raja Haider nudged Shahnaz with his foot. "Stop play-acting. Get up."

Coming first to her knees, she stopped to wait for the passing of a wave of pain, then used the end table to push herself to her feet. Her head spun, and she had to press a hand against the wall to stay upright. Her eye caught a small movement as Zainab, curled into a fetal position at the end of the sofa, kicked her body behind it.

"Useless." Her brother-in-law stomped off toward the bedrooms.

Limping to the sofa, Shahnaz patted Riffat, then sank to the floor and lifted the two-year-old into her lap. It took soft words and much caressing to convince Zainab to unclench her muscles. When Noshaba scuttled back into the room, she gathered Riffat into her arms and nursed her. Blessedly, they shrank into the silence.

With the children in their arms, the women iced their bruises. Shahnaz's left eye was closing and her jaw on that side swelled so much it was difficult to speak. She could not imagine chewing. The two of them did, slowly, clean up the broken bits. Shahnaz spent much of the time on the floor, holding Zainab and picking bits of glass from the threads of carpet. Noshaba swept. As soon as she could, Shahnaz took Noshaba's proffered arm, invited Zainab to take her other hand, and hobbled back to her room. Noshaba found her more ice to place against her face and heat for her hip and then left her to put the children to bed.

It was in the shadows of their room that Naseer found her. He was livid, speaking through clenched jaws as he paced the room. "My sisters met me at the door. I can't believe he did this." He perched on the side of the bed and pushed her hair back from her face. She flinched.

"Oh, I'm sorry. I didn't mean to make it worse."

She reached out for his hand. "You haven't." Though her left eye was almost shut, Shahnaz could see with her right that her husband's face was seamed like that of a man twice his age. The sinews in his arms looked like steel rods. As he stood and began again to pace, she watched his fingers flex, form fists, and then flex again.

"Tell me what happened. I need the details." He stopped at the end of the bed.

She sat up, lowered her legs carefully over the edge of the bed, and in words that missed their consonants in her attempts not to aggravate her split lip, described what had occurred. Her husband's hands grasped the teak bedstead as he leaned in to catch her story. When she finished, he thanked her, strode to the door, and snapped it closed behind him.

She cried then that she hadn't been able to stop her brother-in-law, that her life had suffered its own earthquake. Would her furious husband be hurt as well? Was this a sample of her future?

When Naseer returned, an hour later, she searched his face for any marks but could only see those deepened lines across his forehead. "Tell me, please." She pushed herself to a sitting position against the head of the bed.

His shoulders sagging, Naseer dropped his weight into their chair and sat with his hands hanging between his legs. "I apologize for all this. I should've protected you better. I didn't think it'd come to this. I didn't imagine my father would be sick, and I thought it would be years before *he'd* be head of the household. Oh, Shahnaz, I'm so sorry."

She shook her head and winced. "Ah...It isn't your fault."

"Whose fault is it? God's?" He laughed that sardonic sort of cackle that wasn't funny at all and flung his body back against the chair. "I don't believe in that sort of God, the one who smites us when we err and brings famines and earthquakes to test us." He looked up at her, eyes brimming with tears. "I told him you were *my* wife and I alone could discipline you. I tried to use his language, his beliefs. But he's so drunk with power, he wasn't listening, can't hear any arguments but his own. He's asked that you wear black and cover your face, and he wants me to make you stop working.

I argued with it all, but I had to compromise. He is…much as we don't like it…he is head of the house. So, I said you'd cover, but you had to keep working."

Naseer allowed one side of his mouth to turn up. "The only other choice is to leave the house."

Shahnaz struggled to take it all in: wearing black and speaking through a veil. If she refused, she'd now be disobeying her husband as well as facing more beatings from her brother-in-law. This was it, her nightmare come alive. She closed her eyes, hoping the salt of her tears wouldn't exacerbate her wounds. He was kind to suggest they move, but how could they desert his sisters? And Noshaba? And Maryam? These women were family. "Thank you for giving us that option. I need to hold on to it. But, until we know what's happening with Sohail, I couldn't move away and abandon the others."

His eyes filled with tears and he crossed the room to kiss the top of her head.

"My parents asked me, before we wed, if I could willingly obey." Shahnaz wadded up the sheet in her hands. "I told them I could. How very naïve of me. I'll resent every minute of covering." She thought again of the men whom she had served in her father's home and who had dismissed her like trash. Yes, she knew that feeling of resentment.

Naseer sat down on the edge of the bed and took her hand. "I know. I see your joy in choosing and wearing bright colors. It comes in unexpected moments, when you don't know I'm looking and you're laughing with your colleagues at pick-and-drop or when I visit the office and see how you light up the dull room." He leaned back, using both arms to balance on the bed, and stared at the wall. "I've been so protected by Abu, I never really thought about a future with Raja Haider in charge. How naïve of me. This is the tradition. It's how we've always done things. I don't know how to make it better, if we stay. I just don't know."

Early the next morning, the one slated for Sohail and Maryam to travel to Islamabad, Shahnaz stared at her closed purple eye, blackened cheek, and crusty lip in the mirror and probed around her eyes to make sure no bone chips or breaks were evident. It all hurt with an endless aching, but even the damage to her hip hadn't gone through to the bones. She supposed she should be thankful for that small blessing. When she emerged from the bathroom, limping, she felt a mixture of anger at Raja Haider, worry over the safety of Noshaba and the children, concern over how she should behave at work, and embarrassment.

Naseer winced and took her in his arms. "I'm so sorry, so sorry."

She felt the tears come into her eyes and, as she reached to whisk them away, a shot of pain. She must remember to keep her hands off her face unless she was very, very gentle. Standing up straight, she savored her anger and a peculiar sense of righteousness. "He's not going to be a god to me. I refuse to accept that his beliefs are right."

Naseer held her shoulders, his touch light as a feather. "We'll fight this. I'll think of something."

She slipped her arms into her black abaya and buttoned it from her chin to her feet. It allowed only the edges of her red shalwar pants to show over her black shoes. The coat, seen in the mirror, diminished her, made her indistinguishable from the background shadows in the room. She grimaced as she swung the sequined black dupatta over her head and pinned it so no hair showed. Even its soft fabric irritated her swollen face. It was with a growing depression that she took a last glance at this dark image of herself.

Naseer donned his brown wool vest and stood behind her. "You're still a beautiful woman, Shahnaz."

She caught his eyes in the mirror and looked down. "Thank you."

"And you don't have to put on the abaya until you leave the house."

She nodded, looking up at him. "I know. I wanted to see myself as others will see me." She paused, turning from side to side. "I suppose I should focus on the fact that I'm warm, but mostly I'm angry." She pushed a bit of hair under the dupatta.

Naseer patted her shoulder. "Shall we go?"

She followed him out of the room.

All three of the Khan sisters were clad in black for the morning meal and all were silent. So, he'd extended his decree to all of them. Nooran shot a pained expression at Shahnaz. With a quick look at Raja Haider, now seated in his father's place at the end of the table, Shahnaz slipped into her place next to Nooran and squeezed her hand. She felt a small piece of paper push into her palm, so she bent her head as though praying, and read it. *I called Ammi.* Shahnaz squeezed Nooran's hand again and then served herself a Pakistani omelet. Insh'allah, she would be able to chew it and the chilies would provide her with some zip. Looking at the severe line of girls between herself and Raja Haider, she hoped the chilies would strengthen them as well. What a profound effect this man had had on the household in only a week.

Before exiting the house, the girls gathered before the door to secure their hijabs. Each carefully pleated and pinned her black dupatta so one long end of material crossed over the bridge of the nose and was secured with additional pins on the other side. Only their stricken eyes could be seen as they sent supportive messages to each other. Shahnaz broke the silence. "C'mon. Let's go." She was amazed at how muffled her voice sounded, even to her own ears, and tried to resign herself to that diminution of personhood.

Usually the Peace driver tooted his horn when he reached

their driveway, their servant opened the gate, and the two chatted until she reached the car door. Today, Wali saw her as she opened the house's door and jumped down from the cab of the vehicle to take her canvas tote and open the car door for her. She thanked him and prepared herself for a day of people sympathizing with their eyes and their actions—as well as their words.

As she walked in the door of the office, several pairs of eyes scanned her apparel—and swollen eye—and conversation stopped for long moments. It seemed she picked up the Pied Piper's entourage on the way to her desk as a string of women followed her upstairs to the supervisors' room.

Arjumand, usually so forward, took Shahnaz's hand and asked softly what had happened.

Shahnaz had rehearsed an answer. "Raja Haider, Naseer's older brother, has asked all of us to cover." She smiled, touched her face, and added, "And he won't tolerate my being late or shirking family duties."

Irum brushed Shahnaz's temple. "How can you never be late? You know the trouble we have sharing vehicles. None of us gets home on time every day."

"I'll do my best." She stopped, wanting to make this simple and hoping to turn attention to something else. All the sympathetic eyes and murmurings made her want to cry, which she was determined not to do. Not here. Please, God, not here.

And then the tears started. "Please, everybody pray for Sohail to get better—soon."

Irum hugged her, someone handed her a tissue, and the women dispersed to their desks. When they were seated side-by-side, Irum leaned close. "I'll pray for Sohail and for you, and that Raja Haider learns to value who you are and what you do."

Shahnaz found her friend's hand and squeezed it. Then she struggled to get a tissue up to her running nose before its cloth covering absorbed the wetness.

As Shahnaz was gathering folders for the day's supervisory visit, Amir stuck his head in the door, looked about as though checking whether it was safe, and came in with his schedule chart. "Shahnaz, could you stay in the office today and help me with the records? Arjumand can take over the supervision you have scheduled."

She smiled at this obvious attempt to make things easier for her. "I'll be happy to help, Amir. But tomorrow I really have to go to Dharian Bambian."

He nodded. "Of course."

—••—

A small ray of light penetrated Shahnaz's gloom when she talked later on the phone to her mother, who sympathized with her daughter's pain at her new mode of dress and her ambivalence about obedience to the requirements.

Ammi proposed non-confrontation. "You're smart, Shahnaz, you'll figure out how to live under these rules."

"But I'm straightforward. I don't want to work around rules. I want to change them. That's what you and Abu taught me to do."

"Yes, I know. And now you need to try something besides argument."

"I can't lie."

"I didn't mean that."

"Oh." Shahnaz was not at all clear on the alternatives, but before she could question her mother further, she heard whispering at the other end.

Ammi spoke with some annoyance. "Rabia wants to talk to you."

"Oh, Shahnaz, it's all arranged. I'll marry Javed later this spring, probably in May, and the engagement party will be Friday,

March 30. You have to come down to Islamabad. You have to! Oh, and Naseer, too, of course."

Shahnaz took a deep breath. "I'll try my best."

Rabia ordered her not just to try but do it. "You know, there's talk of his going to London. What do you think of that? I may take an airplane for the first time in my life. I can see all the sights. I mean, *London*!"

Shahnaz heard the exclamation points on her sentences, and while she couldn't muster great enthusiasm, she tried her best to sound happy for her sister.

"Oh, and I did ask those questions you insisted on. Auntie says his sisters adore him, he wants a wife who'll make his home a welcoming place, and he likes banking because numbers don't lie—or something like that. See? He's going to be a fine husband! It's all working out perfectly."

Shahnaz could imagine her sister dancing about the room and didn't know what to say. Would it work out all right? Maybe numbers don't lie. Perhaps his bank staff reconciled the in-flow and out-go of rupees every day, but relationships weren't that clear cut. Did his sisters "adore" him or just obey him or ignore him? And had Rabia thought about how it would feel to be so far from her family? She'd even be far from *his* family and certainly from the support of people she knew and could count on. It wouldn't be Shahnaz's choice, for sure, but then, her current uncomfortable situation was nothing to strive for either.

A few bits of good news accompanied the need to travel south to Islamabad. She could take a couple of vacation days to be with her family, go to the engagement party, and help Maryam care for Sohail. It felt like such a release, the excuse to leave the confines of Raja Haider's dominion, and when she shared the news over dinner, she was a little embarrassed at the excitement in her voice.

Naseer said he'd be able to come down for the weekend and

join her. Raja Haider said the rest of the family would remain in Muzaffarabad. After that pronouncement, he scanned the faces of his sisters and sister-in-law and laid out his orders. "You, Shahnaz, will, of course, wear black and cover at all times when non-family members are present."

She thought of protesting that she would only be with women, and wouldn't need to cover at all. But it occurred to her that she hadn't asked if the party would be segregated or not. Ah, yes, better to be quiet. The time for arguments would come. She stared at her plate.

—•●—

There was a buzz of conversation two weeks later when Shahnaz entered the foyer of the office around lunchtime. Thankfully, she was sure it wasn't her face causing the commotion, as make-up covered what was left of the bruises. Irum threw her dupatta over her shoulder as she walked quickly to greet Shahnaz. "Have you heard?"

"Heard what?"

"The girls from Jamia Hafsa. You know, the madrassa next to the Red Mosque in Islamabad. The girls who took over the children's library. They've kidnapped three women, accusing them of being prostitutes."

"I don't understand." Shahnaz took Irum's arm and moved them out of the traffic flow. "Didn't the government do anything about their take-over? I haven't heard a thing about it, and it must be six or eight weeks ago they moved in."

"Nobody's talking. I mean, maybe the government's been negotiating, but none of us has heard about it. Nothing's in the papers."

"What about the head of the school or the leaders of the mosque?" Shahnaz was confused. Wasn't someone in authority dealing with this unlawful set of activities?

Irum shook her head. "All we know is that the girls are serious about their demand for Sharia law. It seems they're making themselves the arbiters of who's obeying the law and who's not."

A new burden settled on Shahnaz's shoulders. Here were these girls taking aggressive steps that could get them into serious trouble and change life for all the women in Pakistan. Like the students, all women would probably be required to wear black and cover in public. They might even be restricted to their homes unless accompanied out by a male relative—like the Taliban had done to women in Afghanistan. The thought made her sick with fear. Would the government agree to institute Sharia law? Did these young women understand what they were asking for? President Musharraf must be in a quandary. It would be hugely unpopular for him to order the police or the army to fight young women, yet he certainly couldn't agree to their demands.

When the cook announced that lunch was ready, the group moved into the dining room/conference room, found seats around the table, and helped themselves to the steaming keema and rice. With a thrill of disobedience, Shahnaz unpinned her hijab. Raja Haider need never know. To her, she argued, these men and women were family, and at least at meals, she was going to show them her "family" face.

Amir came to lunch late, more pensive than usual. "This kidnapping business. What a sense of power these girls must have."

One of the men stopped his naan midway to his mouth and then set the bite back down. "Yeah. Imagine what their clerics and teachers are telling them. Very clever of the men to put girls up to these actions."

Irum picked at her rice, her color rising. "I'm scared for the girls. You can just feel the violence in the air."

Shahnaz looked from one friend to the next. She thought the

authorities should make the girls leave the library, make them obey the law of the land. Here was that issue of obedience again, but now Shahnaz was surprised to find herself in favor of it.

The room was quiet for a moment, and then Amir spoke. "I can't believe that most Pakistani authorities—and even clerics—want to throw out our legal system and institute Sharia law."

"I agree," Shahnaz said, "but in a conservative madrassa like Jamia Hafsa, the girls have to obey their teachers and prayer leaders or they'll be beaten or sent home."

Irum leaned forward. "I don't like the girls' methods. They're using violence and not caring what anyone else wants."

Several people nodded, and Amir grunted. "I can't see a good ending."

Aware that her shoulders were clenched, Shahnaz realized it was from fear of what Sharia law would do to her life and the lives of the women she served. Tonight she was going to reread the Qur'an, get a better grip on its ideas of violence, especially toward wives.

When she reached home after work, she searched for her copy of the Holy Book, an English translation, which she understood better than the Arabic original, and found Sura Four, verse thirty-four, which told men: "If you experience rebellion from the women, you shall first talk to them, then (you may use negative incentives like) deserting them in bed, then you may (as a last resort) beat them. If they obey you, you are not permitted to transgress against them." The italics had been added by the translators, who also provided a footnote explaining that "God prohibits wife-beating by using the best psychological approach...Similarly, God provides alternatives to wife-beating: reasoning with her first, then employing certain negative incentives. Remember that the theme of this sura is defending the women's rights and countering the prevalent oppression of women. Any interpretation of the verses of this sura must be in favor of the women." A sense of justification ran through her, stopped suddenly by the realization that Raja Haider's version of the Qur'an wouldn't have the italics or the footnote. Once again, it would be his interpretation against hers. This was becoming very personal.

—•—

When Shahnaz arrived at her parents' house the day before the engagement party, Rabia was a whirlwind of joy and excitement. She grabbed Shahnaz in her arms and danced her in a circle, which had the effect of tearing Shahnaz's dupatta where it was pinned. When she protested, Rabia let her go. "Oh, you should take it off anyway. You're in our house."

"I will, if you'll give me a moment."

Ammi scurried into the foyer and embraced her older daughter. "It's so good to see you, my dear. We are in such a to-do with this engagement party. There's so much to be done." With her fingers, she traced the area around Shahnaz's eyes. "Much better, I think?"

"Yes, Ammi." It was such a comfort to be home, not to worry about whether a word might incite a beating or to brace herself for an argument. She separated from her mother's embrace. "But this party—isn't it at Javed's house? You didn't move it here, did you?"

Ammi pulled her dupatta off and flung it back over each shoulder, making sure it was an equal length on each side. "No, no. But plans seem to change daily. I can hardly keep up." To Shahnaz she looked more flustered than ever before. As if in answer to this thought, Ammi shifted her eyes toward Rabia and shook her head so surreptitiously that Shahnaz was sure she was not to probe further in Rabia's hearing.

The young woman in question pulled at Shahnaz's arm. "Come on, you've got to see the shalwar kameez I've had made. It's the most brilliant mustard gold with red and black embroidery. It's to die for! Right, Ammi?"

Ammi patted Rabia's arm. "Yes, dear, it's lovely. Why don't you show it to Shahnaz and give her some time to freshen up?"

Rabia kept up a constant patter of awe, astonishment, excitement, and bliss as she pirouetted up the stairs. While listening with one ear, Shahnaz allowed her mind to wonder what was upsetting her mother. It could be any or all of the things that had bothered her to begin with—the other family's arrogance, insensitivity, social status—or something new—expectations of their family for the dowry, removal of Rabia from Islamabad soon after the wedding, or a different issue. It didn't seem like something she could solve without more information, so she turned her attention to admiring the engagement attire.

The shalwar kameez Rabia drew out from the closet must have cost a small fortune. It looked like a family heirloom, the sort of intricate embroidery on soft shimmering silk that was done by older women for brides in a time when hours of hard work were expected for this sort of garment and women sat in the dimming light of their windows, squinting to focus on the tiny stitches. "Oh, Rabia." Shahnaz's fingers crept up to her cheek. "It's exquisite. I don't know when I've seen such delicate needlework or felt such fine silk." She let the fabric slip like water through her fingers. "I'm sure you could pass this fabric through a ring."

Rabia grinned. "I know. And I get to wear it Friday. It fits perfectly." She held the chest of the kameez in both hands, looking down at the embroidered bodice and feeling it with her thumbs.

Shahnaz unpinned her dupatta and unbuttoned her abaya. Each garment slipped to the bed, and she felt herself emerge from a cocoon. Patting the bed, she invited her sister to sit down and chat. "Tell me what's going on. Ammi seems, I don't know, nervous."

"Oh, it's nothing. You know Ammi." With her back to Shahnaz, she tucked the outfit back into the closet.

Shahnaz watched her sister, waiting for more, until the silence was embarrassing. "Well, yes, I do know Ammi, and usually she's not skittish. At least, I don't think she was like this at my wedding. Something's upsetting her. What is it?"

Her sister donned an annoyed expression, one hand on her hip. "I suppose you'll find out soon enough. It's just a little thing, but Ammi's blown it way out of proportion."

"Okay. What is this little thing?"

Rabia collapsed into their chair, leaning back and extending her legs. She fiddled with the fringe on her dupatta and glanced at her sister. "It's you."

"Me?" Shahnaz sat up straight, searching the conversations she'd had lately with Ammi. Her mother knew she'd been beaten, that she was working to reconcile obedience with her own desires. She'd agreed it was the right thing to do.

Rabia pointed to Shahnaz's black clothes. "It's that."

"My clothes?"

"The business of being so conservative, really."

"I don't understand."

Rabia let out a burst of air. "The party won't be segregated. Everyone will be on the lawn, and the buffet will be outside, too. See, Javed's family socializes with lots of international people, bankers and politicians, and the party will have lots of important people. I told them everyone being together was fine, but Ammi's worried."

Shahnaz paused before answering. A month ago she would have checked in with Sohail and Naseer, and this would have been easy. Now she wasn't so sure. "I...I don't know what to say." A wave of sadness swept over her: would Raja Haider forbid her from sharing this time of happiness with her family?

Rabia jumped from her seat. "Shahnaz, don't ruin this party. You've got to come or Ammi'll never forgive me! Can't you just not tell anyone?"

Shahnaz smiled for an instant at her sister's naiveté and then rested her forehead on her palm to think. She would tell Naseer right away and see what he could do. She wouldn't lie. That was not an effective strategy and it would mean that Naseer would have to lie as well. Besides, the family would find out, one way or another. "I'll see what I can do; I'll try, Rabia. Oh, I really do want to come."

—••—

"Naseer, what did he say? Can I go to the engagement party?" Shahnaz paced the length of the TV room, clutching the mobile against her ear. She had told her husband of the issue on Thursday afternoon, and he'd promised to do his best for her, but Raja Haider was not due home until late that night and she'd received no call back. Now it was nearly two o'clock on Friday and she still didn't know.

"Shahnaz, I've tried. I talked with him last night and appealed again this morning. He's adamant. He threatened to forbid your working. I had to compromise and agree you wouldn't go into mixed company tonight. I'm sorry."

She could hear the traffic in the background with lots of car horns beeping, and she imagined the swirling dust through which he walked home from Friday prayers. It was a tie to reality when her world seemed to be disintegrating. "This is too hard." Her voice quavered as her tears started again, and she reflected that she was crying far more often these days than any other time in her adulthood.

"I know. I'm angry, frustrated, unhappy—for you and for me. I don't want to run to Ammi or bother Abu. I'm almost sorry I asked Raja Haider. Maybe if we'd just gone together, it would have worked. But now, well, we can't."

She caught the sound of his jagged breath as he climbed the hill. Tears streamed down her face. How would she tell Rabia...and Ammi?

After punching the END button on the mobile, she sat for many minutes on the couch, allowing herself the time to mourn and then rehearse possible things to say. With a sigh she went to find her mother, who was in the girls' bedroom trying to calm Rabia down about the list of people invited to the party. Someone must have been left off, and Rabia was near hysteria. Shahnaz hung onto the door handle, debating whether she could bow out until this fit was over, when Ammi spied her and ordered her to come in. Together they talked Rabia down from her pique by assuring her that her friend would be invited to the wedding. Ammi would call and explain. Her friend would not feel slighted.

It was perhaps twenty minutes later when Rabia collapsed on the bed, turning her red eyes toward Shahnaz. "Did you talk to Naseer? It would be the last straw on this perfectly horrible day if you can't come." She stared into Shahnaz's eyes. "That's it, isn't it?"

Shahnaz heard the register of her sister's voice climb precipitously. Better to get this over with. She glanced at Ammi, whose hand covered her mouth. "I can't go. I'm so sorry. You know I don't want it this way, don't you, Rabia?" She sat down next to her sister and put her arm across her shoulders.

Rabia shook off the attempt at comfort. "This is just like you, Shahnaz. Everyone will ask 'Where's Shahnaz?' as though I don't matter, only you do."

Shahnaz flushed with anger and hurt. It was too much: being forbidden to celebrate with her sister and being repudiated by that same sister. As she stood up, intending to find sanctuary, she heard her mother snarl at Rabia, "You stop this mewling right now. It's Shahnaz who needs our sympathy, and I'm tired of your theatrics."

Rabia opened her mouth in astonishment.

Ammi pulled Shahnaz into an embrace. "You mustn't take this to heart. I know you're sad, and I will be, too."

Shahnaz cried on her mother's shoulder, thinking that she was a perfect example of disempowerment right now. Fear shot through her, increasing the tears, as she knew forbidding her to work was next. It was hard to breathe. She had to stop this avalanche that was burying her dreams. She would pray, many times each day, for help. Maybe she and Naseer should move out of the house. But how could she abandon the others?

When Naseer arrived that evening, he brought the news that Shahnaz was to go to the hospital early and enjoy a special meal with his parents. He, himself, would go to the engagement party as her emissary and take notes on all that was happening so he could tell her all about it later in the evening. He looked rueful. "I know it's not the same as being there, but I promise to do my best to see it through your eyes."

The tears came again, but she blinked them away. "Thank you."

With a heavy heart, she helped Rabia dress, greeted her female cousins and friends who came first to their house, and watched her husband dress in his best embroidered kameez. It was the color of a café latte that was largely cream. Before the family left, Naseer escorted her to a car rented for the evening and drove with her to the hospital. He waited until the delivery service brought their dinner, set out the plates, and served the meal. With a smile and a bow, he left Shahnaz with his parents for a quiet evening together.

Maryam kept up a continual patter of conversation as she fed Sohail. No one mentioned that the man diminished each day or that he ate almost nothing. Even the bites of rice she cajoled him into eating were difficult for him to swallow. Only sips of lassi slid down comfortably. Shahnaz felt comforted that he looked often at her and turned up the right side of his mouth in his best smile. Unfortunately, it looked more like a grimace, which Shahnaz noted only to herself.

It wasn't long before Sohail was exhausted, and Maryam and

Shahnaz sat without talking to allow him to drift into sleep. After he nodded off, Maryam dragged her chair close to Shahnaz's and patted her daughter-in-law's knee. "I want to tell you a story. It's one I haven't shared with my children."

Shahnaz was surprised and touched. She bent her head closer so their whispers would not disturb Sohail.

"You've noticed, I'm sure, that I rarely talk about my day. It's no business of my children what I do. None at all." She leaned forward to tuck the blanket under Sohail's arm.

Shahnaz held her breath, wondering what was coming next.

"When we were first married, I taught school. Did you know that?"

Shahnaz shook her head.

"Well, I did, until Raja Haider was born. I know I was supposed to be fulfilled by having a baby, but I wasn't." She pursed her lips for a moment, and two vertical lines appeared in her forehead, just above her nose. "I missed all my students and the other teachers, and I got to thinking I needed more to my days than a baby and home. So, I visited with the people at the education ministry who contract for textbooks. And in these years, I've written forty-five of them. What do you think of that?"

Shahnaz covered her mouth to silence the astonished "ah" that was surprised into being and then hugged Maryam. Whispering into her ear, she said, "I'm astonished. How did you do all that work with no one finding out? Did Sohail know?"

Maryam chuckled. "I was a little nervous at first, not being sure of his reaction, but he's proud of me and has supported the writing all along. He's brought me books for research, sometimes going all the way to Lahore or Karachi, and he's connected me with people on provincial textbook boards so I know what others are doing." She pushed threads of his hair off his face. "He's a good man."

Shahnaz held onto this movement of love. "Why haven't you

told your children?"

"At first, they were too young. And then I decided this was my secret, not public information."

"I think I understand, but don't you receive recognition for all this work? Certainly you've earned it."

Maryam patted her knee again. "My husband and the education ministry have given me recognition—and God, perhaps; that's enough."

Shahnaz sat back to muse on this revelation. Was Maryam saying she was on Shahnaz's side and would fight for her to be able to continue working? Was she suggesting Shahnaz must not talk to Raja Haider of things about which he would disapprove? Perhaps Maryam was saying Shahnaz could be quiet and get more of what she wanted. She needed to discuss this with her husband. "Ammi, is it okay if I tell Naseer?"

"Yes, dear, I think it's time he knew."

Shahnaz looked down and fingered her skirt. "Ammi, I'm pregnant again. I'd like to keep it quiet as long as I can, until I'm sure everything's okay."

Maryam clasped Shahnaz's hand. "I understand."

8

It was a little after eight the next morning when Shahnaz's mobile rang, showing Maryam's number. She and Naseer were sleeping in since Shahnaz had left her in-laws about midnight and had fallen asleep well before her husband had returned from the engagement party about three. When she looked groggily at the phone, she hoped it wasn't bad news.

"Ah, Shahnaz. Please, could you put Naseer on the phone? His must be turned off."

She pushed herself into a sitting position, alert to the anxiety in Ammi's voice. "Yes, certainly. He's right here."

Shahnaz held the phone out to her husband, who was beside her in bed wiping the sleep from his eyes. He raised his eyebrows, and she shrugged her shoulders to say she didn't know the reason for the call. A wave of fear broke in her chest. The news was bound to be bad.

"How is Abu?...Oh, no...Yes, I'll make the calls." Naseer pushed his legs over the edge of the bed, dropping his phone hand to his lap. "He's slipping away. It won't be long now. I'm to tell my siblings." He slewed his body around to face her. "Could you check with your mother to make sure my brothers and sisters can stay here with your family? Our cousins already have guests, it appears, and while Ammi can remain there, the rest of us can't."

Shahnaz laid her hand on his arm. "I'm so sorry, so very sorry. He seemed awfully tired last night, but I've kept hoping he'd turn a corner and improve. I guess it was not to be." She waited a moment for a reaction and then patted his arm. "I'll just be gone a minute." Noiselessly, she slipped on her robe and went to find her mother.

Within hours, on this gray Saturday, the Khan family piled their small suitcases in the foyer of Shahnaz's parents' house and made their way to the Islamabad hospital. In the small dark room, they took turns sitting next to their father's bed and saying goodbye to the man who no longer responded to them. His daughters cried as they held their mother's hands. His sons stood vigil. At one point, Zainab turned over her grandfather's hand to check for the sweets it often held and looked confused and angry when her father pulled her away. Noshaba, carrying the baby, crept in and out of the room, bringing food and tissues as the need arose. About ten at night, Shahnaz and Noshaba took the children and their sisters-in-law home to bed, leaving the men to support their mother.

Just before dawn on Sunday, Naseer woke Shahnaz to say that Sohail had died. As he sat on the edge of their bed, he reported that his father's raspy breathing had simply ceased. Maryam would not leave his body, but he and Raja Haider had come back to the house to pack up and have breakfast before they took the body to Muzaffarabad for burial.

At the morning meal, everyone crowded into the TV room, sitting on chairs or the floor around the large red cloth that held the plates of omelets and chappati and the bowls of fruit. Shahnaz felt deflated, like an abandoned balloon. Coming after the blow of missing Rabia's engagement party and the happiness of sharing Maryam's secret, this weekend felt like a series of aftershocks with the ground no longer trustworthy beneath her.

As she rose to check for fresh tea, Shahnaz heard Raja Haider clear his throat. Oh, no, not this morning. Looking up, she saw his eyes focused on his youngest sister, Rizwana. Shahnaz tensed as she looked at the thirteen-year-old in her spring-like shalwar kameez with its large violet iris in a verdant garden. There was such hope in that pattern, a sense that alongside death comes new life.

"I presume you have appropriate clothing with you, Rizwana?" His voice held no sympathy. "Just because I didn't comment on this in the hospital, don't think I haven't noticed you haven't worn black on this trip."

She looked hard at her fingers. "I...I..."

Shahnaz felt her hand crawl up to her face. Surely Raja Haider would not punish this young girl—not today.

Noshaba, clad in black, said, "We'd just started the laundry when Naseer's call came, and all of Rizwana's black clothes were wet. Since we'd be with family this weekend—in the hospital or here, I hoped she could be excused."

All around the red tablecloth, family members fell silent. Shahnaz's Ammi looked at Abu, but did not speak. The Khan women tensed as they awaited the inevitable chastisement. Shahnaz wondered that Noshaba had dared to attempt an explanation and watched, hand on cheek, as her sister-in-law continued to feed small bites of omelet to Zainab. Zainab had grasped her mother's skirt, and while she chewed obediently, her eyes opened wide in the fear that often characterized her face as she stared at her father.

"This is a matter of respect—to Allah, to my father, and to me. Surely one of you has clothing you can loan Rizwana." Raja Haider scowled as he looked from one female to the next.

Shahnaz knew that a part of the girls' resistance to the command to fully cover was their refusal to purchase more than one black abaya and one solid black dupatta each, but no one was going to wave that flag in Raja Haider's face.

Noshaba carefully wiped her hands of the oil that always stuck to chappatis. "I'd have loaned her one of mine, but she's already several inches taller, and it wouldn't be suitable. I'm sorry, but there didn't seem anything we could do yesterday but hurry into the car." Without looking at him, she proceeded to clean her daughter's hands just as thoroughly as she had done her own.

All eyes switched back and forth from the busy, apparently unconcerned Noshaba to the raging Raja Haider. His mouth opened and closed as if gaining momentum for a bold speech, and his body seemed to swell. He scanned the group, casting a long glare at Rabia, who was covered in bright yellow and red tulips, the kind of extroverted pattern that reminded one of a Van Gogh painting.

"Don't look at me," she said, "I don't have anything black to loan."

"Obviously." He scanned her from head to toes. "Modesty does not seem to be a trait you embrace."

"What an awful thing to say!" Her chest heaved. "My fiancé doesn't believe that. He thinks I'm perfect."

Shahnaz could see Rabia's color rise from neck to cheeks.

"Then you're fortunate, for I wouldn't allow you to marry into my family."

Rabia leapt to her feet. "And I wouldn't live with someone as obnoxious as you." She flipped her dragging dupatta over her shoulder and flounced out of the room.

Naseer scratched his head. "I'm afraid we're stymied on the black clothing. Perhaps we can let it go just for the trip home?" He stopped, holding his brother's eyes. "Would you like to call Ammi to see how soon we can leave or shall I?" He appeared calm, though Shahnaz knew what he had said constituted just as much rebellion as the girls' reactions. She willed herself to lower her hand and adopt her husband's calm.

Raja Haider pointed his finger at the younger women. "You

may not leave this house showing colors." His baritone voice stretched a little higher than normal.

In a shaky voice, Ammi spoke. "I may have something appropriate." She struggled to her feet, using her husband's shoulder as a prop. "Rizwana, come along and we'll look in my closet."

As her mother opened the door, Shahnaz reawakened to the fact that she had meant to ask for more tea and followed her Ammi and Rizwana out of the room. Her body flooded with relief that a solution had been found.

After a few words of instruction to the cook, she returned to the hall and debated what to do next. She could go back to breakfast, an action which held little appeal, try to find Rabia, though soothing her would sap more of her limited supply of energy, or she could go pack. Desperately, she wanted some quiet time to get command of her anger and give in to her powerful grief.

Rabia erupted from the downstairs bedroom. "I've got a few things to say to that man."

Shahnaz grabbed her arm and pulled her back inside. "Not now. Calm down."

"How can you live with that insufferable bull-headed jerk?" Rabia paced to the windows and turned back, hands waving. "He thinks he's God's gift to us all, that none of us would know how to behave if he didn't tell us! He's ruined this weekend for me, absolutely ruined it, and I can't believe you're agreeing with him!"

Shahnaz put her finger to her lips to quiet her sister and, when Rabia was within reach, caught her sleeve and drew her down onto the bed. "I know this should've been your weekend, and I'm really sorry we've brought our family trials here. Sohail's death has rattled all of us."

Rabia's face relaxed an iota. Shahnaz was sure she was at least listening.

"Even Raja Haider is shaken by it. He's got his father's mantle of obligations, and it's weighing on him." She thought this all sounded reasonable, though it had come out a little preachy, and she didn't believe it excused his actions. Oh, she knew he would grieve for Sohail, but he'd also rejoice, albeit quietly, at having his way in this family.

From the sharp drawing together of her eyebrows, Rabia was having none of it. "His being the oldest is not the issue and you know it. Abu has authority but he doesn't abuse it. Raja Haider's mean, Shahnaz, that's all there is to it: he's mean. He's a mad bee that stings everyone in his way."

Shahnaz sighed and felt her body droop. What to say? She was filled with grief for Sohail and had no desire to defend her brother-in-law. "I don't know why he's so angry."

"You shouldn't let him get away with this."

Shahnaz barked a short laugh. "Rabia, do you think I can change thousands of years of male behavior just because I *want* to?" She had a vision of hundreds of angry men standing one behind the other in a line that ran backward into the mists of time.

Rabia glared at her sister. "You've stopped even trying."

Shahnaz looked at the floor, feeling humbled. She hadn't initially bowed to Raja Haider's proclamations; she'd argued. Until the beating, when she'd cowered at his feet. What had happened to the strong-willed woman she'd once been?

—•—

It was nearly noon when the caravan was ready to leave Islamabad. Raja Haider had arranged for a vehicle to transport the body, his mother, and his wife and children. Sohail's car and driver would take the five youngest Khan siblings, and Naseer and Shahnaz would ride in Peace's double cabin pick-up along with others on the organization's staff who had taken the opportunity for a weekend in

Islamabad and were now returning to their posts in Muzaffarabad. Shahnaz's parents would come later in their own car.

After expressing their sympathy, the Peace staff sharing the truck relaxed into napping, providing Shahnaz the opportunity to exchange details with her husband. They reminisced about Sohail: what they so admired, the things he said that showed his wisdom, how much he was admired in forestry circles, how this stroke had changed everything. After a long silence, Shahnaz told her husband about her conversation about Maryam's writing, which brought a sad smile to his face, and he replied with a story about the engagement party.

"Rabia was magnificent, you know." Naseer's face softened with a smile. "She relished every moment of being the center of attention. She has this special way of walking, a sort of model's strut. When she came through the archway, everyone stopped talking, right down to the hired staff, and all eyes were on her—like paying homage to a queen."

"I'm so glad she had her day. But...but did a lot of people ask about me? She was so worried that the conversation would be about me, and that she'd be forgotten."

Naseer patted her arm. "Several people asked, and I said you weren't able to come but wished the couple well. I'm sure some people gossiped but not around me. Truly, it was Rabia's night."

"Good." She sat back, comfortable in the middle seat and with the knowledge that her absence hadn't caused any major problem. Then she found new tears in her eyes. Would her future be filled with these disappointments, these pleasures forbidden? Why did Sohail have to die? Would she be able to carry this baby to term? Was God testing her ability to obey, seeing how far she could stretch without breaking? Did He want Raja Haider's ideas to prevail? "Naseer, do you think your brother will forbid me from attending Rabia's wedding? I don't think I could bear that." Shahnaz looked down at her hands, just peeking out from under the black dupatta. The fear of such isolation gripped her lungs and made it hard to breathe.

"I don't know."

She saw him look out the window, anguish on his face, and sought a compromise. "I want to be a part of it, but I guess, if I had to, I could stay in the women's tent. But I don't want to be left out of the conversations and picture-taking. I'd feel that I was no longer a part of my family, that I was shunned." Her tears spilled over, dropping on the black shawl. Embarrassed at the thought of her co-workers seeing this emotion, she glanced around, saw that they slept, and lost herself in desolation. God, she prayed, please tell Raja Haider to follow his father's footsteps and please bless this new baby with a long life.

"Insh'allah, he'll see that his restrictions are too severe." Her husband echoed her prayer, but the hesitancy in his voice belied his words. After staring out the window for a few moments, he turned back to Shahnaz. "There's another side to my brother, one I saw for a few minutes last night. A white-haired man came into the hospital room, leaning heavily on a cane. Raja Haider immediately went to him, offered his arm for support, and helped him to a chair. He was so gentle as he asked who the man wished to see and then guided him to the right room. Maybe he saw Abu in the man. I don't know. So often he's gruff and unfeeling, I forget his compassion."

Shahnaz pictured the scene, forcing her brother-in-law into this role. Working to breathe more fully, she willed herself to recover optimism. Maybe he'd show such compassion at home. And then her mind jumped back to Rabia and the party. Was Rabia going to find compassion in her new family? Shifting her weight to turn toward Naseer, she said, "Tell me about Javed. What did you find out?"

Naseer looked at her for a moment. "I think he'll become a politician, eventually. I had the feeling he was working the crowd.

You know, introducing himself to everyone of stature, everyone he might need in the future. With me, he lectured about banking. He seems obsessed by the best way to run a proper Muslim bank. He didn't bother to ask about me, and I'm afraid he has me categorized as a no-count underling." He smiled. "Perhaps he's right."

"Oh, no, he's not. You're worth a hundred Javeds."

This time, he managed a sad smile. "Oh, Shahnaz, there's so much over which I have little power. I couldn't help my father get better. I've failed miserably at protecting you. I don't feel I'm worth a hundred of anything."

She felt her breath catch. Naseer had Sohail's temperament, his calmness, thoughtfulness, and caring that made it safe to share feelings, safe to obey in the confidence that he wouldn't ask too much. "No, no. You care about people, even those you don't know very well. You put them at ease. I can't imagine you lecturing a guest at a party, especially on a topic the guest isn't interested in."

"I suppose you're right about the guests, but I wouldn't be honest if I agreed to the rest." He smiled at her, fleetingly, as he shifted position.

She put a hand on his arm. "Tell me about Javed's sisters. What are they like and what do they think of him?"

"I don't know much. They were involved with their female cousins. I did hear your Ammi tell Rabia to mind her tongue around Sumeela, who made several snide remarks about Javed being immune to feelings. Who knows if that's true."

Shahnaz grew silent. She hoped Rabia was doing the right thing, marrying this man. Insh'allah, God would watch over her—though God seemed to be acting in perverse ways these days...

—•—

Sohail was buried alongside his parents in a small village outside of Muzaffarabad. Following tradition, his sons had ritually washed his body when they arrived home on Sunday, wrapped it in clean white sheets, and laid it on a charpoy, a bed of webbing usually stored in the servants' quarters. The men stayed with him through the night. Maryam refused to sleep and wandered in and out of the bedroom. Early Monday morning, a large group of male relatives, friends, and colleagues arrived to accompany the body to the cemetery. Maryam cried out and as the vehicle took the body away, she drooped into Shahnaz's arms. Shahnaz led her to the couch where she could hold her as she sat, weeping.

Later, when the graveside service had ended, relatives came to the house bearing food and condolences. By tacit agreement, Shahnaz stayed with Maryam in her bedroom, greeting the female guests, repeating over and over the events of the last month of Sohail's life, and escorting each group out to admit newcomers. Sohail's daughters were in their bedroom to receive the younger female guests. Noshaba took the responsibility of ensuring the guests had something to drink and to eat, and Shahnaz was certain that Noshaba would be moving like a wraith to check on the male guests in the living room—not inserting herself in the conversation or even entering the room but instructing the cook and driver to fill guests' needs. Every twenty minutes or so, she appeared at the door of Maryam's bedroom and invited the female guests to have more tea or soda or come to the courtyard to fill a plate with food.

Mid-afternoon, a large contingent of women from Peace came to pay their respects, and after they had spoken with Maryam, Shahnaz excused herself and took her colleagues into the garden. Following their expressions of sympathy, Shahnaz asked about her Lady Health Workers and who was watching over them. Irum had taken several, Arjumand the others. "Who has Bibi?"

Irum answered. "I do. She's fine."

"Could you tell her I still want to take Kameela to Islamabad—

if her husband has agreed?"

"She said he was coming around." Irum smiled. "Don't worry. I'll let you know what's happening."

And then the conversation turned to the latest activities of the girls at the Jamia Hafsa madrassa, the ones who had taken over the library. Goodness, Shahnaz thought, are they still in that building?

Irum caught her up on the facts. "Remember those three women the girls kidnapped? Two of them seem to be mother and daughter, the third a cousin or neighbor, and one of the younger women has a baby. Anyway, the girls claimed that they'd been watching the house and the women they've kidnapped were prostitutes. We all heard bits of information—like the girls have set up a Sharia court and found the women guilty and feel justified in killing them. I don't know if that's true. But the kidnapped women came out onto the library's porch last night and, in front of TV cameras and lots of media, cried for forgiveness and said they'd never behave this way again."

One of the others continued the tale. "They looked distraught, like they hadn't bathed in days or changed clothes. They also looked exhausted, so perhaps they hadn't slept."

Shahnaz was confused. "Why is this going on so long? Why isn't the government stopping them?"

Arjumand answered. "Nobody knows. But imagine what people would say if they sent the army or policemen to attack black-clad girls. Everyone would object. And, well, the government would be moving against Islam."

Gul, their finance assistant, took up the story. "Justice Chaudhry would have stopped this. He'd have figured out a legal way, but since Musharraf removed him, there's no help from the Supreme Court." She shook her head, looking down at the ground, and moved a small stone with the side of her shoe.

Shahnaz felt a wave of nausea as her body temperature rose

in the heat of the afternoon, a problem begun—only a little—with this pregnancy and enhanced by the extra layers of cloth in the abaya she had put on in case men wandered into the garden. "Shall we move inside where it's cooler?" she asked the group. "My room's just over there, and it'll be more pleasant."

The eight young women crowded into the shadowed bedroom and spread themselves across the bed and on the arms and seat of the chair. Noshaba came to ask about drinks and then disappeared to fill the order.

Irum asked, "How are you all doing—you, Noshaba, your sisters-in-law?"

It was a loaded question, and Shahnaz wondered for a moment if she should turn it off or answer it honestly. She decided to lean toward honesty about family affairs, even in the big group of her fellow staff. "We're all so sad: Sohail was the central pole holding up the family tent, and it feels like the canvas has collapsed. And...well, I'm afraid we're all a bit worried about what Raja Haider's going to do." She looked down at her hands as they crushed the fringe of the dupatta, wondering where her self-confidence had gone.

Gul responded, reaching out to touch Shahnaz. "You can't leave. We need you. You encourage us. You're our role model. The Lady Health Workers listen to you. They're all worried about not having you to back them up."

Murmurs from several other staff seconded these sentiments.

"Thank you, so much." Tears gathered in her eyes as she drank in the support of these women. "You know I want to stay on. But I'm pregnant again. And so much has changed here. We'll just have to wait and see."

When the Peace contingent left—in time for pick-and-drop at the end of the workday—Shahnaz and Noshaba shared the process of cleanup. For a while they discussed who had come, what foods had arrived, and the odd places people had left used glasses, but when the back rooms were restored to order, Shahnaz fell into a chair in Noshaba's bedroom, settled the baby on her lap, and asked her sister-in-law to sit for a moment as well. "Noshaba, you've been wonderful these last few days. You're taking charge in a lovely way—making sure we're all tended to." She paused. "Thank you."

Noshaba, still in her hijab, tucked her chin to her chest. With her head covered in black, she disappeared against the bed's stark headboard. "It's nothing. I'm only doing my job." She snuck a look at Shahnaz's face and then stared back at the bed so that Shahnaz saw only the dark mass of her sister-in-law's covering.

Shahnaz leaned forward to touch Noshaba's arm. "I was especially thankful that you explained to Raja Haider why Rizwana wasn't wearing black. That was very brave of you."

Noshaba returned a shy smile. "You started it."

Shahnaz started. "Me? I didn't say a thing in that conversation."

"No, not then. It was before. You were willing to take my punishment that day you were late coming home. It made me think about my responsibilities to the other women in the house, and I've been reading the sayings of Mohammad—Peace Be Upon Him—to try to understand. Do you know that, in his last sermon, our Holy Prophet said, 'Treat your women well and be kind to them for they are your partners and committed helpers'? That's what I want to be—to Raja Haider and to all of you."

"Insh'allah, I will be your helper as well." Shahnaz picked up Riffat and kissed her on the forehead and cheeks.

—◆•◆—

So many guests flooded the house in the days after the funeral that Shahnaz felt she'd taken on a full-time job of giving orders to the cook, serving guests, and cleaning up after others. The refrigerator was stuffed with food from those offering condolences, which was helpful as extra people often joined the family for dinner. Over and over, she and Noshaba combined leftovers from multiple dishes onto a single platter and reset the table and tea tray.

On the Thursday less than two weeks after the funeral, it was something of a relief to have only one extra couple for dinner, Maryam's brother Tanvir and his wife. This uncle had a constant twinkle in his eye, a handlebar moustache that was waxed upward into a smile, and a neatly trimmed beard, perhaps an inch long. His stomach pressed against his kameez as though proclaiming his pleasure in eating as well as in life. He held a high rank in the finance ministry and loved to prattle on about politics and government. After the fifth or sixth repetition of his surprise and sadness at Sohail's death and an appropriate pause, he turned the conversation to current events. From his deep-voiced regrets, his register rose. "So, have you all been following the story of the Minister of Tourism?" He looked around the table with some hopefulness. "Ah, no, I can see. Well, that's to be expected, I guess. It all happened last weekend and you were busy with other things." He took a large bite of chicken karahi, chewed for several moments, and then licked his fingers. "It seems she has been in France and was persuaded to try sky diving."

Raja Haider blew out his lips. "Puh. Silly thing for a woman to do. What does she want from sky diving?"

The uncle stared at him for a moment. "Yes, well, seems she wanted to try it and got herself tied to a French instructor and jumped out of a plane. I've always wanted to do something like that. Imagine being upstaged by a woman."

Raja Haider interrupted the flow again. "She should've been stopped."

Tanvir looked again at Raja Haider and then at the others as though checking whether he should go on. When Shahnaz stole a glance around, she saw most everyone focused on their dinner plates.

Tanvir cleared his throat. "Hmm. Well, Nilofar Bakhtiar wasn't stopped. And when she landed safely, she hugged her instructor. Caused no end of a ruckus."

"As it should," Raja Haider said. "Such a public insult to the words of our Prophet—Peace Be Upon Him. She should never have been given a minister's job, and she should be punished for touching an infidel—and a man, to boot. Disgraceful."

The uncle pointed his finger at Raja Haider, sitting as he was at the head of the table. "I don't know where you got your backward ideas, nephew, but it's time you updated them." He stuffed another bite of chicken into his mouth and chewed noisily. "And you do interfere with the telling of a good story. I don't know that I'll tell the rest of it."

With a glance at Raja Haider, Naseer smiled at his uncle. "Tanvir Uncle, I, for one, want to know what's happened."

"Good lad." Tanvir shot a swift glance at Raja Haider, then scanned the others at the table. "You remember all this to-do going on at the Red Mosque in Islamabad?"

Several people nodded.

"Turns out the clerics there have held Sharia court and issued a fatwa against Nilofar for intimate touching. They want her killed." He cleared his throat, popped in another large bite. "You wouldn't believe the flap." He shook his head, wiped his mouth with the back of his hand, and swallowed. "And what does our leader do? Hmm?" He lifted his eyebrows and looked around the table. "Musharraf has ordered protection for *her*, which is fine, but not a word does he utter criticizing the clerics, not a comment denouncing the fatwa."

Shahnaz heard him tut-tut several times to himself and felt her nascent optimism fade. The pendulum was swinging backward with a vengeance. As Raja Haider and Tanvir debated what might happen and what *should* happen, Shahnaz found her mind cycling back to her life a year ago. She had been so confident, proud of her job, honing her diplomatic talents during the day, spending evenings with a mixed group of friends and wearing colors. Now she stared with envy at Maryam's sister-in-law, who was dressed in an embroidered, bright blue shalwar kameez which she would display with ease as she walked out the door.

When the relatives had gone, Shahnaz carried the baby toward the corridor to the bedrooms, meaning to walk her to sleep. She was stopped by a call from Raja Haider: all members of the family were to meet in the living room.

Maryam and her younger children fanned out across the chairs and couch, with the youngest boy, Qadir, on the floor. Raja Haider stood, hands clasped behind him. His black beard appeared to have grown at least an inch since Shahnaz had last focused on it, adding to the heavy seriousness of his face. She settled the baby in her lap.

"I've made some decisions," he said, looking solemnly at each one in his audience. "Shahnaz, you'll give notice to Peace tomorrow. You're needed here at home. Noshaba cannot be expected to tend to the children and guests on her own."

She lowered her eyes, unable to look any more at her brother-in-law. His eyes gleamed as he moved his pawns about. It was inevitable, she told herself. She had known this was coming. But the knowledge did not make it any less of a blow. So much for Kameela's prosthesis. There'd likely be no sustained push against thalassemia. And poor Fatima would probably die.

And then there was her own baby. Not much morning sickness this time. Maybe that was a good sign. Oh, she wanted to see Dr. Irshad so badly, to make sure she was okay. She inhaled through her teeth. The man of the house had forbidden the women to see male doctors, and she didn't know of a female gynecologist.

"Nooran, Sadia, and Rizwana." Raja Haider sounded as though he was reading an attendance roster, and Shahnaz emerged from her thoughts to look at her sisters-in-law.

Each of the young women looked up and then sideways at each other.

"You are expected to finish your education, as Abu wanted, and then you'll help at home until I've arranged your marriages." He sighted down his nose, as though he was shooting daggers of daring at each of them. "Do not develop any inappropriate expectations about *careers*."

This last word came out like a sneer. Shahnaz glanced at Nooran, so dedicated to medicine, and saw a face downturned and hands stiffly clasped. The baby began to fuss, so Shahnaz lifted her up to a shoulder and patted her back.

"Jamil, you're twenty-three. You have two years to establish yourself as a certified accountant. You've been spending far too many evenings outside this house, and from now on I expect you to study here in the evening. I'll find you a proper wife when you are twenty-five. I'm thinking of your cousin Nayyar."

Shahnaz watched Jamil. She'd thought of him as cocky prior to this evening, a young man out to satisfy his desires with little, seemingly, in his way. Being restricted to the house was going to clip his wings. Who knew what would happen if he married his first cousin. Was thalassemia prevalent in the Khan family? Shahnaz realized she didn't know.

Raja Haider shifted his gaze to his youngest brother. "Qadir, I'm expecting better marks this spring than you showed us last year. You will complete high school with an impressive set of test scores. Do you understand?"

The shy slip of a young man nodded as he stared at the carpet.

"Look at me." Raja Haider's order reverberated like a lion's roar. "Ammi wants a doctor in the family, and that will be you.

Understood?"

Qadir glanced up at his brother and nodded, more slowly than before. Then he turned to look at Nooran, whose jaw was hanging down. He shrugged one shoulder. "Sorry."

No one spoke. So much to mourn, Shahnaz thought: Sohail, the man and the family patriarch, her own work, Nooran giving up medicine, the fun taken out of Jamil's life, and all the poetry that Qadir would not write.

Into the thick silence came Maryam's clear tones. "You seem full of instructions for others, and I want to point out that you're not following the wishes of your father and me."

Raja Haider glared for a moment at his mother. "I'm doing exactly what you sent me to school to learn: how to behave as a proper Muslim."

"We didn't choose a madrassa so you could ignore the progress we've made in the last thousand years or try to recreate a time that never was. Mohammad—Peace Be Upon Him—recognized the talents of others and encouraged them to use those talents. Shahnaz is a supervisor, well respected. Nooran will make an excellent doctor. I can see no reason why these young women should be denied their dreams. And young Qadir loves language. I can't imagine him poking at bodies."

"You've heard my decisions."

"Yes, I have, and I don't agree with them." She stood to face her much-taller son. "When I read the Qur'an, I see requirements to honor your parents and to 'lower your wings to them in humility.' You're dishonoring the explicit plans of your father."

Rising to his full height, Raja Haider glared downward at his mother. "You've chosen Sura Seventeen, mother, and ignored Sura Twenty-Nine where the Qur'an says that if parents hold up an idol as a god, sons must not obey such parents. You and my father have made a god of education."

Maryam's body slumped. "He's dead not two weeks and already you've erased his humanity." With a heavy tread, she walked to her room.

As the door shut, Raja Haider said, "I've given you my decisions. Now go."

━•━

Upon reaching their bedroom, Shahnaz sank into the chair, lacking the energy to unpin her dupatta. "Must I resign?" She willed her husband to stand by the compromise he'd made with Raja Haider to allow her to work.

Naseer moved about quietly, putting his wallet on the bedside table and hanging up his vest. Then he sat on the arm of the chair and began to massage the back of Shahnaz's neck. "I'm afraid so...I'm sorry, but he's in charge now."

Shahnaz pulled away from his hand. "So, you're going to let him do this to the family? To me? You'll let Jamil marry his first cousin?"

He dropped his hand. "There's no point to arguing. I can't win. I wish I could. You know that, right?"

"I'm not sure anymore. I thought we believed in the same things—that women could work, that first cousins shouldn't marry, that my job is important to me. What happened?"

Naseer rose and went to sit on the bed, his elbows resting on his knees. "Those ideas came up against reality, I guess." He looked up, just for a moment, and then stared at his hands. "Families are headed by fathers and then eldest brothers. That's the way it's always been...I love my family. I can't abandon it, and I can't support Ammi, my sisters, Jamil, and Qadir; I don't make enough money. We just have to obey."

She felt a chasm opening between them, and her anger erupt-

165

ed. "Won't you stand up to him? Argue against these decisions?"

"What am I supposed to say?" He pushed himself to a sitting position. "It's his duty to make decisions for the family, and according to his view of Islam, these are the right decisions." He rose and moved into the bathroom.

Shahnaz felt her chest constricting, her anger growing like an inflating balloon. "Don't you run away and hide. Come out here and thrash this out with me."

He slammed the door.

——•◦•——

Mid-morning found the girls together in Noshaba's bedroom—five young women and Noshaba's daughters. Two aunts had come earlier to offer condolences and had just left with Ammi to find and admire old photographs. The men had dispersed to work or, in Qadir's case, to wander. It was a moment blessedly without guests.

Nooran was sitting cross-legged on the bed, picking at bits of lint on her kameez. "I really wanted to be a doctor. Here I studied science all these years, and now I can't put it to use." She looked up quickly at Noshaba. "I'm sorry if I hurt you. I don't mean any insult. But I'm so disappointed."

Shahnaz sat on a wooden chair with her hands clasped, holding herself together. "Me, too. You'd make a great doctor; you're so caring. And we'd make a terrific team, really make a difference for women." She was furious with Naseer for abandoning her to the dictates of his brother and afraid she'd unleash her anger on this sympathetic group if she said any more. It would just make them all feel worse. She needed to talk to him, but he had turned his back on her last night and snuck out this morning when she was in the shower.

Slow nods moved like a wave around the room.

Noshaba stirred on her solid chair. "I'm sorry I failed you." She spoke so quietly Shahnaz had to turn her head to hear.

Shahnaz put her hand on Noshaba's. "It's not your fault. None of us blame you. None of us." She looked around for confirmation.

Nooran straightened her spine. "I wish Abu was here. He wouldn't let this happen."

As Rizwana started to speak, Shahnaz saw the curtains sway, felt the floor roll, and heard the bricks in the walls grind against each other. Instantly, the girls leapt to their feet and ran for the door. Someone screamed. Noshaba and Shahnaz grabbed the children and followed the others into the garden. As Shahnaz cuddled the baby into her body, she saw the wall into the girls' room, the one between hers and the already wrecked end bedroom, crumble forward. New chunks of concrete joined the old, burying the budding plants. Ammi staggered from her bedroom, wiping dust from her eyes, and gaped at the new losses.

———•••———

After several hours of working with the family's cook and driver to rescue clothing and useable furniture, clean up broken crockery, and organize a girls' dorm in the room that had been Sohail's study, Shahnaz slipped off to her bedroom. She needed privacy for her phone call to Amir. Earthquake or not, Raja Haider was sure to follow up. Finding herself unable to focus on resigning from Peace, she pulled the chair near the door, the better to escape in the case of another quake, and sat, staring at the bedroom wall. Would it fall with the next shock? After several deep breaths and a verbalized order to herself to "Do it," she found Amir's number in her contact list and made the call.

Amir answered on the second ring, expressed his condolences, and left several seconds of empty air.

"Amir, I'm so sorry, but I have to resign from Peace. I'm needed here at home, especially now as we're mourning my father-in-law. I'm...I'm so sorry." She could see his kind face and sad eyes.

More empty air. "I'm sorry, too. I know this is a difficult time for you, and maybe there's a middle ground. How about giving you a three-month leave of absence? You could be home throughout the mourning period and then see how things settle out. Insh'allah, by the end of that time, the family will let you return to Peace."

She felt a frisson of excitement, like a lifeline had been thrown to her drowning person. Here was an opening for her, a door ajar. Would things change in the Khan household in three months? Only God knew. But she could hope, couldn't she? Wait. If she agreed to this, it would fly in the face of Raja Haider's order to her. Or maybe not. She did call to resign. She couldn't control the fact that her boss had refused to accept the resignation. Well, her inner critic argued, she could refuse the offer. Certainly Raja Haider would expect that. Her body slumped over as she contemplated refusing. No, she decided, this offer could not be turned down. Something *might* happen.

Sitting up straight, she accepted. "Amir, I think that's a brilliant idea: a leave of absence until mid-July. And thank you so much for understanding."

He hemmed and hawed, obviously embarrassed.

"Please, while I'm on leave, would you follow up on a couple of things?"

"Sure."

"One of my Lady Health Workers, Bibi, has a daughter who lost a foot. Could you talk with her husband and convince him Kameela can come with me to Islamabad—when I'm back—for fittings for a prosthesis? And, please, do take over the Thalassemia campaign. It's so important."

"I'll do my best."

The next hour passed quickly with a visit from the wife of one of Sohail's fellow ministers. Shahnaz felt like she was floating, buoyed by the happiness of possibilities. She answered the proffered questions and engaged in polite conversation, all with her mind ablaze—she might be able to go back to work. So many doors had been closing on her lately, it was time for a window to open somewhere.

She told no one until Irum came to visit late in the afternoon. They had tea together in the bedroom and managed to let the other women know they wished to be alone.

Seated next to her friend on the bed, Irum brought the topic up, with a slight flush on her face. "Amir told me you'll be taking a leave."

Shahnaz beamed. "He was so kind to offer, and I was overwhelmed by such happiness. Insh'allah, it'll work out."

Irum smiled. "We've talked about you a lot. Amir says he relies on you and is so impressed by what you do with the Lady Health Workers."

"I bet he also compliments you."

Irum blushed fully with blotches appearing on her face. She looked at her hands and then at Shahnaz. "Yes, he does...Oh, he's so wonderful. Every day with him makes me want even more to spend my life with him."

Shahnaz embraced her friend. "When will you speak with your parents, Irum?"

Irum drew back and sat tall on the bed. "We've planned to tell both sets of parents next month. Insh'allah, they'll agree to the families' meeting. Oh, Shahnaz, pray for us."

"Of course I will. I'm so pleased." She smiled in real happiness for her friend. But when she looked beyond Irum to the black abaya hanging in the bathroom, she wondered if Amir would be as generous to his wife as he was to his employees. What did they know of his family's ideas about the role of women?

9

The forty days of mourning passed slowly, with many visitors trailing in and out of the house. For the first time, Shahnaz spent whole days in Maryam's company. To begin with, her mother-in-law spoke wistfully of Sohail and of how much she missed his tranquility. Then one day, well into May, she told Shahnaz, privately, that she needed something to keep herself from dwelling on death and loss.

As they sat in the dining room over cups of tea, Maryam stirred her already cooling brew. "I've tried to see the best in people and write texts that inspire children to be curious, help others, and move forward to productive lives. Now I seem to be reliving the past, stuck in my own problems, helping no one." Her worried frown sat atop a gray face; her deep brown eyes looked dull. She stopped her spoon and stared at the wall ahead of her.

Shahnaz laid her hand softly on her mother-in-law's. "We're still in the days of mourning, Ammi. Aren't they for just this kind of reminiscing?"

Slowly, Maryam turned her head and smiled. "Yes, dear. Of course they are. But I think I need to take a positive step forward." Sitting up straighter in her chair, her words tumbled out. "The

Ministry has asked me to write a series of English texts for the primary school, following this new national curriculum, and I do believe I'll accept."

Shahnaz felt her own energy surge. "That's perfect. Oh, Ammi, I know children will love them." It would be such a lifeline for her mother-in-law, she thought with a pang of envy. And a lifeline was what they both needed. With a guilty feeling that she should celebrate for Maryam and not grieve for herself, she looked up to see her mother-in-law scanning her face.

"You know much more about this younger generation than I do, and your English is far more fluent. Would you be willing to write with me? There're only maybe thirty lessons for each class—stories, poems, essays—followed by exercises. We could split them down the middle or we could each specialize. What do you say?"

Shahnaz caught her breath and exhaled slowly, seeing herself at this dining table with large pads of paper and a box of pens—or maybe a laptop—writing. She'd liked English at school, enjoyed writing the occasional story. The books would keep her connected to children, and she'd be working in a way that helped others. But in that mind's eye view of this future, she didn't see any patients. Ammi would be there. They'd talk and argue and discuss, but other than that, Shahnaz saw herself sitting alone in the room whose windows seemed hazily crossed with bars. She knew she had to refuse the offer, and also that such a refusal would add to Ammi's sadness. "I'm so honored that you think this highly of me. I want to agree because I'd like to work with you, but..."

Maryam's smile faded. "I was afraid there was a 'but' coming."

With a blush, Shahnaz nodded. "I'm sorry. I'll help you in any way I can. Maybe at night and on weekends I could brainstorm with you or read drafts or edit. But, well, Ammi, I love my work at Peace. I want to be out in the world, working with Lady Health Workers. I want to see every Kashmiri baby born healthy. Writing feels like it would close me into a private world, and I can't do that. Do you understand?"

Maryam leaned over and caressed Shahnaz's arm. "Yes, certainly. So, I think I'll go ahead and negotiate with the Minister. And you and I will figure out how to negotiate with the current regime in this household, a task that'll be much more difficult than facing government bureaucrats." She paused and leaned back in her chair. "How are you doing with that baby you're carrying?"

"Well, I think. No morning sickness like the last time. I would like to see a doctor."

"Don't your Peace colleagues know of a female doctor?"

"Not around here. I asked."

"Perhaps we should ask others as well. Like your mother?"

—◆•◆—

While Ammi publicly mourned and privately bargained with the Ministry, Shahnaz and Noshaba shared the management of the household, the direction of the cook, driver, and gardener, and the child care duties required by two demanding youngsters. Ammi seemed relieved to give the household to their generation and drifted out of the house on several afternoons, announcing to Noshaba that she needed to "take care of a few things."

The temperature was rising daily as spring grew toward summer, and Shahnaz spent more and more time in the garden. It eased her perpetual worry about earthquakes, but the major reason was the freedom of the open air. The jacaranda tree had already unwrapped its purple flowers, dropped the petals, and pushed out its leaves, so the bench at its base was well sheltered from the sun. One afternoon, Noshaba had taken her out behind the bedrooms to the acres that had once held the family's orchard. Sohail had planted cherry, plum, and apricot trees there early in his marriage and had tended them like children. The family had the benefit of fresh fruit, and Sohail had given a good deal away as part of his zakat, his charity.

When she looked at the field, Shahnaz saw simply a mass of weeds, old plastic bags, and piles of garbage. Noshaba said it had been hard to watch people cut down the trees, and she, like Sohail, wanted them to grow again. Neither she nor Shahnaz saw an interest in trees in any of Sohail's sons, at least not yet.

On this gray-blue morning, Shahnaz strolled along the flowerbeds of the house's inner garden, pointing out the various plants to three-month-old Riffat. The gardener had put in lots of purple, yellow, and white pansies, and Shahnaz picked a deep violet one for Riffat. The baby giggled when Shahnaz flicked her cheek with the blossom and then let her crush it in her hand.

Soon Shahnaz was humming and patting Riffat's back as the baby eased into sleep, freeing her mind to run on. What this family needed was an infusion of life. Of course, they needed to observe the proper mourning period. But just look at the pleasure that Riffat felt at the color and touch of a pansy flower. Like her mother-in-law and the baby, everyone needed to explore and create. She, alas, was stuck—looking and feeling drab, taking care of someone else's baby, afraid to celebrate her own pregnancy lest it be bad luck, serving endless cups of tea, unsure she'd be able to return to Peace, and knowing writing books wasn't right for her. And then there was Naseer. Since Raja Haider's pronouncements, he'd grown quiet. Oh, he was unfailingly polite, but he often stayed out late, sat without speaking through dinner, and disappeared into their room right after. She'd tried to reach him, even tried to rouse him to anger by declaring she needed to return to Peace. He'd merely patted her and said, "You know you can't."

As the sweat bubbled up on her forehead, Shahnaz found her way to the bench and settled Riffat across her legs. Here was an uncomplicated love. Riffat pumped her arms and legs in excitement when Shahnaz appeared. Unconditional joy. She sighed. Riffat was not her child, and she was afraid for the one she carried. If only she could see Dr. Irshad. But that would lead to more argument and who knew what punishment.

The muffled sound of Shahnaz's mobile broke her reverie. As Riffat was now soundly asleep, Shahnaz pulled it from her shalwar pocket and walked several steps away for a quiet conversation. It was Rabia.

"Shahnaz, I need you to talk to Ammi. She cannot make up her mind about important things anymore! Now it's the flowers for my Mehndi. I told her I want lots of yellow and white, and she's worried that people will comment on the absence of red. Please, will you talk to her? You didn't have this problem. Why do I?"

Shahnaz smiled wistfully, wishing again for the days when this kind of thing constituted a problem. "Is it simply an issue of color or more than that? I mean, does the florist say there's trouble in finding enough gladiolas and roses at the end of May? That's supposing you don't want marigolds."

"Oh, no. Marigolds only for the neck garlands—that's traditional. But tall, distinguished glads in the flower baskets with lots of greenery and yellow roses and white tuberoses filling them in. And no pink. That's the point. *No pink!*"

Shahnaz chuckled. "So, no red either? Or just not *all* red?"

"Well, a little red shows passion and that's good. Maybe in the table decorations—but not in the vases around the room. You see, don't you?" Her voice was nearing the hysterical range.

Shahnaz broadened her smile. "Yes, I see. Is Ammi around?"

"Yes. Praise God. I'll get her. And, well, thanks."

Shahnaz could hear the retreating sound of pounding feet. She reflected that things had changed since she left that house. It used to be Rabia who could wrap Ammi around her little finger;

now that young woman was appealing to her sister for help.

"Shahnaz." Her mother sounded relieved. "How nice of you to call Rabia. Is everything all right? You don't usually phone at this hour."

How like Rabia. "Ammi, we're fine here. I've just put the baby down for her nap, and since we have no visitors, I thought I'd call."

"So nice of you. We're at sixes and sevens around here." Her voice dropped to a whisper. "Your sister is driving me crazy. Everything's a crisis, and since she changes her mind every day, I'm forever having to call the florist or caterers and even the man I'm renting the tent from for the Mehndi."

"Why a tent? It should be warm enough the last weekend in May, and that's a month before the monsoons."

Her mother sighed. "It's Rabia. She's convinced the monsoon will start early this year just to ruin her marriage weekend."

Shahnaz laughed so hard, the baby stirred. "It's more likely to be terribly hot and stuffy in a tent."

Her mother chuckled, just a little. "Oh, we'll have them open the sides if that's the case."

"I hear from Rabia that today the issue is flowers."

"So she said, starting at breakfast this morning. I hadn't even had my tea when she charged into the dining room to tell me she had to have only yellow and white. Shahnaz, it's not that I mind the colors. It's that last week she had decided pink enhanced her skin tones and made her look more delicate. Then yesterday someone told her it was insipid and I think she said Javed hated it, though why he'd do so, I have no idea. I had settled all the plans with the florist and now she says I must change them. It wasn't like this for your wedding—so much saner then. Now we're in a tizzy all the time. I do wish you were here to calm her down."

"Oh, Ammi, as though I ever could." Shahnaz was charmed by the positive attributes she had been given in the time she had been absent from her mother's house.

"Well, you've talked me out of my desire to throttle her, and that's all to the good. Perhaps now I'll manage to speak with the florist. Insh'allah, I can placate him by increasing the order."

"Oh, Ammi, see? You've got it all settled."

Her mother sighed. "And have you settled what will happen with your family at this wedding?"

Shahnaz could imagine her mother fluffing her hair while waiting for the response. "No, not yet. Everyone knows about it, of course. I guess I don't want to ask and be disappointed. I think if it's undecided, there's hope for me to be a part of everything."

"Insh'allah."

Shahnaz felt her mood lighten as she tucked the mobile back into her pocket and relaxed on the bench. She had helped *solve* a family problem instead of creating one, not a position she often held in the Khan household. All decisions, even the small ones like what to serve for dinner, were tainted by the worry of whether Raja Haider would approve. He questioned just about everything, as though he couldn't trust Noshaba or her to act with forethought and wisdom.

Of course, they did sometimes decide things that they thought it possible Raja Haider would disapprove. Not often, but when it was necessary. There was the issue of Sadia, for example, who—to be honest—weighed more than she should. She'd fainted when walking up the hill from school, sort of crumpled in the road. It was that first stifling day in May, and she was dressed too heavily for it. It also was the time of her period, which left her weak. Down she'd dropped, to be found by a couple who made their driver stop. The woman (and, thankfully, not the man) moved Sadia onto her back, cradled her head, and sprinkled water on her face. When she woke, the woman insisted she get in the car and be driven home. Shahnaz and Noshaba hadn't discussed their decision with Raja Haider, but they'd agreed that the Khan driver should pick up Sadia each day after school. Shahnaz had argued that they should tell Raja Haider, thinking he couldn't object. Noshaba had thought he would refuse the privilege, as he believed they should all sacrifice in this time of mourning. Had they "solved" the problem or created yet another one? She didn't know.

Unfortunately, it took little time to discover that Raja Haider thought that their solution for Sadia was a bad idea. Only a week into the pick-up routine, he wanted the car during his lunch hour— right at the time school closed. Later that afternoon, he paced the living room in front of the women. "Here I'd made a breakthrough in obtaining verbal permission to begin the rebuilding of our home and needed the driver to take me quickly from office to office for signatures before anyone left town. And what do I hear? And from the driver, of all people. That he was taking Sadia home and I'd have to wait." He stopped, glaring at the two women. "I understand you'd given him this order. Am I correct?"

Shahnaz watched his hands, now on his hips, anticipating an unexpected slap at her face if she wasn't tracking their whereabouts.

Noshaba answered, facing off against him. "Yes. She fainted in the street, and we felt it was unsafe for her to walk home alone in this heat."

"I see. And why wasn't I consulted?" He raised arced arms from his sides as he glared at one and then the other of the women.

Noshaba shrugged a shoulder. "I thought it was women's business, a part of running the household."

Shahnaz swelled with pride in Noshaba for responding while feeling guilty at the same time for allowing her sister-in-law to shoulder the burden of Raja Haider's anger.

Raja Haider simmered as he worked out his next move. "Now you listen to me, Noshaba. I expect the car to be available when I need it. No more transport to school. You hear me?"

Out of the corner of her eye, Shahnaz saw Maryam enter the room and walk to her son's side. "What's this about, Raja Haider?" She spoke clearly, without fear.

He turned to face her, mouth half open.

Shahnaz thought he looked like a looming vulture.

"It's not your concern, Ammi. I'm fulfilling my duties in this house."

"Hmm. Do I have to remind you that we're in mourning? You're filling the house with anger instead of sadness and respect. Why?"

He looked her up and down, his squinty eyes spitting fire. "With all due respect, Ammi, I'd appreciate it if you would cover *all* your hair. Bits are showing around your face. It's not appropriate modesty."

She stared back at him with those same dark eyes, open wide. "As I'm sure you know, the Qur'an says that elderly women do nothing wrong by relaxing their dress code, provided they don't reveal too much of their bodies. Showing a few strands of hair can hardly be said to be revealing much. I think my age and widowhood give me the option of not covering at all, but in deference to you, I continue to do so." Her compact body stood firm and erect.

Raja Haider's chronically high blood pressure, combined with his anger, suffused his face with red. The capillaries seemed to be preparing to explode. "I've been meaning to discuss your responsibilities in this house for some time, Ammi, and I haven't out of deference to our mourning. However, now I must say that you are overburdening Noshaba. I expect you to..."

Noshaba broke into his lecture, placing a hand on his arm. "Please, excuse my interruption. I..." She stuttered as his hand closed into a fist. "I don't feel overburdened, truly. With Shahnaz's help, we're doing fine. Please, if you'll permit it, I'd like to manage the house and give Ammi time to mourn."

Raja Haider stared down at his wife and beat his fists together, then transferred his gaze to his mother.

Before he spoke again, Maryam clasped her hands behind her back in the form of a commanding officer. "On another topic, I'd like to talk about my plans. I'm not comfortable keeping important matters secret, and there's something I need to tell you. Shall we sit down?" She moved to the sofa, settled into its softness, and patted the cushion next to her. "Come. I don't wish to get a stiff neck from looking up."

Raja Haider eyed the younger women for a moment, flicked his wrist in a dismissive gesture, and sat on the edge of the designated seat.

Shahnaz captured Noshaba's hand and led her into the hallway, just far enough to be out of sight of those in the living room. She put a finger on her lips, and the two women stood absolutely still. A shiver of excitement frisked its way up Shahnaz's spine.

"What is this issue, Ammi? I have many things to take care of this evening." His tone was annoyed, dismissive.

"Why don't you sit back, son? You look uncomfortable and, really, this couch is a place to relax."

"With all due respect, I don't wish to sit back. What do you want to say?"

"I want to tell you a story."

He groaned.

"No, no, it's not long." She paused. "Do you remember the letters I wrote to you when you were away at school?"

"No."

"I used to enclose little stories, sometimes about the family and sometimes just fanciful tales. Perhaps you recall Yaqoob the hoarse duck whose siblings made fun of him or Sofiya the little girl who was always late to school?"

"Vaguely."

"Hmm. Well, those were stories I wrote for Kashmir's primary

Urdu textbooks. I tried them out on you to see if they'd work for the right age group and, if they did, I put them in my books."

Noshaba leaned close to Shahnaz's ear. "I remember those stories from school. I loved them."

Shahnaz squeezed her hand and tiptoed closer to the ongoing conversation, staying near the wall so as not to be seen.

"Oh, yes, your *books*." He spit out the last word.

Shahnaz wondered what he knew about them. Naseer certainly had no clue. But Raja Haider sounded angry. She moved a step closer.

"All total, I've written forty-five books for the primary grades and now I've contracted to produce new English texts for classes 1 through 6. I signed the papers today. This is something Sohail and I talked about a lot. Your father loved reading my stories as much as I loved writing them. I want to dedicate this new series to him."

Shahnaz felt tears swamp her eyes. Noshaba dropped her head against Shahnaz's arm and entwined their hands. Not even Raja Haider could overrule such a heart-felt tribute, could he?

He cleared his throat. "I hated your books. And you know how I feel about women working. Find another way to honor Abu."

"I can't imagine a better way. I intend to write, insh'allah, about things like our forests and wood crafts that Sohail held so dear."

A long silence ensued, and then the couch squealed, signaling someone had risen. Shahnaz assumed it was Raja Haider.

"In my household, no woman earns money. No woman goes out in public alone. It's too boastful, too risky. We will honor my father by acting in all ways according to the Qur'an."

Shahnaz heard Maryam's answer, as clearly as a gong being struck. "Our prophet—Peace Be Upon Him—was proud to send his wife out to work, as was your father. As I recall, the wife of the prayer leader at your madrassa directed the girls' school, didn't she?"

"Ammi." Raja Haider separated the syllables. "I've told you

181

my decision. Your working destroyed this family years ago. It will not do so again."

"What do you mean?"

Shahnaz heard his sharp intake of breath.

"You sent me away so you could work. Abu told me about the books. He would have let me come back, but you insisted I return to that madrassa. It's a little late to regret it."

"No, no. We sent you away to give you the best education. I didn't insist you had to return. Sohail and I discussed it when you complained. I remember that winter break like yesterday. We thought you were having a temporary bad spot—when that friend of yours left school." She sounded confused.

"You seem to have conveniently forgotten any number of other times I was unhappy. Apparently, you were so involved in your books, you had to get rid of me."

"No, no. I cried each time you left. Sohail talked with your teachers and the prayer leaders to be sure you were okay. We wanted you to have the best education possible. That's why you were there."

"Well, the tables have turned. I learned surrender to Allah and proper obedience to my superiors. Now I'm making the decisions."

Heavy silence filled the air. Shahnaz realized she was holding her breath and let it out slowly so as not to be heard. For a moment, only the sound of a bird hooting from the garden tree splintered their peace.

After a full minute, Maryam audibly sighed. "When Sohail's father died, Sohail tried to behave like his father. It didn't work. We both had jobs, for one thing, and he had to adapt to the circumstances. Now you—well, you want to change everything, recreate some era that never was. That won't work either. We're all mourning Sohail, and it feels as if you're taking him away with all these dictates. Please, move slowly and leave some of my husband."

"I loved my father."

"I know."

A few seconds into a new pause, Shahnaz picked up the soft whoosh of a Raja Haider footstep on the carpet. She poked Noshaba. "Tea. Hurry." They stepped softly from the hall into the kitchen and were arranging cups on a tray and chatting when Raja Haider strode by, heading for the bedrooms. A moment later they heard Maryam's shuffling feet when she moved past the kitchen toward her bedroom.

When the door to the garden—and the bedrooms—had closed behind the two combatants, Shahnaz leaned her hip against a counter and let out a long breath. "Whew, we were almost discovered. Let's make tea for Ammi. She must feel awful." She got down another cup and saucer and then paused against the counter. "Do you think he really won't let her write?"

Noshaba finished setting up the tea tray. "I wouldn't be surprised."

Shahnaz folded her arms. "Excuse me if this question offends you, but what attracts you to him? What do you admire about him?"

Noshaba paused, staring at the wall. "He protects me. It's like Allah has given me a shield to keep me safe from prying eyes, from the harm that comes from men."

"Goodness. I don't feel threatened by men—at the office, on the street. Usually I feel honored and respected, like at work, with Amir, the other supervisors, even the district and provincial authorities." Not, of course, by Raja Haider, but she kept that to herself.

"Not me. My father lectured a lot about men's lust. He said if I showed even a little bit of hair, a man would feel the right to possess me. I'd be leading him on. I've covered since I was eight."

"Eight." Shahnaz shook her head. "Didn't you mind?"

"Well, it was strange at first. But it was just the way I dressed." She paused to pour the hot water from the kettle. "I thought it was romantic."

"Romantic?" Shahnaz was astonished.

Noshaba blushed. "I was keeping myself hidden for my husband, saving myself for him. I would belong to him and no one else."

"Yes, I see."

———•·•———

That evening, troubled by the day's events, Shahnaz hung up her shalwar kameez, her back to her husband. "Ammi told Raja Haider about her books today, and he forbade her from writing."

Naseer grunted as he untied his shoes.

Shahnaz closed her closet door and turned to watch him. He banged his shoes together and rose to take them to his closet, next to hers. The shadows on his face seemed deeper than usual, and she wondered if he was growing his beard. "I'm scared—for her, for me. Like a trap is closing around us. Will you talk to him? Please?"

"Stop pushing me." Naseer slammed his closet door and faced her, hands on his hips. "You think I like this position, caught between you and him? Well, I don't."

His hefty accents on each word said not to pursue the topic, but Shahnaz couldn't help herself. She put out her hand to touch his arm. "Please, we have to change his mind."

He shook off her hand and stomped across the room to the chair. Collapsing into its softness, he looked up at her with anger—and perhaps fear—in his eyes. "I agreed, with reluctance, that you could take a leave. Why isn't that enough for you? Why do you have to force this issue?"

She kneaded her hands. "It's just that now—well, he seems to be slamming so many doors shut. Someone needs to stick a foot out and keep the doors open."

"You want to work. I get it. You're saving lives. You're applauded by your bosses. You eat up the praise and glory of it all. How about thinking of me? I'm in mourning, for goodness sakes. Isn't that draining enough without having to fight your battle?" He jumped up and paced across the room, speeding up as he turned and re-crossed the space. "I hate coming home these days. If it isn't you, it's my sisters whining about the rules. Frankly, that's what we're all learning about these days, obedience."

"Naseer, please listen." She took a deep breath. "It's not just us, it's our daughters I'm fighting for, too. I want them to grow up healthy and able to study what they want and work. Don't you—"

"Stop it! Stop right now. You will obey, Shahnaz, and our children will learn obedience. Have you got that?" He looked her up and down, glaring. "Get my shoes out. I'm going for a walk."

—•—

After the men left for work and the children left for school on the last official day of mourning, Noshaba wandered toward Shahnaz in the garden, slowing to peek in windows. "I...I need to talk to you. Don't go away."

Shahnaz stopped in the act of settling Riffat on a blanket on a shady square of grass and watched Noshaba's receding back. Why the worry of being watched? And where was Shahnaz supposed to be going, anyway? They were the only two family members at home. The baby grunted, fussed, and jabbed her arms and legs into the air. She was just not going to nap and allow them the time for an adult conversation. With a sigh, Shahnaz picked her up again, murmuring to her that she should sleep as her aunt was badly in need of quiet. Instead, Riffat arched her back and screamed her unhappiness. Shahnaz began the slow walking and patting that usually helped calm the baby.

Noshaba reappeared with a pail and shovel and Zainab trailing behind. The child stamped her feet and begged for the toys, and her mother insisted she could have them when they reached the pile of dirt next to the fallen bedroom wall. The gardener had abandoned that part of his domain, having been told that workmen would be coming soon to start the renovation.

When she made it back to Shahnaz, a slightly bedraggled Noshaba took the baby into her arms and sat on the bench to try breastfeeding. "She didn't eat much this morning; perhaps she's just hungry."

Shahnaz stood, watching and thinking that little was going well in her life at this moment. She couldn't even convince a baby to sleep. Then she heard the unmistakable explosion of diarrhea and was assailed by the sharp smell. Not wanting to take the baby into the children's small, hot room, she said, "I'll get the wipes and another diaper. Wait here."

When Riffat finally slept, Noshaba laid her on the blanket and collapsed onto the bench next to Shahnaz. "I hope she's emptied out. I can't imagine what's made her sick. Did anyone give her water?"

Shahnaz shrugged. "I don't know. What a bother that it's still contaminated." She, too, hoped this was a one-time event. The poor baby was exhausted.

Noshaba shook out her dupatta, sent the end over her left shoulder, and folded the edge more comfortably under her chin. She snuck a glance at Shahnaz, then focused on the ground. "Last night...Raja Haider was so angry...about a lot of things—his father's death, his sisters resisting covering, and his mother challenging his authority." She looked up, her eyes pleading. "He is one of the truly Faithful, so much a Believer; he quoted the Qur'an about his duty to honor his parents and told me what his teachers said that meant and where he feels he must part from Abu's ways and Ammi's desires."

"Yes? Then what?" Shahnaz swallowed her anticipation.

Noshaba braided the fringe of her dupatta. "This is hard to

say. But I can't hold onto it alone."

Shahnaz covered Noshaba's hands with her own. "I promise to keep it between us, unless you tell me I can speak of it."

Closing her eyes, Noshaba inhaled slowly. "Okay. Here goes. Usually we each undress in the bathroom. You know, as we're getting ready for bed."

Shahnaz waited, conjuring up possibilities.

Noshaba stared at her slowly plaiting hands. "This is so difficult...He wasn't thinking of what he was doing, and he took off his kameez. It was horrible." She pulled the edge of the dupatta with its tangled fringe over her face.

Shahnaz automatically put her arm around Noshaba's shoulders, mentally reviewing images of his body: was it misshapen somehow? Had it lots of hair? But wouldn't she have known of those things from touching him while they made love?

Noshaba sobbed. "His back and chest are covered in scars of burnt flesh."

"What?" Shahnaz's jaw dropped and her hands fell to the bench.

"I drew back from him and screamed. It's awful, like he was systematically tortured."

"Who would do such a thing?"

Gulping air amidst her sobs, Noshaba went on. "He said he never wanted me to see. He apologized and pulled on his kameez. Then he sat on the bed, his back to me, and in a monotone told me it happened at the madrassa. Some older boys singled him out. They'd pull him out of bed in the middle of the night, order him to clean their room or wash their clothes or do push-ups or lie still with eyes closed. Often, they had him strip and commented on his skinny arms, lack of pubic hair, or small member. When he wasn't fast enough in a job or stopped for a rest, one of them spurred him on with a burning cigarette. How he hated them. My poor husband.

He suffered so, and I never knew."

Shahnaz was stunned. How could boys do this to each other?

Noshaba turned to her. "He was gentle to me last night. It was different, like I was coupled with a wounded soul, a tender man."

Shahnaz contemplated this new image of Raja Haider, bullied by other boys, prevented from sleeping, believing he was abandoned by his parents. Poor boy. And now a bitter man. Probably she should make allowances for all he'd suffered, understand that his violence now was a part of his fighting back for the burning done to him. But "allowances" didn't mean accepting his decrees. In fact, maybe she could use what she'd learned. Perhaps, just now, he was vulnerable.

Buoyed by this possibility, she hung around the living room to intercept him as he entered the house after work. After all, she was a strong woman and a kind one. She could show him her caring and persuade him that her work came from that same compassion. She could point out to him that her work was a part of God's work. Surely, that would make a difference. Her stomach grew jittery. It had to be today. His mood might not last and, she thought with embarrassment, Naseer wouldn't be home until late. He'd hate this. All he'd see was more disobedience.

When Raja Haider came through the doorway, he looked calmer than he had in days and, perhaps, distracted. By the time he'd leaned his briefcase against the wall behind the door, Shahnaz had risen from her seat at the dining room table and planted herself in his path to the bedrooms. "Can I get you a cup of tea?"

Raja Haider swung his head around, shaking his arm as though it needed unfurling from the weight of his papers. "Uh, sure."

She turned to walk to the kitchen. "There're some new notes and a few cards from today's visitors, if you care to look, on the end table near the door." Sneaking a peek over her shoulder, she saw him reach for the pile and begin to flip through them. Good, she thought, he'll stay for a few minutes. The tea will help him relax, and I'll speak.

When she returned with the hot mug, she found her brother-in-law seated on the couch, reading a note from the pile on his lap. His face was a pale version of itself, his body relaxed. A small tic hiccupped under his eye, but, all in all, she thought the time was right. She knelt at his knee. "Your tea."

He looked up at her in mild surprise, as though he'd forgotten her presence, and accepted the mug. Then he returned to the note he'd been reading.

"Excuse me, Raja Haider, but may I have a word?"

Slowly, eyes fixed on the paper, he moved the note to the couch and looked back at her. "What is it?"

She slipped onto the couch, perching on its edge and leaving ample space between them. "I feel Allah has called me to compassionate work for our people, and..."

"No, you may not return to Peace. Bringing in Allah—even by his proper Arabic name—buys you nothing." He picked up a business card, flipped it over, and discarded it on the growing stack.

"I...I thought if I explained how Peace is doing God's work you might..."

"No." He allowed the sound of the vowel to linger in the air between them. "Now go."

—◆•◆—

When the family gathered for dinner that night, Raja Haider ate little and said nothing. As though uncertain of what to make of his silence, the family spoke in whispers; Shahnaz kept looking from Naseer to Ammi to Noshaba to Raja Haider, trying to sort out what was going on. Her husband didn't seem upset, only lost in his own thoughts. Finally, Ammi broke the silence, her head tilted to one side like an inquiring sparrow. "Son, what do you wish to say?

The suspense has everyone afraid to speak."

Raja Haider cleared his throat, appraising his audience. "All right. Perhaps it's time." His gaze stopped for a moment on Zainab, who buried her face in her mother's side. He reached over and put his hand on her head and let it graze over her hair.

Shahnaz stared, amazed and worried.

He pushed back from the table, took a deep breath, and addressed them. "I talked today with my friends in Lashkar-i-Taiba."

Ammi leaned into the edge of the table, her eyes narrowed. "About what?"

"About a lot of things I don't choose to go into." He swept his eyes around the table. "I'm going to the Red Mosque in Islamabad. I leave tomorrow."

Shahnaz flashed on all those young women in black with their long sticks. "Is that where you went to school?"

Naseer answered, drawing all eyes to himself. "Yes, in the boys' madrassa associated with the mosque, Jamia Faridia."

More pieces of the jigsaw puzzle of Raja Haider fell into place. Of course there'd be a boys' madrassa associated with the mosque as well as the girls'. And probably the activities of the girls would be supported by the boys. After all, the boys were much more likely to be out watching the neighborhood for potential wrongdoers and asking people about their jobs, where they were going, and why. It made sense that the boys were the eyes and ears of those girls holed up in the children's library.

Ammi's voice interrupted her puzzle-solving, a voice heavy with suspicion. "And what will you do there?"

Raja Haider lifted his head and locked eyes with his mother. "I'm joining a number of Believers to push for Sharia law. This will show that I, too, am properly committed to Islam." He paused, and with a fresh breath, plunged ahead. "I took a leave from work this afternoon and will travel to Islamabad tomorrow. I expect the household to honor my instructions in my absence." He transferred his gaze from face to astonished face around the table.

Noshaba sobbed. "But you may be killed."

He looked down his nose at her. "I'll be on Allah's jihad. Do not question His directions."

Noshaba shoved her chair back and ran from the room, roughly rubbing her nose with her dupatta.

Maryam broke the prickly silence. "I don't think this is a good decision."

"It's not yours to make. It's mine."

"Yes, and you're an adult. But you're also my child whom I don't wish to lose."

Shahnaz felt the concern sent from her mother-in-law down the long table, as well as the panicky trail left by Noshaba.

"I'll simply help them sort out how Sharia law can become the law of the land, and then I'll return."

Maryam sighed deeply and shook her head. "There's nothing simple about it."

Shahnaz swelled with ambivalence. She didn't want Raja Haider killed, but with him out of the house, Naseer would be in charge. There was a chance he'd loosen the rules. As she strove to contain her excitement, Raja Haider reached beneath his chair and pulled out the blueprints, which he handed to Naseer. "These, brother, are yours. See that they are followed."

Naseer was slow to reach for the papers, but when he held them, he nodded once to his brother. "I understand."

10

On the Saturday after Raja Haider's departure, Shahnaz was reading to Zainab and Riffat in the living room when she heard the front door opening. Hoping to see her husband, Shahnaz looked up and started to smile. Nooran stuck her head around the door. "Are you alone?"

"It's just me and the babies."

"Good thing." And she slipped through the doorway, a vision in blues and greens, shimmering like a mermaid emerging into sunlight.

Shahnaz felt her mouth open. "Oh, my!"

"You're not going to tell, are you?"

"Goodness, no. And who would I tell anyway?"

"Noshaba, for one. And—well—Naseer."

Shahnaz thought about her husband for a moment. "Oh, yes."

Nooran flopped into a chair and dropped her books on the floor. "I'm sick of the hijab getting in my eyes when I look through the microscope and finding its material wet with water or acid or who knows what. And our temporary buildings are so hot inside. It's not as though everyone in my classes has never seen me this way—they all have. It's not revolutionary."

Shahnaz grinned and, with a sense of pure impishness, blew a kiss to her sister-in-law.

When they sat down to dinner a few hours later, the room pulsed with animation as it hadn't done in weeks. Jamil and Qadir were the last to slide into their chairs and received a long look from their mother. "You're late for what reason?" It was her mock angry voice.

Jamil gave a soft punch to his brother's arm. "This kid's been writing pathetic Haiku poems, so I had to show him what a good Haiku was like."

Naseer stifled a smile. "Then you'd both better give us your best shots."

The two erstwhile poets looked at each other. The younger one grinned, the older one shrugged a shoulder.

"I'll go," Qadir said.

"He skipped town Friday,
Captured some fuzz the next day.
Now he's in hiding."

"A paltry attempt." Jamil drew a scrap of paper from his pocket, looked at Naseer, and took a sideways glance at Noshaba.

"The roaring Haider
Abandons his pride and snares
Policemen instead."

Naseer coughed and Shahnaz watched him smother his laughter.

Ammi tilted her head. "I'm afraid you'll have to explain. What has Raja Haider to do with policemen?"

The boys turned pleading faces to Naseer, who sent them a quelling look. "I was going to tell you later, Ammi. We heard about it on the news this afternoon. The girls from Jamia Hafsa captured four policemen earlier today, men who'd been guarding them so no one would hurt them."

The sound of a sob invited all eyes to Noshaba. "What has he done? Oh, what has he got himself into?"

Ammi put her hand out to rub Noshaba's arm. "I can't believe he's involved in this. Nor can I see him a party to hurting policemen who were there to help."

"But now they have guns," Noshaba said.

It was hard for Shahnaz to decide where to look—at an empty plate, at other family members, or at Noshaba.

Naseer pulled his lower lip into his mouth. "I'm sorry you heard about it this way. We should have taken more care in giving you the news." He shot a grim look at the Haiku perpetrators, who stared at their plates, and then turned back to his upset sister-in-law. "I'm afraid there've always been guns. The papers suggest there may be an arsenal in the basements of the mosque and the madrassa."

Through the tears streaking down her face, Noshaba peered at her brother-in-law. "I didn't know. Excuse me, Ammi. I must call my husband. I must know he's all right." She slipped from her seat and hurried down the hallway.

"And you two..." Naseer pointed at his brothers. "...will show proper respect to your elders. No more snide comments, even ones disguised as poetry." Looking around the table, he stopped at Nooran and sighed. "Young ladies, you *must* cover. It's Raja Haider's order, and I promised we'd obey his rules in his absence."

Shahnaz turned to her husband to see his eyes daring her to object. Then she felt a sharp pain on her left foot where Nooran's heel had thumped it. "You told."

Naseer shook his head. "No, Nooran, I didn't hear it from Shahnaz. I had it from a servant."

Shahnaz stared at her hands.

Later, alone with Naseer in their bedroom, Shahnaz tried to be solicitous, to bridge the crevasse that separated them. She whisked her husband's dusty shoes into the bathroom and cleaned them with a damp cloth before stowing them in his wardrobe. Taking out the vest he had just hung up, she located the clothes brush and stroked the garment's back.

From behind her, she heard Naseer's annoyed voice. "There's no need to act the servant. I understand why you didn't tell me Nooran had shed her abaya. I even acknowledge that loyalty among women is proper—sometimes. But I do admit, I'm having trouble telling whose side you're on."

She moved to him, taking his hands into her own. "I didn't mean to be disloyal to you. Truly, I didn't. I thought maybe you wouldn't mind Nooran in colors. It'd be like old times." Scanning his face, she saw a fleeting tenderness in his eyes and a determination in the setting of his chin.

He extracted his hands and allowed his body to sink into their chair and his head to fall against its back. "Raja Haider made it clear he expected me to uphold his rules." He focused hard on her face. "Do you think it was easy for me to agree? I knew these issues would come up. But how could I refuse?" He paused. "And he told me you spoke to him about working—after you'd discussed it with me and I'd asked you to leave it be."

Shahnaz sank down onto the bed, hating where his monologue was leading.

Assuming the dignity of a judge, her husband continued, "Shahnaz, can't you see you've put me in an untenable position? How can I ask my sisters to obey if I can't command my wife's obedience?"

She hung her head. "I thought I had a chance, that he'd listen if I put it the right way, that I could take the burden of argument from your shoulders."

"Oh, don't use me as an excuse. You did this for yourself."

She looked up, examining his shaking head. It was unsettling to feel this distance between them. It was awful to suspect she was wrong in not obeying. After all, she'd been angry, justifiably so. Yes, God asked Muslims to surrender multiple times each day, and she did this willingly in prayer, but she couldn't simply surrender to these men on earth. It all came back to this definition of obedience. Was she only able to obey when it was abstract, when it made no difference in her life to do so? Or was she right not to surrender in this case? Were her husband's beliefs moving closer to his brother's, close enough that she lost her comfort in being with him?

"Why did you agree to enforce his rules?"

"Because it's my place to obey my older brother. Whether I like it or not." He pointed his index finger at her and used it to emphasize his words.

"But you don't believe in them."

He jumped up and took two angry strides to face her. "I gave my word."

She saw his hand form a fist. Her mouth dropped open, and she stared at him in horror. He wanted to hit her. Her gentle husband. "There's no need to punish me further."

Naseer's eyes shifted downward to his hands. He shook out his arm and turned away.

For a moment, she ran her fingers over the embroidered flowers on the bedspread, gathering courage. "And what about Rabia's wedding?"

He groaned. "You'll all cover. Surely you know that?"

She gulped. "Do we have to stay in the women's tent?" To her own ears, her voice wheedled like a small child's.

He walked over to stare into the night. "Yes, you do."

The kernel of hope that, with Raja Haider gone, the house would return to the days of Sohail's presence faded to a speck and was gone.

The following morning, she was surprised to find Irum at the door. Her brown shalwar kameez with the black embroidery deepened the worry lines on her pinched face. They'd not spoken in some time, with all the family turmoil, and Shahnaz was embarrassed not to have inquired how the visit had gone with Amir's parents. "How good to see you. I'm sorry I haven't called. Come in, come in."

Shahnaz ushered Irum to the garden, bringing the children with them. Riffat was pleased to lie down on her stomach and practice flying while Zainab clung to Shahnaz's clothes, thumb in mouth, looking from one adult to the other. Shahnaz apologized. "Noshaba's in bed, I'm afraid, so I'm watching the children." She patted her niece's soft hair and then shifted her body to face Irum. "How are things?"

Irum pulled her dupatta further forward on her head, making blinders that shielded her face. "I've come to say goodbye."

Shahnaz's hand rose up to her face. "Oh, Irum. What's happened?"

"You haven't heard?" She glanced sideways at her friend.

Worried by the fact that Irum would not look directly at her, Shahnaz leaned forward to see her downcast eyes. "No. What is it?"

Irum focused on the tired grass. "I've repeated the story so many times, I thought everyone knew." She pressed imaginary wrinkles from the skirt of her tunic. "You see, my parents did meet Amir and his parents, and they didn't dislike them. But...well, his father's a farmer, not a professional, and my father thought I could do better. I kept arguing that Amir had a professional position, that he would be promoted, and my father was listening, but then..."

"Then what?"

Concentrating on the browning lawn, Irum continued in a monotone. "Amir and I went up to Bagh last Friday—Wali was driving—and after the opening meeting we stopped for a picnic."

Shahnaz imagined them sitting on one of those brilliant mountain slopes of thick grass and stately trees.

Irum folded her hands. "We were laughing at something one of the parents had said at the community meeting, sharing a mango, when four teenaged boys stalked toward us. They were very angry. They screamed at us, called me a prostitute—it was horrible—and one of them pulled my earrings from my ears. See?" She pushed the dupatta back to show the jagged scars and then drew it forward again. "Those were all I had of my sister."

Shahnaz took Irum's hand. "I'm so sorry."

Irum sniffed. "But that's not the worst. They beat Amir, as though they wanted to kill him. Wali waded in, ordering them to stop, but two of the boys restrained him, and it wasn't until Amir was unconscious—and so bloody—that they backed away."

"Will he be all right?"

Irum grimaced. "Physically, yes, I think, though his face will be scarred." She bit her lip. "I thought that would be the end of it. I thought, naively, the worst was over when we got Amir to a doctor. But the nightmare had just begun."

Shahnaz's left hand unfurled onto her cheek. "What happened?"

"Apparently the boys went to their imam, who decided that it's the presence of organizations like Peace that have brought immoral behavior into Kashmir. They've demanded that we fire all women staff. I think they'd be pleased if we shut our doors."

"We can't agree. Please say Peace didn't agree."

"All the senior managers are here from Islamabad, meeting with the imams. People from a number of organizations are closeted together to prepare a counterproposal. You can guess what's in it: only women can share a car, all women staff will be driven home before dark, no woman will share office space with a man.

That sort of thing."

"And *you*. How bad is it?"

Irum wiped away angry tears. "My father's come to take me home. He's livid, convinced I'm ruined. He's waiting in your drive-way while I say goodbye."

Shahnaz hugged her, fiercely, unable to find words of comfort. "I'll miss you so much."

"And I'll miss you." Irum faced Shahnaz, a frown pulling her lips down at the edges. "Marrying Amir is out of the question. I'm to be married this weekend to my cousin. It's unlikely that I'll be allowed to visit you again."

Shahnaz couldn't meet her friend's eyes. "Insh'allah, you'll find happiness with him."

"Insh'allah. I wish it wasn't conceived as a punishment. I wish it were Amir. But I must accept that Allah knows best in all things." Her hand trembled as it fixed her dupatta more firmly about her face. She looked so pale Shahnaz thought she might be in shock.

"Shahnaz, there's more bad news. That baby with thalassemia, little Pervez, died last week. And Bibi told me the father's broth-er is betrothed to his mother's sister. The family is insistent that Allah would not bring them illness from another wife." She found Shahnaz's hand. "One last thing. Remember Fatima? Her baby was stillborn, and she's very weak."

As they rose to exit the garden, Shahnaz despaired. So many losses. She was sinking in quicksand.

———•———

As Shahnaz had predicted, that last weekend in May, Rabia's wedding weekend, proved to be hot and dry, with the tarmac on the road south to Islamabad shimmering and dust rising in clouds as cars passed on the shoulders. The Khans' two-car caravan bumped slowly along, prepared to drop Shahnaz and Naseer at her parents' home and the rest of the family at their cousins'. Right until the last moment, it wasn't clear whether Noshaba would join them. Caught between wanting to stay home—as her husband had instructed—and wanting to be closer to him, she packed and unpacked her suitcase, muttering alternatively "I must go" and "I shouldn't go." Eventually she climbed into the car with her daughters, not intending to enjoy the parties, which she said were frivolous, but to support her husband's jihad.

Shahnaz tried to sleep along the route, hoping she could find her way to an oblivion that stopped her picturing the flock of black crows they would resemble at this wedding, the bucket of her self-esteem emptying drip by drip, the shrinking of Noshaba into a two-dimensional version of her already small self, the erasure of Irum from her work "family," her worry that she hadn't yet found a doctor, and the upcoming eruption of her sister's anger over having a wedding marred by miserable relatives.

Rabia tore open the door in greeting, yanking so hard that the inside handle smacked the hallway wall. Shahnaz winced at the noise a second before her sister pulled her into the foyer. "You've got to see my clothes! Come on, come on. They're hung all over my room, and you've never seen anything so beautiful, I promise. And take that abaya off—I don't want to see one more minute of it than I have to." With a hand on the banister railing, she turned back to her brother-in-law. "Honestly, Naseer, I can't believe you're making her wear that thing. It's archaic!"

Shahnaz glanced at her husband, whose lips managed a rueful curve. He waved her up the stairs. Feeling a little ashamed of her sister, yet pleased to be valued so much by someone, she stood between the two. "All right, all right, I'll follow you. Give me a minute." She hung the abaya on a coat hook in the hallway and unpinned the covering across her face.

Halfway up the stairs, she spotted her Ammi, looking mildly deranged, peering out from Rabia's room, the one that used to be Shahnaz's as well. Several spikes of hair poked out from Ammi's head, and she waved a white cleaning rag as though wanting desperately to surrender. Looking at her younger daughter, she shook her head. "Such a theatrical production we have here, complete with prima donna."

Suspiciously, Rabia stopped, one hand on her doorframe. "What's a prima donna?"

Feeling a tiny surge of energy, Shahnaz gave Rabia's back a push, sending her stumbling into the room. "It's someone way too full of herself."

Then she hugged her mother. "It'll all be over soon."

Her mother smiled.

"I am *not* full of myself. It's my wedding, and I have a right to be excited." Hands on her hips, Rabia dared her mother and sister to contradict her. "Frankly, I think I'm taking this abaya business very well when we all know your covered face is going to ruin all the pictures. I've decided it's your problem that no one will know who you are, and I'm not going to let it cut into my pleasure."

Shahnaz tried to shake off the feeling that she was a sad burden to this family. At least, she vowed to hide it. "So, take me on a tour of these fabulous clothes you have."

Spread out across the bed lay a royal blue silk kameez decorated with yellow and gold sequins and embroidery in a paisley pattern. The dupatta was gossamer fine, with matching decorations, and the shalwar an identical gold. It made Shahnaz think of the rajas and ranis in museum pictures, and she moved to finger the material. "It *is* gorgeous." She felt a twinge of envy.

Rabia danced from foot to foot. "See? Told you they were superb. That one's for the Mehndi." Pulling again at Shahnaz's arm, she pointed to the outfit hanging on the mirror. "Now, look at this one!"

Shahnaz gave in to her sister's tug and turned to see the clothing for the Walima—a blood red heavier silk with a woven pattern on the bodice that followed a tribal tradition hundreds of years old. The dupatta, a lighter weight silk of the same deep red, had a border in the pattern. Running her hands gently over the material, Shahnaz was certain it was all hand-done. The pantaloons flared at the bottom, according to the fashion for weddings, and they, too, sported an embroidered hem. "I'm awed, Rabia, truly."

In a momentary oasis of calm, Rabia glowed. "Javed's the oldest son, you know, and his family believes he should have the best." Then she giggled. "I guess that means I'm the best, doesn't it?"

Shahnaz turned to her mother and rolled her eyes.

Ammi shrugged her shoulders. "She's been like this for weeks."

When they finished the required exclamations over all the new clothes, Ammi persuaded Rabia to settle down for a cup of tea in the dining room. In the kindly voice of a liege lord, Rabia allowed as how it would be permissible to include Naseer, so Shahnaz went to find him.

Reaching for a mug of steaming tea and a chocolate chip biscuit, Rabia poured out more details to her sister and brother-in-law. "Javed's been promoted." She looked from Shahnaz to Naseer and back again. "He's going to manage a large branch of the bank in Lahore." She extended her exhale so long on the city's final syllable that her listeners knew that city ranked near to heaven in her esteem.

Feeling restored by her sips of tea, Shahnaz encouraged her sister to say more. "So, you'll be moving to Lahore?"

"Um hmm. Javed's already found a house for us, and his mother has helped with the furnishings. He says it's very fancy, with no expense spared." The pride showed in her posture as she swayed slightly from side to side and ended up as tall as a flagpole. "Javed told me he thinks his next promotion will be to London." Again, the awe was evident in the breath that entered unbidden into the pronunciation of the city's name.

Shahnaz noticed that her mother's eyes remained on her tea mug as she slowly moved it from table to mouth. She turned to her radiant sister. "It sounds like you're excited about moving away."

"Of course! This is like a dream come true. I mean, Javed says Lahore has a much better social life than Islamabad. He has lots of relatives there who know everyone worth knowing. And Javed says I'll like entertaining because he's found us a wonderful cook who knows all the best recipes and can make anything I want."

Shahnaz, already weary of the onslaught of "Javed says," plugged gamely on. "And will you mind being far from home?"

"Me?" Rabia squealed. "Not at all. Javed says I'll be so busy with all I have to do to finish the house and entertain that I won't have time to miss Islamabad."

Shahnaz saw hurt in her mother's eyes from this blithe dismissal of home and parents. "And your friends and family here?"

Rabia waved the question away. "You can come and visit. It'll be a fabulous chance to get away from your crumbling house."

She glanced at her husband to see how he was taking the description of his home and saw that, thankfully, he had his hand in front of his mouth, hiding a smile.

Naseer set down his empty teacup. "It looks as though we'll be able to start rebuilding our 'crumbling house' this summer actually, so if it gets too hot for you in Lahore, say next spring or summer, you'll be able to come visit us in the mountains."

Looking from one of them to the other, eyebrows knitted together, Rabia paused a moment. "Yes, perhaps."

—•—

Shahnaz felt like a disconnected witness to the blur of activities that marriage weekend, an almost invisible shadow lingering at the periphery of the expensive show. Through thin separations between tent flaps on the night of the Nikah, she watched the comings and goings of more than two thousand people as they gathered on the lawn of the Faisal Mosque. Turning to scan the crowd in the women's tent, she was accosted by the heat of all the milling bodies and the noise of the animated conversation. She picked out all three of the Khan sisters, as their black coverings leapt from the colorful crowd. Being only with women, they could have dispensed with the abayas, but they'd decided to accumulate as much sympathy as possible, hoping people would speak to Naseer. They must be having as hot a time as she was, having kept her abaya on in the hope that Naseer would invite her to join him in the central tent. No luck there. Noshaba hadn't come to the festivities. She was pacing the house and phoning Raja Haider's mobile every few minutes.

Thank goodness her cousin Talaat from Detroit had once again flown into Pakistan and was staying in their house. She needed Talaat's optimism. Letting her eyes wander about in search of the ivory silk shalwar kameez Talaat had designed for the occasion, Shahnaz felt an easing of tension and a growing excitement. Surely Talaat's clothes stood out among the colors of the crowd, if not by their style: the bodice was sleeveless, the neck deeply vee'd, and the fit skintight. Embellished with small pearls, the kameez had to be turning the heads of everyone in the place. Modest it was not.

When Shahnaz found her, blessedly within the women's tent, she was surrounded by a bevy of cousins. Threading her way through the guests, Shahnaz stopped to greet those she knew and heard Talaat's light bantering and laughter like a nightingale's song decorating the evening air. When she arrived at her cousin's side, Talaat used her right arm to pull Shahnaz close. "So good to see you. We haven't had a moment to talk since I arrived." Looking at the circle of relatives, she hooked her arm around Shahnaz's. "You'll excuse us, I know, as we catch up with each other?" With a smile to each, she took Shahnaz's arm and propelled her out into the warm evening air. "Phew. Even the fans can't keep me from sweating, and I'm about to stain this dress. It's still cool in Detroit, and I'm not used to this heat. But enough of my complaints, tell me how you are."

They walked in step along the road fronting the mosque. The crow and the dove, Shahnaz thought, as she avoided the droppings from the horses that had pulled the groom's carriage. "This is sort of a difficult time for me."

Talaat snorted. "That's an understatement. We've got you hiding in the women's tent, your sisters-in-law complaining about their restrictions to anyone who'll listen, and Naseer speaking little and looking pained. What's going on?"

"My brother-in-law is camped out at the Red Mosque pushing for Sharia law. He left us with strict instructions about our behavior, which fueled the family's uproar. His wife's scared he's going to die."

Talaat stopped and turned to Shahnaz, a frown creasing her brow. "Not to make the scene even worse, but in your shoes, I'd be worrying he's going to come out of there with Taliban fervor and an even harsher view of Islam, one that restricts women to the house."

"I...I know. I hate this. I hate *him*. It's so hard. He's my brother-in-law and I should respect him and obey him, but I don't want these rules. I want to work. I want my freedom back." She sensed she was wailing and fought to control her tone. "It's all mixed up. I'm supposed to discipline my sisters-in-law for things we all believe are right. Naseer's enforcing all of Raja Haider's rules, and here I am pregnant and forbidden from seeing a male doctor."

"Wow. That's extreme." They walked several paces. "Are there women doctors you can see?"

"There aren't up north. I've asked Ammi to look around in Islamabad, but she hasn't found anyone yet."

"She will." They strolled another few steps. "And if Raja Haider dies? Will you—and Naseer—continue these restrictions in some weird honoring of his memory?"

The question stopped Shahnaz's words. She stood in the road, staring into the muddled sky, wondering what she would do. "Please God, not that."

After giving her cousin a hug, Talaat took her hand and pulled her back into motion. "I can't figure out Pakistan. Each time I come over, the country seems more conservative, more unable to decide to be a part of the world. We can't let it move backwards, we just can't. It's so different in the States. Even in the aftermath of September eleventh, when Muslims were viewed as the enemy, most of us have a sense of possibilities open for the future." Her wooden heels clacked decidedly against the pavement. She chortled. "I've forgotten to tell you, in the stress of this visit, I have personal news, one of those 'possibilities:' I'm to be married next winter."

Shahnaz whirled her head around to see her cousin's shadowy grin. "You're full of surprises. Come on, tell it all."

"After your wedding, Abu went ballistic about my needing to marry. He couldn't stand the fact that you—being younger than I—were married first, and then when he heard Rabia was to be married, well, it was the last straw. So, I found three men among my acquaintances that I thought would be tolerable husbands, and who came from families my father would find acceptable, presented him with the list, and here we are."

"Talaat, you're amazing. And who is this paragon?"

"His name is Asad Khan—no relation to your Khans, I'm afraid. I've known him forever, and I think we shall suit. He admires me and my fashion designs, and I like his style. He's handsome and urbane, wears designer clothes with a flair, has a wry sense of humor, and just before he gets to seem staid and boring, let me say he loves to hunt. I think of him as a modern-day Mohammad Ali Jinnah. We shall do. We shall do."

"I should think so." Shahnaz couldn't imagine marrying a man as rich and elegant as the first president of Pakistan. How elevated Talaat must be in social status in the States. And how sure she was of her own ability to succeed at whatever she tried. Shahnaz recalled the feeling. She'd once believed in herself that way.

——••——

It was almost dark when their car reached Muzaffarabad the day after the Walima. Noshaba had spent the trip sobbing that her husband wouldn't talk to her, that he was going to die, that her babies would have no father, and that—basically—the world was coming to an end. In their confusion over their mother's distress, both children fussed, cried, and demanded attention. Shahnaz spent every last bit of her energy on them and on keeping her temper when she wanted to wring Noshaba's neck. Upon arrival at home, Noshaba crawled into bed, her face to the wall. Even her crying children couldn't bring her to her feet, and the brunt of childcare landed heavily on Shahnaz. With Maryam's help, she calmed the children, put them to bed, and sought refuge in her own chamber, telling her husband she was sorry but she couldn't talk.

The next morning, with the children in tow, she told Maryam that she feared for Noshaba's health. "She's not eating, and I've only been able to persuade her to take a cup of tea today. The children don't understand why she turns away from them. I'm not getting anywhere. Please, Ammi, will you talk to her?"

Maryam set her pen down on the dining room table, where she looked to be writing notes, removed her glasses, and pinched the bridge of her nose. She stared a moment at Zainab who peeked at her from behind Shahnaz, thumb poked resolutely into her mouth. "She always was one for punishing herself, that Noshaba. I'd rather throttle that son of mine for scaring all of us like this, but he isn't taking my calls. Let's see what we can do." She pushed herself up with both arms and stood still as though rolling up her proverbial sleeves.

"They did let the policemen go, didn't they?" Maryam asked as they passed the kitchen.

"Yes, unharmed." Shahnaz shifted Riffat to her left shoulder and reached to open the door to the garden.

"Thank goodness. Though I don't imagine that's the end of this nonsense. Perhaps Raja Haider will talk them out of further action."

Shahnaz felt her eyebrows rise with the naiveté of this comment. "Do you really believe he could—or wants to?"

Maryam sighed, shoulders slumping. She stopped to look up at Shahnaz. "He was such a positive little boy, sure of himself, convinced he could do anything, with God's help. I hardly noticed as his optimism faded. I guess I misread a lot about him. I even thought his judgmental pronouncements were a stage he was going through." She paused. "You're right to call me on that. I must be realistic. It's far more likely that this whole affair will only be resolved by people dying."

"Yes, I'm afraid so."

Shaking her head, Maryam covered the few remaining meters to Noshaba's bedroom door and knocked. Shahnaz and the children trailed behind.

Hearing a tearful "come in," the three generations of females made their way into the darkened space. Noshaba's long hair spread willy-nilly across her pillow. A box of tissues sat askew on the edge of the sheet and bobbled as she struggled to sit up.

Maryam walked around the bed and dropped down on it. Shahnaz and the children remained at the foot. Having drawn her hand across Noshaba's brow, Maryam began to straighten the sheets and collect the wadded tissues. "My dear, I simply cannot let you continue like this. You have children who need you and a husband who is relying on you to keep the house going in his absence."

Noshaba brought a fresh tissue to her suffering nose and let her arm drop to the bed. "I'm afraid for him."

Maryam patted her hand. "And probably afraid for yourself. Now, I want you to listen to me." She gripped Noshaba's hand. "In Sohail's family, widows are always taken care of. You and your children have a home here for as long as you'd like. Do you understand?"

Noshaba nodded.

Shahnaz worried. That was Sohail's house. How could Maryam be sure she herself would have a home if Raja Haider returned and found she was writing?

"So, now that that issue is taken off the table, let's talk about your husband. I want to know exactly what he's told you. We know you've talked to him but not much about what he's said."

Noshaba's watery voice said, "He doesn't want me there."

"A wise man." Maryam rubbed Noshaba's hands between her own, as though infusing them with life and energy. "I wouldn't want you there either—a lot of bickering, women and men threatening violence, guns being collected—I'm surprised you'd want to be in the midst of all that."

"I should be at my husband's side." She withdrew her hand and reached for a tissue.

"When he calls for you, child. Not until then. What does he say he's doing now?"

"Last week he said they'll continue these actions until Musharraf agrees to Sharia law. Which could be forever." Then she turned on her side and buried her face in her pillow.

"Noshaba, look at me. He won't be there *forever*." Maryam brushed the soggy hair away from Noshaba's eyes. "It may feel like every day lasts forever, but that isn't true...What has he told you they do all day?"

"Just pray and go to meetings."

Maryam looked up at Shahnaz. "I think we should push Naseer to find out more."

Shahnaz nodded, unsure herself what her husband knew—and what he was keeping from the women.

"And now, Noshaba, you must get up and shower and dress. We're all going to the Sangam Hotel for tea. We'll sit outside on the terrace, enjoy the river running by, and your daughter can watch the men filling sacks with sand and loading their donkeys."

"I cannot. I cannot." She rolled her head from side to side.

"You'll do it for me, for Shahnaz, and for your daughters." She turned her stern schoolmistress look on Noshaba and pulled her up to a sitting position. "I think some lavender-scented soap is in order." Taking the small hand of her granddaughter, Maryam walked toward the door. "I know you remember just where my special soaps are, don't you?"

Zainab nodded, her thumb traveling up and down with her head.

"Then we'll get them for your Ammi and be back in a few minutes." At the door, she stopped and looked back at Shahnaz. "Be sure she doesn't crawl into that bed again."

———•———

After their sojourn outside the family walls, Noshaba and her daughters all took naps, allowing Shahnaz and Maryam time to talk. Choosing the quiet of the living room, Shahnaz sat back into the crook of the couch, against an arm, and invited her mother-in-law to take the other end. "Ammi, I feel so closed in. What can we do about all this?"

"I don't know. We've gone from one grief to another these past weeks. When I can capture some perspective, I try to convince myself we're doing the work all families must, after a death. Ours is just more dramatic than most."

Having only these few weeks' experience of grieving, Shahnaz could only nod agreement. "I haven't had a chance to tell you, but my friend Irum has left Muzaffarabad. She and my boss Amir were the NGO employees who—"

"He was the man beaten by those boys?"

Of course, Maryam's grapevine had relayed the news. "Yes. It looks like the NGOs around here are going to tighten the restrictions on female employees."

Shahnaz sipped her tea and settled the cup in the saucer. "You may not want to tell me—and I'll understand if that's the case—but are you writing?"

Maryam stared at her for a moment, head cocked to the side, as if debating how much to reveal. "It's not that I don't trust you. I don't want to wind you up in another tangle with Naseer."

"Ammi, we all need to share with someone. How about if I start? My mother is looking for a woman doctor for me. I feel all right, and as far as I can tell the baby is okay, but I so want a professional opinion."

Maryam smiled. "Insh'allah, this pregnancy will be fine."

"Ammi, you know I respect your confidences, and if it makes any difference to you, well, Naseer's pretty much locked me out of his thoughts."

With a rueful smile, Maryam divulged that she had almost finished the first book. "I can't bear having nothing but worry to occupy my time. Writing is a necessary escape."

Shahnaz closed her eyes. "I know what you mean. I hate waiting, wondering what will happen, doing so little." She stared at the door, seeing a ghost of her former self beckoning. It glowed with an infectious smile, an aura of energy, and the brilliance of greens and golds.

11

By June, the air had settled into its summer role of heavy blanket. As was true on so many hot nights, on the twenty-third the family lingered in the living room after dinner. It was simply too draining to sit outside or in a stuffy bedroom—and they were trimming their use of electricity to match their significantly reduced family income. Sohail's co-workers had donated a considerable sum to the family, but without his and Raja Haider's salaries, the adults worried this would not be enough to live on. Without any explicit discussion, everyone eschewed air conditioning, except when the family gathered in this room.

Jamil turned on the television to Geo News. "Hey, look. It's Lal Masjid, the Red Mosque."

All talking ceased as eyes were riveted on the TV. The camera spent a few minutes on the black-clad girls, clustered on the library's porch proclaiming they had broken up a prostitution ring run from a local acupuncture clinic. They paraded a group of perhaps nine mostly Chinese men and women before the camera and then sent their prisoners to the bowels of the building. The broadcast shifted to the mosque's prayer leaders. As Abdul Aziz and Abdul Rashid Ghazi boasted of cleaning up Islamabad, the camera panned across a group of men. There, in clear view, was Raja Haider.

"Look, it's him. How stupid can he be?" Jamil pointed to the screen.

Naseer sat forward on the couch scanning the group of men with their dark beards and serious gazes. "I don't like this. Not only is it clear to us that Raja Haider's there, this video clip will show the police, the army, and the intelligence services that he's one of them."

Loosened from Noshaba's grasp as she covered her face with her hands, Zainab toddled to the television and stuck her finger on her father's face. "Abu?"

Shahnaz looked at Naseer and then at her sister-in-law. Being closest to the television, she moved to kneel beside the child. "Yes, dear. Now, come sit in this chair with me."

When the Geo News report ended and the family had absorbed the stories on every other English and Urdu channel, Naseer assured them all that he'd try to call Raja Haider that night or, if he couldn't, early the next morning.

As they reluctantly dispersed, Shahnaz saw Maryam shake her head. "Why is he doing this? What does he have to prove?" The older woman held on to the back of a chair for a long moment and then moved slowly toward her bedroom.

Fortunately for their level of stress, Raja Haider answered his mobile just before midnight. Since reception was better in the garden, Naseer stepped outside. Shahnaz sat on the step into their room, knowing she couldn't sleep until this call was over. Sensing movement to her right, she looked up to see Noshaba quietly opening her bedroom door.

"Yes, yes. We saw you on television...Hmm?...I'm not sure what to say. Mostly we're worried for your safety...I don't support prostitution either...In fact, I have lots of concerns about this action. Like—how do you know that these acupuncturists were doing anything other than acupuncture?...Uh huh...So, a couple of boys from

Jamia Faridia saw something suspicious, and that's enough?...Okay, okay. It's not enough for me, but I accept that. Have you thought about the pressure that'll come because those kidnapped are Chinese?...You honestly think that'll *help* your cause? More pressure on the government?...Frankly, I'm afraid it'll provoke retribution...I guess I'm sorry you're ready for it, too. We need you here, you know. Noshaba's crying and scared most of the time. Renovation will be hit-or-miss without your guidance. Are you sure, very sure, you want to remain in the middle of this?"

Shahnaz rose to put her arm around her sister-in-law.

When Naseer clicked his mobile shut, he dropped his arm and let his shoulders droop. As he turned to see his audience, he shook his head. "He won't come home, not now. He sees this as a test of his faith, a test from God. I'm sorry, Noshaba. I'll keep calling, keep talking, but I'm afraid the future is in God's hands."

Shahnaz helped her crying sister-in-law into her room, murmuring platitudes and hoping to reassure her. It was some time before she found her own bed and could discover sleep.

——••——

The next morning, Shahnaz began her day in the garden steeping in the heat, idly watching a sleeping Riffat draped across her skirt, and letting her mind wander. Already, by nine o'clock, her face streamed rivulets of sweat as she leaned back against the jacaranda tree. Much of her clothing was damp across her lap, yet it was too much effort to pick up Riffat and go inside where it was cooler. She looked about languorously, thinking to herself that she had to figure out something to do besides stew about Raja Haider, Naseer, unborn babies, and obedience. Even making a shopping list was better than wishing her brother-in-law would disappear, worrying if the husband she loved would come back to her, or rehearsing her next speech to get Noshaba out of bed. The ringing of the phone in her pocket roused her with a start. She dug in to pull it out. Ah, she thought when she saw the incoming number, it was Rabia.

"Shahnaz, you really have to come visit us. I'm having the best time! Lahore's awesome and we're out to dinner or a party several nights a week. Javed knows *everybody*! Last night we went to the home of the president of his bank, which you wouldn't believe. It was huge and decorated like a palace. There were servants all over the place offering drinks, passing around appetizers, serving dinner. You know. They were everywhere. And the president said Javed's an excellent manager. How about that? 'Excellent,' he said. Really. Javed says that he may be sent to London as early as this fall. Wouldn't that be incredible? Then you could come visit me in England!"

Shahnaz pictured Rabia pacing across her air-conditioned sitting room, a half-drunk mug of tea on the table, her dupatta trailing and her arm waving with this recital of her delights. A sudden wave of jealousy flooded over her. Why did Rabia get all the gifts while she suffered? She was instantly appalled at herself for the thought. "It sounds like you're having the time of your life. But London? That's so far away."

"Yes, but who wouldn't want to go? Javed says he'll be in a training program with people from several countries—and England, of course, so we'll have a whole network of people to socialize with. It's what I've always wanted!"

London, Shahnaz mused, a perfect escape. But not for me. I'm committed here, like it or not. "Have you told Ammi?"

"Yes, and she's already cried and said it was so-o-o far away. But you wait; she'll come around, and I'll bet she and Abu come for a visit. You'll come, too, won't you?"

Shahnaz pulled the sodden material of her pants away from

her skin. What to say? "Not an option, I'm afraid."

"What do you mean?" Rabia probably had a hand on her hip.

"Rabia, we don't have the money. You know I'm pregnant. And I don't have the energy." Shahnaz dropped her head back against the tree.

"I don't understand you. This is the chance of a lifetime, and you're turning it down?"

Shahnaz sighed. Her dream was comprised of comfort in her husband's love, bearing a healthy child, going to work each day, and watching the maternal and infant death rates slide downward. Flying off to England wouldn't get her any of those.

A more subdued Rabia spoke into her ear. "Will you come visit me in Lahore? Javed's going to be away for a week or ten days at the end of July, and I could show you around."

Shahnaz groaned, torn between the idea of escape and her family responsibilities. "I don't see how. You know what we're going through here. Haven't you made friends with some of Javed's relatives? You could spend time with them."

There was a considerable silence before Rabia answered. "Not really. His cousins haven't been exactly friendly. I mean, they invite us to dinner but then—well—they talk to Javed. I understand, of course. He's *their* cousin and they've known him forever. But they could've invited me last week when they went to this great new spa to have manicures and pedicures. Javed says they just didn't think of it and I shouldn't worry."

"But you are worried."

"Well, yes." It sounded like she was telling a secret. "Do you think they don't like me?"

Rabia sounded like the ten-year-old Shahnaz remembered whose schoolmate had told her she was "stuck up." "Insh'allah, you'll find your niche." And may I be so blessed as to find mine.

When Shahnaz closed the phone, she dropped her hand to the

bench. Her inner critic cried out that Rabia was her route of escape from this house, her constant childcare duties, a husband who chastised her, and rules that chafed her. How could she have said no?

As Riffat began to fuss, Shahnaz picked her up. "You, too, little one? Unhappiness must be catching."

—•—

Over the next two weeks, Naseer called his brother every night. After a couple of hours of television news broadcasts, when the family went off to bed, he disappeared into the garden, mobile in hand. Each night, bedroom doors stood open and listeners eavesdropped. Shahnaz listened in her search for a personal reprieve, fearful that the government would agree to adopt the protesters' stringent definition of Sharia law. With a simmering anger and growing panic, she watched the calendar days pass.

Noshaba listened to the phone calls in quiet desperation. Her husband wasn't answering her calls, so Naseer was her only chance for connection. As the days passed, she pretended to be more interested in her children, put more food on her plate, but her kameezes hung from her shoulders and her shalwars stayed up only because of the strong elastic at the waist.

The brothers spoke only once more over the next ten days. Raja Haider explained he had to attend meetings or exercises or prayers that made talking on the phone very difficult. And, no, he did not wish to return home. He was doing important work.

On July 3, the television news had the family glued to their seats. Some madrassa students had snatched weapons from the police deployed in a nearby building, and the government leapt into action. Troops and paramilitary cordoned off the mosque and Jamia Hafsa. They wouldn't tell reporters what their orders were, though it was clear the government was going to bring this stand-off to an end—and soon. The troops bristled with guns, rolls of barbed wire unfurled around the buildings, sand bags were heaped to form protective guard posts within which uniformed men pointed heavy weapons. Raja Haider's mobile was turned off. Noshaba was distraught.

The next morning, Jamil flipped the television on during breakfast, and first one and then another of them sidled into the living room. The government had imposed a curfew in the G-6 sector around the mosque. During the night, the army had trucked in more barbed wire and sand bags; they'd closed off nearby streets with guard posts and sentries, ensuring only residents could enter or exit.

In an attempt to moderate what could turn into a full-blown disaster, the government offered free passage out—through regulated checkpoints—for any unarmed student or adult who wished to leave. At the same time, they announced that the army would shoot any armed militant on sight.

Noshaba's whimpers turned to sobs and then wailing. As Shahnaz tried to calm her, Naseer headed out to the garden for a call. Only a few moments later, he returned and shook his head at Shahnaz, who continued her quiet assurances to her sister-in-law. "Naseer will keep trying to reach him. He'll argue that he should take advantage of the amnesty, that there will be a better time for the push for Sharia law. He'll say whatever he can to convince Raja Haider to leave." She looked up at her husband's gloomy face and then at the television pictures of tanks rolling down the deserted roads of the residential area.

The television remained on all day with Noshaba refusing to leave the room, clicking from channel to channel in search of her husband. Shahnaz hovered near her, keeping watch over the children and growing more and more annoyed at the constant repetition of the same short tapes. A newsman complained that the government was severely restricting journalists in an attempt to keep the number of onlookers to a minimum. By evening, the news was grim. Gunfire had been exchanged. At least sixteen people had been killed, the reporter said, perhaps one hundred and forty injured. The prayer leader, Abdul Aziz, and his wife, the director of Jamia Hafsa, tried to leave, both dressed in burqas, but they were discovered and held by the authorities.

Maryam waved a hand at the TV. "If the imam is bailing out, surely Raja Haider won't stay." But her eldest son still had his mobile off, and none of the TV snippets showed him coming through a security gate from the mosque to the street. Late reports claimed that the abandonment of the mosque by its senior religious leader had opened floodgates to about twelve hundred. But since no one would admit how many had been inside, it was unclear how many remained.

Maryam threw up her hands. "They have the madrassa's director locked up. Why won't she tell the enrollment in her school? They have the prayer leader. He must be able to estimate the number left inside. Does he want them to die?"

Naseer, who had been pacing behind the couch, pressed his hands onto her shoulders. "We don't know who's telling the truth. From what I heard at work, the police have estimates of enrollment from hundreds of girls to several thousand and numbers of adults that range from a few to hundreds. They don't know who to trust."

Around midnight, Maryam struggled to her feet, pushing against the arm of the couch to reach her full height. "I can't take even one more repetition of these scenes of tanks and soldiers. My knees are stiff from being locked in the same position. I'm going to bed believing my son is out of there."

Shahnaz transferred her arm from Noshaba's shoulders to her elbow. "Come, let's head for bed as well."

With Naseer on one side and Shahnaz on the other, Noshaba shuffled toward the hall. She sniffed back tears. "Call him again, please."

And as the hot breeze ruffled the leaves of the jacaranda tree, Naseer rang his brother one more time. No answer.

—••—

For the next few days, the Khans—and the rest of the world— saw students hurl hand grenades from inside the mosque, the army demolish the wall that separated the mosque and girls' madrassa from the street, and heavy explosions light up the complex. The television blared continuously as Musharraf extended the amnesty and militants swore that they would die rather than surrender. No one knew how many children remained inside. The government broadcast a death toll of nineteen, then twenty-four, while Assistant Prayer Leader Ghazi, still inside, claimed it was seventy. A delegation held last-minute talks with the militants—who, by that time, had ousted Ghazi—to no avail.

Finally, on the morning of July 10, the family watched in horror as the TV played and replayed a tape of the mosque exploding under government fire and shadowy men in uniform storming into the ruins to free any remaining women and children and capture the militants. The army offensive had begun in the wee hours, and as the day progressed, the channels repeated the same few pictures of the smoking ruins of the mosque and Jamia Hafsa with their weapons caches, splotches of blood, and blackened walls.

Noshaba began the day in tears, which ballooned into hysterics and her collapse in her room. Shahnaz calmed her down, staying until she slept, and then tracked down Naseer and Maryam in her bedroom. Having no luck contacting Raja Haider on the mobile, they had called Maryam's brother Tanvir to beg him to use his influence to find his nephew.

Naseer paced the room. "It'll be chaos in Islamabad, with people searching hospitals and morgues, but Tanvir Uncle can find him, if anyone can. He knows senior army men."

Ammi's dupatta had slipped back on her head, and tendrils of hair waved about her face. "I'm so afraid he's been killed. My son, my talented son. Such a waste." Tears slipped down her cheeks, which she swiped at with her fingers. Turning to Shahnaz, she sighed. "How's Noshaba?"

Shahnaz shrugged her shoulders. "Sleeping. She's exhausted and scared and..." A noise made Shahnaz swivel around.

Noshaba stood in the doorway, a suitcase dangling from one hand and Riffat cradled in her other arm. "I'm going to Islamabad to find my husband."

Naseer strode toward her. "Let me take your suitcase. Come, sit for a minute."

Confused, she allowed him to take the case and lead her to the bed.

Dragging up a chair, Naseer faced his sister-in-law. "I can only imagine what you're going through, and please believe we're with you. We have a plan."

Maryam, still seated in the second chair, explained, "We're going to enlist Tanvir Uncle to find Raja Haider. He knows all the right people, and, insh'allah, he'll locate your husband."

Noshaba's head turned from person to person, her face uncomprehending.

Shahnaz knelt beside her and clasped her hand. "You remember Ammi's brother. He tells us wonderful stories over dinner and makes us laugh." Noshaba nodded. "Ammi says he's the best person to track down Raja Haider, better than any of us because he has friends in the right places."

Naseer took up the persuasive patter. "We all want news of him. I promise to keep calling. Our cousins in Islamabad will scour all the lists of those granted amnesty, those in hospitals, and so forth. Noshaba, what this all means, though..." He bit his lower lip. "...is that you must wait here until we know where to go."

She shook her head resolutely. "No. I must be with him."

Shahnaz exchanged looks with Maryam and Naseer. Maryam rose and peered down at her black-clad daughter-in-law. "Noshaba, it is I who am in charge of the females in this household, and I forbid you to leave until we've located your husband. Do you understand?"

A white-faced Noshaba nodded slowly, clutched the baby to her chest, and ran from the room.

Maryam sat down heavily. "I didn't like doing that, but we can't have her lost in Islamabad as well. Shahnaz, please keep a tight watch on her."

"Yes, Ammi." And as she turned toward the door, she decided it was once again time for tea.

—••—

When Shahnaz and Zainab awoke from their mid-day nap, they went to find Noshaba. Her bedroom was empty, and she wasn't in the main house or the garden. A search of her room showed her suitcase was missing and a swift interrogation of the cook revealed she and the baby had truly gone. A nervous Shahnaz hastily called Noshaba's mobile and then Naseer's. Both were turned off. Clutching the frightened toddler, she hunted for Ammi only to remember that she was running errands.

First things first, she chided herself, and she instructed the cook to fix a snack for Zainab. While the child chewed and watched her every move, Shahnaz rang her mother-in-law.

Maryam moaned. "That silly girl...I'll be home in a half-hour."

Shahnaz debated her options and called Noshaba every few minutes. No answer. She yearned to move, take the car, steal a helicopter, hop on a plane. Something. Zainab clutched her skirt and ran beside her as she strode around the garden. The walls hemmed her in, the child pulled her down, and her heart pounded with excitement.

When she caught the sharp scrape of the driveway gate opening for the car, Shahnaz rushed to the front door, grabbed the sides of Maryam's arms, and spilled out her scheme. "I know where she'd go—the sports stadium, where government people are stationed with their lists, and Jamia Faridia, the boys' madrassa. I know Tanvir Uncle can go there, but he's chatting up police and army friends. Please, Ammi, let me go find her. I can enter where only women are allowed. I'll be dressed like the students and teachers, and women may tell me more than they'd tell a man."

Maryam paced the living room, her younger children massed just inside the door. "Let's try Naseer again."

Shahnaz pressed her to use her own mobile, guessing Naseer more likely to pick up when he saw his mother's number, but he did not. Neither did Noshaba. As she shifted Zainab from hip to hip, Shahnaz's heart pounded with excitement and the elation of release. Maryam simply had to give her permission to search. And, when Noshaba was safe, she'd see a doctor. Her Ammi would certainly have found one by then. Shahnaz was nearly four months along, better than last time. But this morning there'd been spots again in her underclothes.

Maryam stopped to face Shahnaz. "All right. I'm making the decision: you should go. While you pack, I'll check on the times today's buses left Muzaffarabad and arrived in Islamabad. Maybe, just maybe, if you take our driver, you can catch her at the station in Islamabad." She started toward her phone, then turned back. "And you'll see a doctor?"

"Yes, Ammi."

Shahnaz hurried through the garden to her bedroom, Zainab

clinging to her chest. The monsoon's charcoal clouds coalesced in the sky. She raced through packing and the donning of her black coverings, talking nonstop to the toddler. She would take only two shalwar kameezes. Did Zainab think the green flowered one would be good?

Zainab nodded.

Shahnaz's inner voice told her to "Hurry, hurry. Beat Noshaba to Islamabad. Get away before Naseer comes home."

Saying goodbye turned into a battle. Zainab clung to her, the child's face awash in tears. Shahnaz knelt to set the child on her feet. "Sweetie, I'm going to bring your mother home, insh'allah. I'll come back, I promise." She hugged the sobbing child.

"No go; no go." Zainab stamped her foot.

Shahnaz pushed sodden hairs out of the child's eyes. "I won't be gone long. You can play with your aunts. You'll like that."

"No, no." Both Nooran and Ammi shushed her, to no avail, so Shahnaz pulled her again into her arms.

"Me go too. Me go too." The toddler's nose dripped onto Shahnaz's dupatta.

Making eye contact with Maryam, Shahnaz shrugged her shoulders. "I could take her. She could stay with my mother while I search."

"It's too much for you, too much. Nooran, you must take charge." Maryam assumed her commander pose, and her daughter reached for the now angry child.

The toddler pummeled Nooran's chest and kicked her, screaming to go along.

As a few drops of rain splashed on the pavement, Maryam waved Nooran into the house and pushed Shahnaz toward the car. "Go. Do what you must." When she stepped backward into the doorway, the rain intensified, and she brushed droplets of water from her clothes.

With the noise of the child's tantrum filling her ears, Shahnaz slipped into the seat behind the family's driver. She gritted her teeth as the rain beat down on the vehicle, and seized the safety handle above the door, determined to hold tight for the trip. Closing her eyes, she listened to the driver recite his customary prayer that Allah guard them on this journey. The car shifted into gear.

The journey turned into a nightmare. A landslide partially blocked the road up one of the mountains. The driver of the van in front of them, loaded with passengers, misjudged the slope of the scree. Shahnaz stared in horror as the top-heavy vehicle canted to the left and then rolled slowly off the cliff. It was several hundred meters down to the river. There would be bodies, more dead bodies. Like Lal Masjid. They were crowding into her life.

12

At six in the evening, when they slid into Islamabad's bus station, Shahnaz was still shivering from the nearness of death, knowing it would haunt her dreams. There was no sign of Noshaba, just a heavy smell of spent gas, sweaty bodies, and oily water. Unwilling to give up her search, she told the driver to drop her at the sports complex and wait in the car. The large arena was almost deserted, holding only small bands of disconsolate relatives in dripping garments. She approached one group after another, asking about Noshaba. People shrugged their shoulders or shook their heads. One black-clad woman looked much like any other, they said, and many had babies. After a third stop at the boys' madrassa, which was curtained from view by the thick rain and well-guarded, Shahnaz collapsed back against the seat in defeat. She'd take shelter with her parents for the night.

As the driver set the wipers to high, she called Maryam to report her lack of progress. Maryam clucked in concern that Naseer was still not answering his mobile, which was odd, but low among Shahnaz's concerns. In fact, the longer it took to connect with him, the more time she had to search. She knew he'd hate this action of hers, and she knew she had to do it. So, she set Naseer aside—

he'd probably just misplaced his phone anyway—and asked herself again: where was Noshaba? Her mobile was off, so either she didn't want to be pressured to return or it had been taken from her or lost.

Shahnaz's mother welcomed her with a "Praise God" and anxious questions. "Are you all right? Is there word of Noshaba or Raja Haider?"

Shahnaz shook her head as she hung up her soaked abaya and unwound her dripping dupatta. "Nothing yet, but I need to make a couple of calls. Have you heard anything?"

Her mother wrung her hands. "No. I keep watching TV, and it's awful, these children dying. Abu doesn't want you going places alone."

"I'll speak with him in a moment, Ammi. First, the calls."

"Wait. Before you go. I found a female doctor."

"Bless you. After I find Noshaba, I'll see her. First things first."

In the privacy of the downstairs bedroom, she reached Tanvir. "Any news?"

"No, nothing." His voice sounded dull, drained of its usual energy. "Can't figure this out. Grilled my cousin at Kashmir House. He's supposed to have the names of all dead Kashmiris and all the Kashmiris in custody, and he swears young Haider isn't listed. Spoke to a police captain who was thoroughly irritated at being found, and he corroborated Haider wasn't in jail. Denied all knowledge of Noshaba. You don't suppose Haider gave them a false name, do you?"

"I wouldn't think so. He's proud of his role."

Tanvir grumbled, "I hope Noshaba's someplace safe."

And the conversation shifted to plans for the following day. They agreed to try the sports complex early the next morning, so he could speak to as many men as possible while she questioned women and girls. This evening, Tanvir would call a couple of generals at home.

As she was grilled by her Abu over dinner, Shahnaz privately sifted through Noshaba's options. She might have gone to Lal Masjid. It was cordoned off, supposedly empty, and the sector was under curfew, but a black-clad figure might be able to sneak in under cover of darkness or hover on its periphery.

With great tact, she persuaded her reluctant father to drive her over in the heavy darkness and pelting rain to see how close they could get to the mosque. Their car was halted as they turned onto Shahid-e-Millat, the road that cut the sector in half and passed what had been the side of Jamia Hafsa. The bedraggled army officer at the checkpoint blocked the road with his body, his AK-47 placed across his chest. He strode to the driver's side and, when Abu rolled down the window, dripped water from his hat into the car. He demanded identification and when they admitted they didn't live in G-6, he ordered them to turn around. The wind ripped at the trees behind the soldiers, tearing off twigs and leaves and driving them to the ground.

Whispering, Shahnaz urged her father to ask where the army sent people who broke curfew. The officer had already stepped away, hurrying toward the tarp pitched behind the sand bags, but he stopped and swiveled to announce they were jailed at the Aabpara police station, which was not accessible to non-residents. While her father backed around, Shahnaz phoned Tanvir to have him check to see if Noshaba was in that station. By the time she and Abu had made their way around the perimeter roads of the sector, which were replete with men in uniform and empty of women, and returned home, the answer was back: Noshaba was not at Aabpara.

With a depletion of adrenaline and a growing exhaustion, Shahnaz retreated to her room and called her husband. It was the right thing to do, the brave thing, but she knew the conversation would be unpleasant. No answer. She could crawl into bed now, have some hot milk. No. She called Maryam, who related that Naseer had just come in from a business dinner. He'd misplaced his mobile and retraced his steps from the day to find it.

When Ammi handed him her mobile, Shahnaz spoke at once. "I'm sorry I left without talking to you. I couldn't reach you. Ammi and I both tried. She agreed I could come, and I'll be with Tanvir Uncle. I'm afraid there's no news yet."

There was silence on the line and then the sound of a deep breath and a crying child. "Ammi, I'm going to the bedroom for this call." Then she caught only the sounds of his footsteps on concrete and the squeak of their bedroom door. "I understand why you've gone, and I don't like it. The capital is crawling with armed men. It's no place for a woman, especially one who's pregnant. I want you home tomorrow. I should be the one to conduct the search."

Shahnaz gritted her teeth. She'd never openly disobeyed before, but she couldn't bear slinking home like a disciplined dog curling its tail between its legs. She had to find Noshaba—and see the doctor. "I'm sorry, but I can't. I promise I'll be with Tanvir Uncle, I'll be covered. But only I can search the bathrooms and the women's section of the police stations. Only a woman can speak to the mothers in the hospitals." He had to see how important it was for her to do this, he had to!

He cleared his throat. "Shahnaz, I'm asking again that you come home. No, not asking. It's my order, and I expect to be obeyed." His voice exuded decision, worry, and ferocity.

Her fingers crawled to her cheek. She didn't want to disobey. She didn't want yet more trouble with her husband. But staying could be a life-or-death matter for Noshaba, who hadn't her own knowledge of the capital or experience out in the world. Seeing the doctor could be a life-or-death matter for their baby. Hating the action yet believing in its justification, she chose words that hid her intent. "I understand. I'll stay with my parents tonight." And Shahnaz folded her phone and slipped it into her purse.

As Shahnaz dressed for bed, her mobile rang, showing Rabia's number.

"You need to come visit, Shahnaz. You really do."

Shahnaz sank into the room's chair, annoyed at yet another person about to make demands on her. "Not possible, I'm afraid. We're—"

"No one cares about me anymore!"

"Oh, for goodness sakes, of course I care, and I'm sorry you're so lonely. But, really, that hardly compares with what's going on here. Raja Haider is missing. I can't find Noshaba. Naseer is—"

"You don't care."

Shahnaz allowed her head to drop into her hand and sighed. "Okay, I'll play. What's going on?"

"Well, Javed's made rules. I have to pin my dupatta on my shoulders or pin it to cover my head. He hates messiness. And his relatives are all standoffish, like they don't approve of me." A whine had squeezed into each word.

With a deep breath to sustain her through the inevitable "Javed says," Shahnaz asked, "Does Javed know what's going on?"

Her sister's voice dropped into that of a peeved adult lecturing a child. "He says I should devote myself more to him and recognize I'm not the center of the universe. I think it's very mean of him. I know I'm not, but he doesn't understand my energy and how lonely I am. He has all these people at work and relatives who fawn all over him. I have no one."

Shahnaz tried some worldly wisdom. "Life delivers different sorts of gifts, and being lonely may be what God thinks you need."

"Thanks a lot."

"Rabia, they're your family now. Work it out."

Shahnaz rubbed her aching forehead. She pictured her sister's long dark hair falling across her face, her nose sniffing back tears. "Listen to me. You're capable and educated. You know your own mind. Insh'allah, you can build the life you've dreamed of."

Rabia huffed and puffed—and hung up.

Shahnaz sighed again and shut her mobile. She was going to bed—now.

◄•►

The next morning, Tanvir and Shahnaz entered the sports complex, which teemed with people. Most of the crowd rocked from foot to foot in snaking lines, some milled about the field, and others roosted here and there in the seats spreading upward from the ground. It was a religiously conservative group with lots of long beards, embroidered caps, black abayas, and hijabs. Tanvir immediately pointed to a line in front of a gray-suited official who had a tower of scruffy folders on his table. "I know that man. Insh'allah, he'll tell me the truth. You'll be okay?"

Shahnaz scanned the multitude and decided to begin her questioning with a whispering pair of women and a younger girl, all in black. "Yes, certainly. I'm going to start with those two women just to my right. If I'm not back here when you finish, I'll be moving counterclockwise around the field."

Nervous at what raw nerves she might expose, Shahnaz approached her first quarry. "Excuse me; I need your help. I'm searching for my sister-in-law, who's looking for her husband. Do you know of Noshaba Haider or Raja Mohammed Haider Khan?"

The women shook their heads, and the child, perhaps ten years of age, buried her face in her mother's side.

Seeing fear in the women's eyes and anxiety in their pursed lips, Shahnaz's sympathies were aroused. "Are you missing other children?"

231

The younger of the women, holding on to the child's hand, nodded. "Two. Only this one has found us. The older girls have been taken somewhere, we think, and no one will tell us where." Her voice wobbled as she fought back tears.

The older woman wrung her hands and added, "We've been to the hospitals and poured over the lists of the dead. Praise Allah, my granddaughters weren't there, but where could they be?"

"I'm so sorry. We have such sadness with these people missing." She put her hand on the child's head. "You must've been scared, inside the madrassa and coming out through all those army men. It was brave of you to stay and brave to leave."

The girl nodded solemnly. "I was scared. My sisters wanted me to stay, but I didn't want to die. A big man saw me crying, put down his gun, and said I could leave. He found a teacher, and I came out with her." The child leaned into her mother's abaya.

"It was very kind of him to help you, and I'm glad you came out. Insh'allah, you'll hear news soon about your sisters."

Slowly, she worked her way from one cluster of women to another. So many families had no idea of the whereabouts of their children. Where were they all? The government was saying only a few children had been killed. Supposedly, all those in hospitals or in custody were on the lists.

Of the black-clad girls she talked with, two more spoke of a man who helped them leave. An eight-year-old described a man roaring at her teenaged sister when she'd ordered the youngster to stay. The little girl seemed ashamed she'd left, worried that she hadn't been loyal to her sister.

Her mother kept saying, "There, there," which left Shahnaz guessing whether she'd have preferred her daughter to have stayed. An older girl in another family had been awakened by an argument outside her door. A young-sounding man yelled at Imam Ghazi that he shouldn't use girls as shields. Others had shouted him down. The next morning the girl recognized the man's voice as he encouraged groups of girls to accept amnesty. She thought, perhaps, someone had called him "Haider." Could it have been Raja Haider? Shahnaz wanted to believe it, but thought it didn't fit well with his usual disdain for girls.

By ten o'clock, sweat coursed down Shahnaz's back. The sun beat down without mercy, reflecting yet more intense heat from the shiny seats. As Tanvir inched forward in line, she sought a ladies' room. The scruffy interior looked like the end of a holiday celebration—a couple of squat toilets were clogged, there was no toilet paper, and bits of unmentionable trash were strewn across the floor. She recoiled from the smell as she stepped into the room and hurried to finish her business.

As she stood at the sink, shaking water from her hands, she heard a scuffling noise from the end cubicle. Turning, she saw a petite black-clad figure and gasped. "Noshaba, is it you?"

A child's voice said, "No, I'm Samira." And the child burst into tears.

Shahnaz ran over and hugged her. "What is it? What's the matter?"

The child melted to the filthy floor. "My parents are so angry. They say I've shamed them by leaving the mosque, and they have no money to take care of me. I'm to be married to my cousin, and I'm afraid of him." Tears flooded over the top of her hijab.

Overwhelmed with sadness, Shahnaz crouched beside Samira and took her hands. "How old are you?"

The watery voice answered, "Twelve."

"Twelve." At that age, Shahnaz had been in middle school worrying about required essays and gossiping with her friends. For a moment she entertained visions of secreting this child away, finding her lodging in Muzaffarabad, and paying for her to finish high school. But she knew these dreams couldn't become reality. This child would lead a miserable servant's life if she were pirated away. No one would marry her, no one would love her. So, with a heavy heart, she set about persuading Samira to return to her parents.

Four hours of accosting women and asking questions yielded no news of Raja Haider or Noshaba. Shahnaz was running out of time. Over lunch at her parents, she and Tanvir planned the afternoon. He ticked off a list of men to see. She wanted to try hospitals. Swallowing her guilt for going off without Tanvir when she'd promised Naseer she'd stay with a man, she prayed she'd find Noshaba.

Accompanied by her father's driver, she headed toward the PIMS hospital, where Sohail had spent his last days. As they drove along the smoothly paved Margalla Road, first through F-8, then F-7, she looked up into the thick greenery of the Margalla hills. It didn't seem the sort of area that would attract Noshaba, who'd lived all her life inside houses. As the hills came closer to the road, however, Shahnaz recalled the location of Jamia Faridia, in E-7, in the midst of the homes of military and retired military, where the hills met the Punjab plain. Noshaba had last seen her husband there, and in her current anxious state, she might have returned.

On impulse, she told the driver to make a U-turn and go to the boys' madrassa. Access to Jamia Faridia was still barred, with police and soldiers patrolling the grounds. She couldn't get near the buildings, but presumably Noshaba wouldn't have been able to either.

Shahnaz scrutinized the area. What else would be a magnet for Noshaba? The surrounding houses looked forbidding behind their high boundary walls. Suddenly, she pictured the Buddha tree, a huge pipal that, it was said, Buddha sat beneath as he taught his followers. She'd seen it on a school trip, years ago, and was sure it was close by, reached by a well-worn path. How like Noshaba to flee from men and guns up such a path.

It took only two or three minutes to locate the path, as her father's driver knew the area well. She picked her way through the dust and stones of the path only to see charred fragments of the huge covering tree strewn about the ground. The kiosk that sheltered visitors and information still stood, though one side was crumbling, and the meditation bench had completely vanished. How sad. The tree had been hundreds of years old. She looked about for the nearest shade, wanting to rethink her next steps, and caught sight of a moving shadow flitting across the periphery of the clearing. Not another lost child, she thought, as she moved in its direction, leading with an open hand. "I won't hurt you or capture you. Please, can I help?"

A small voice cried out. And the waif, holding her baby tight, stood half hidden behind a tree.

"Noshaba, is it you?"

The figure backed further behind the tree. "Don't take me back. I must find him. He is my protection. He's my life."

Shahnaz walked gently up to her and floated a kiss toward her right cheek and then her left. "I won't make you go home. I'm here with Tanvir Uncle to find you and Raja Haider. Please, join with us."

Shoulders sagging, Noshaba cried. "I thought I could come to Islamabad and talk with people." She sobbed, staring at the ground. "But I was too frightened by all these men. I've...I've never spoken to a strange man, not ever."

Shahnaz hugged her—and the serene Riffat—privately thanking her father for his advanced ideas. "It's all right now. Tanvir Uncle and I will do the talking." She guided Noshaba toward the car, thinking of how to proceed, and realized they couldn't go hunting now. Noshaba had spent hours wandering about the city and must be exhausted. "You poor thing. If you've been in the woods all morning, you must feel dirty and very hungry." With a sympathetic smile, she gathered the sleeping baby in her arms and led Noshaba down the path. "Come on, we'll go to my parents'. And wherever did you spend the night? Surely not among these trees. The monkeys can be very aggressive."

Noshaba vigorously shook her head. "Not here. I was at a hospital, walking the corridors and asking nurses if they knew Raja Haider. Then I was afraid to leave because of the curfew. I slept a little with the family of a young girl who'd been burned. They were kind and even found me diapers." She stopped and pleaded with her eyes and voice. "Do you know where he is?"

"No, not yet. But I think we should tell the family that we've found you." Shahnaz retrieved her mobile from her purse. "Will you call Ammi, or should I?"

Noshaba shrunk into her abaya. "You, please. She'll be very angry with me."

While she reached into a pocket for her mobile, Shahnaz heard a commotion on the path and saw her driver, now held between two armed policemen, stumbling toward them.

"Excuse me, ma'am, but they think I'm a terrorist." His voice pleaded for rescue.

"Nonsense." Shahnaz strode quickly to the group of men. "Let this man go. He's my driver."

Neither policeman loosened his grip on the man's arms, and the older one picked up the barrel of his AK-47. "Who are you?"

"I'm Shahnaz Naseer, and this is my sister-in-law. We're here from Muzaffarabad to locate her husband."

With a gun pointed at the women, he demanded to see their identity cards. Shahnaz handed Riffat to Noshaba and rifled through her purse for her card. Noshaba just raised scared eyes. Shahnaz glanced at her sister-in-law and immediately answered for her, "She doesn't have her card with her. I'm sorry."

The younger slender policeman elbowed his partner. "Looks like we've got another of the Jamia Hafsa girls."

Handing back her card, the men released the driver and waved

Shahnaz away. The younger man pointed to Noshaba. "You, come with us. Give her back the baby."

With a muffled scream, Noshaba turned and ran.

Shahnaz took up the chase. "Noshaba, don't run away. We'll work this out." Unencumbered by a baby, Shahnaz trapped a handful of Noshaba's abaya and pulled her to a halt. Then she whirled toward the men with their rifles and straightened her arm with her palm held flat. "Don't shoot. We'll come with you, willingly, but I must stay with my sister-in-law. She doesn't speak to men who are not related."

Shahnaz turned to her quivering driver. "Follow us. Call my father and ask him to tell Tanvir Uncle where we're taken." Standing tall and feeling her growing anger, she pulled a chastened Noshaba to the road, conscious of the poised weapons at her back. As the younger policeman yanked open his car door, she faced him, outwardly calm and inwardly quaking. "Where are you taking us?"

The officers looked at each other, passing a wordless message across the car. This time it was the older one who spoke, fluttering his heavy jowls. "Aabpara."

"Our driver will follow. Please make sure he's allowed through the barricades." She felt brazen, demanding obedience of policemen and relying on their surprise at an assertive woman. She liked the feeling.

Again, the older man reluctantly agreed.

She turned to her frightened driver. "You know where we're going, in G-6?"

"Yes, sahiba." He half-ran to their car, and Shahnaz saw his hands tensed on the steering wheel as he watched the women climb into the police car. Shahnaz guided Noshaba's arm, determined to straighten out this misunderstanding.

When the women were escorted through the archway into the main stone courtyard of the Aabpara station, Shahnaz checked out the surrounding offices and holding areas. Lots of men in uniform strode from room to room, no women. She shepherded Noshaba into the small square office indicated by their guards, where they were greeted by a beat-up desk and several mismatched chairs. Dirt scrunched under their feet, and she swiped a tissue across the scarred wooden chair before choosing to sit, hoping to signal to the policemen that she had standards they didn't meet. A glance at the windows let her know there was little likelihood of being seen from the outside. Only where the panes lacked glass or the windows hung open could you see who was walking by.

A police captain, clean-shaven and all business, presided at the desk, shuffling papers. He looked bored or very tired. "A woman will come interview you."

Shahnaz adopted the guise of a humble petitioner. "May I make a call?"

"No." He turned back to his papers.

Noshaba cradled Riffat, her back stiff and eyes panicky. Shahnaz rose slightly and settled her abaya more comfortably. She vowed not to allow these officers to bully her. Time crept by. Sweat ran down her back, and she fretted that all she could do was pat Noshaba's arm, send calming messages through her eyes, and murmur assurances.

The unattractive woman who eventually entered the room had on the same uniform as the male policemen—medium blue blouse and navy trousers—which fit tightly on her plump body. She whisked them into a second gritty room, patted them down, and asked that they unpin their hijabs. After checking Shahnaz's face against her identity card, which had a picture of an uncovered woman, she listened to the explanation of who Noshaba was and how her card had been inadvertently left in Muzaffarabad. Then she dropped into a chair.

"Well, you're too old to be madrassa students, and they don't have babies, but how do I know you're not teachers?" Her voice was tired but not unkind.

Shahnaz leaned forward in her earnestness. "I've been working for the International Program for Peace, as a supervisor of Lady Health Workers. You can call my boss to verify. You must know them. Their main office is in this sector. Noshaba's been home with her children."

"You could have children and still be a teacher." The woman nodded at mother and baby. Then, distracted, she bent over to massage her legs.

Noshaba sat with head bowed. "I'm not a teacher, and my husband wouldn't let me work, even if I was."

Shahnaz said, "We're looking for her husband, and he could verify her identity. He was in Lal Masjid, and perhaps he's here now—Raja Mohammad Haider Khan?"

The woman grimaced, still rubbing her legs. "I suppose I could check. It'd be nice to have something positive happen around here. I'm about dead on my feet—been on duty most of the last twenty-four hours." She placed her hands on the chair seat and hoisted her body upward. "Don't leave the room." After a stop outside the door for a quiet exchange with someone, the sound of her footsteps faded away.

Shahnaz squeezed Noshaba's hand. "Pray."

Minutes ticked by with a constant drone of voices, doors closing, and shuffling footsteps. Noshaba supported the sleeping Riffat on one arm and went through her ring of beads with her free hand, a black mourner bent in prayer. Shahnaz shifted several times in the chair, seeking a comfortable position, until she could bear it no longer and walked to the window. Her stomach was unhappy, and her mind chattered. It was unlikely Raja Haider was in the Aabpara station. Tanvir had checked. So, what next? She couldn't leave Noshaba. The poor girl's cheekbones stuck out prominently and her eyes were sunk so deeply in their sockets, she looked like an unfriendly ghost.

Something that Tanvir had told her popped into her mind: an army friend had reported that all amnesty recipients were questioned at Aabpara. That must mean there were teachers here, and surely one of them would attest to the fact that Noshaba wasn't associated with Jamia Hafsa. What could they lose from such an admission?

Interrupting her ruminations, the policewoman returned and sighed as she dropped again into her chair. "No Raja Haider. We'll put this lady in with the other women, and we'll let you know. You left your phone number, didn't you?"

Shahnaz hurried back to her chair. "Please, madam, you have some of the madrassa teachers here, don't you? The ones who chose amnesty?"

The matron nodded, reaching under the desk to attend to her legs.

"Please, couldn't you ask them if they know Noshaba?"

"Oh, my." She groaned. "I suppose. C'mon." With a touch to Noshaba's shoulder, she headed toward the door.

Noshaba rose but turned to Shahnaz with an anguished look, which Shahnaz took as a plea to come along. However, when she started to the door, the matron ordered her to wait and keep the baby. She held Riffat in her arms and watched Noshaba stumble forward and the matron grab her elbow.

Left alone, Shahnaz paced, patting the waking child, and prayed. If this didn't work, what next? She murmured to Riffat they'd have to go home and get Abu or Tanvir Uncle to intervene, but would the child's mama survive incarceration?

It was about twenty minutes later when the matron returned with a drooping Noshaba and reported that no one knew her. "I'll speak with the captain, see if that's enough for him. Wait here." She pointed to Noshaba's chair, swiped her uniformed forearm across her sweaty forehead, and left.

Noshaba looked like an old crone as she shuffled to the chair and sank down. "They won't let me go. I know it."

Shahnaz pulled her chair to Noshaba's, sat Riffat on her lap, and leaned to touch Noshaba's hands. "Insh'allah, we *will* be going home. You must hold on, just a little longer."

Assailed by a penetrating odor, Shahnaz added, "You don't, by any chance, have another diaper, do you?"

Noshaba shook her head, eyes closed and head bowed.

"I hope the matron has something." She stood Riffat on her lap and scowled at the greenish-brown stain creeping down the baby's legs.

When the matron returned with the captain, they each wrinkled their noses as they came through the door. The captain halted near the entrance, rubbed his nose several times, and then pointed to Noshaba and the window. "Let them go. Just take down their full names, addresses, phone numbers." And he retreated backwards from the room.

Struggling with her smelly armful and a sagging sister-in-law, Shahnaz got the entourage out of the station. The family driver was hovering on the sidewalk, with orders from Shahnaz's father to bring the girls and baby home immediately upon their release. He and Tanvir had been refused entry to the sector and were furious.

Once in the car, Shahnaz let her sputtering father know they were on the way home and then turned to Noshaba. "Now, Ammi. Will you call or shall I?"

Having collapsed against the corner of the seat where it met the door, Noshaba gave a moan and waved a weak hand at Shahnaz, who shook her head and punched in Ammi's number.

"Noshaba and Riffat are with me now, Ammi. Both are fine except Riffat desperately needs a change." Directing a smile toward

Noshaba, she listened to Maryam's relief. "We're on our way to my parents', and we'll get them both cleaned up, fed, and into bed."

"Thank God you found her. Tell me what happened." The words gushed from Maryam's mouth.

So Shahnaz related the events of the afternoon and then handed the phone to Noshaba. "She wants to hear your voice."

Noshaba slowly moved the mobile to her ear, her hand trembling. "Yes, Ammi. I'm okay, and I'm sorry but I had to come." With a couple more refrains of "I'm sorry" and a few goes at "Um hmm," she passed the phone back. Her shoulders slumped, leaving her a picture of physical exhaustion.

Shahnaz took the mobile back. "Ammi, it's me again, and I'm sure Naseer told you he'd asked me to return today to Muzaffarabad."

"He did mention that," came the wry reply.

"I'm sorry if I've caused you worry, but I couldn't leave. I was sure I could find Noshaba. I'll call him soon, but first I need to deal with my irate father and your brother."

Maryam laughed. "Men!"

13

Shahnaz unfurled her dupatta as she crossed the hall toward the stairs. Tanvir had gone home, and she'd left Abu in the dining room with a fresh cup of tea. Her knees were weak with the need to sleep. Did she dare to put off talking with her husband until morning? Two steps up the stairs, a strong cramp grabbed her belly. She bent over.

Not again. Not a second baby.

Raja Haider's voice echoed in her head. This was punishment for working, for leaving home, for being a part of the world that belongs to men. Naseer'd think so, too, these days.

As the cramping eased, she called for her mother.

Ammi bent over the banister, peering down at her. "What is it? Noshaba and the baby are asleep."

"I need you. I think I'm losing my baby."

Ammi's hand flew to her mouth. She hurried down the steps, put her arm around Shahnaz, and walked her upstairs to her old bedroom. Then she disappeared to call the female doctor she'd located.

Shahnaz curled up on the spread, praying for the pain to go away.

The door creaked open. "The doctor's gone to London to visit relatives, but her husband said he'd come when he finished his rounds at the hospital. He's also a doctor. I know, you don't need to say it, he's a man." Ammi wrung her hands. "Surely Naseer won't object, not in this crisis."

"You know he's forbidden it." She closed her eyes with another cramp.

Ammi sat on the edge of the bed and felt Shahnaz's forehead. "I...I haven't told Abu about this male doctor business, and I'm not going to. We'll believe that Naseer will understand and let it pass."

"I'm scared, Ammi." The pain eased, and she licked her lips. "Do you think I can't have babies?"

Ammi pushed a few loose hairs out of Shahnaz's face. "No, I don't. I wouldn't be surprised if all this trauma wasn't to blame. Please don't worry about that. The doctor will be here soon."

"Naseer will be so angry."

"You think he'll blame you for a miscarriage?" Her voice rose in astonishment.

Shahnaz rolled onto her side, fitting around her mother. "Not exactly. He'll be sad about that. It's the male doctor. He'll hate that I disobeyed him—again."

"Oh, Shahnaz. Don't you worry about that." She straightened her back. "He'll have to face me if he's angry."

Shahnaz wanted to laugh. "Ammi, you haven't ever argued, even with Abu."

"No one has threatened my child before."

It was so good to have someone on her side, someone she could speak to from her heart. Once it had been possible with Naseer, but not anymore. "Ammi, can I move home, here, if Naseer divorces me?"

Her mother remained silent a long time, her rigid back softening. She stared at the floor and played with the fringe of her dupatta.

"Your father wouldn't like it. Besides, it's not time to talk about that. Surely Naseer will agree to your seeing the doctor."

Shahnaz groaned in pain as another cramp swept across her abdomen. Like her last miscarriage, the pains rose and claimed all her energy, then fell away leaving her sweating. A shadow of Noshaba's labor. Except Shahnaz was fighting to hold onto this baby, not birth it.

About an hour into her pains, Ammi took a phone call from the doctor. "Are you on your way here?...Oh, dear...Yes, yes, I understand. It's an emergency. But this is an emergency, too...Well, what should I do?...All right, I guess. I'll be here. Please, doctor, come as soon as you can."

"He's not coming?"

"Not right away. He says I should make you comfortable and stay with you. He'll be here as soon as he can."

Shahnaz closed her eyes to ride another pain, trying out the breathing technique she'd taught other expectant mothers. It didn't work. The pains swelled and swelled some more. She fought them and prayed to hold on to this child. But just after two a.m., she staggered to the bathroom for a final time and felt the tiny baby drop from her body. Ammi had to support her back to bed as she sobbed.

When she had cried herself out, she took the cloth Ammi offered, washed her face, and collapsed against the headboard. "Why don't you call the doctor, tell him he doesn't need to come?"

"Are you sure?"

"Yes. I wanted him to save the baby. Now there's no point. Besides, Naseer would hate it. Has...has he called?"

Her mother straightened the bedclothes. "Yes, Abu took the call a bit before midnight. He told him you couldn't talk, you were having another miscarriage."

"What did he say?"

"He...he was angry, said you shouldn't have chased after

Noshaba." She sank down on the bed.

"Did Abu tell him about the doctor coming?"

"I don't think so, at least he didn't tell me that he did."

Shahnaz closed her eyes. "I'd better call, get it over with."

"Not now, dear. You're exhausted, and he'll be asleep. Look at the clock. It's the middle of the night. You wait until morning. If you're sure about this, I'll call the doctor. Poor man will probably be relieved to go home to sleep."

"I'm sure." Shahnaz lay alone in the bed, washed out, cried out, and unable to sleep for the miserable and repetitive mantra in her head: she was a failure at marriage, at bearing children, and at realizing all those dreams she'd had of saving women's lives. It was almost dawn when she dropped into an exhausted oblivion.

Naseer's call woke her a couple of hours later. "How are you?"

"It's over. The baby is gone." No more lying, she promised herself, no more disobedience. She hadn't the strength.

"Again."

She winced. "Noshaba is fine. And Riffat." Had he no sympathy for what she had gone through?

"Good."

Shahnaz vowed not to cry, to take her punishment. She pushed herself up against the bedstead. "They're sleeping upstairs." She listened to the empty line and felt her heart thumping. He must hate her, what she'd done, to be so curt.

"Yes."

She pressed the mobile more tightly to her ear. The tense silence dragged on.

"I'm furious. You purposely disobeyed me. What were you thinking? You could have been killed. You could have gotten Noshaba or Riffat killed. All the pictures of Islamabad show an armed camp with men ready to shoot anything that moves. Did you want to be hurt? Did you want to lose this baby? Is my home so awful you'll sacrifice your life—and our baby's—to be out of it?"

She held the mobile so tightly her fingers ached. Six months ago, Naseer would have been understanding. He'd have consoled her. Now, she cringed from his anger. "Of course not. I was scared for Noshaba. She's so naïve about the world. I was sure I could find her, if I just had the chance. It...it felt like God was with me, guiding my footsteps."

"How dare you use God as an excuse." His voice thundered down the line. "I'm coming to Islamabad. Don't leave your father's house. Do you understand me?"

"Yes." She slid under the sheet. He'd never been this angry, never yelled at her, never lost control like this. All because of her disobedience. She'd meant well. Truly, she had. And now, what? Had she burnt away all the love? Would he divorce her? Abandon her?

Ammi knocked and stuck her head around the door. Shahnaz was stretched out like a corpse.

"Was that Naseer?"

Shahnaz sniffed, turning her head only as far as needed to see her mother. "Yes. I've been ordered not to leave the house."

Ammi moved to the bed. "Perhaps that's just as well. You need to gather your strength."

"He's furious, Ammi. And I don't feel at all well. I think I have a fever."

Ammi laid the back of her hand on Shahnaz's forehead. "Yes, you do."

Shahnaz rolled her head to find a cool spot on the pillow. "Maybe I didn't get rid of the entire placenta."

Ammi pressed her hands to her cheeks. "Oh, dear." Then she turned and hurried out of the room.

As she curled into a fetal position, Shahnaz heard her parents whispering and her father calling the doctor—the male doctor. Too tired to argue or explain, she closed her eyes.

Abu's footsteps jolted her awake. "Ammi will help you dress. We're taking you to the hospital. Dr. Humayan thinks a D&C may be necessary, and the sooner the better. I'll talk with Naseer."

Shahnaz squeezed her eyes shut. Did she have to tell Abu about the prohibition? She'd promised herself no more lying, but she knew what happened from childbed fever. "He's on his way here and may be hard to reach. You know how those mountain switchbacks interrupt mobiles."

Her father paced the room, his mobile against his ear. In some exasperation, he ended the first call to Naseer and tried again. No answer.

Shahnaz took a deep breath. "Abu, before we leave, I must tell you that Naseer has forbidden me from seeing a male doctor."

"But you were going to see one last night."

Kind Abu, she thought. He looked totally confused, like *his* daughter would never have disobeyed. Who was this on the bed?

Shahnaz nodded, head hanging down. "I know. I was willing to disobey when I thought he could save the baby. I can't disobey now."

Abu tapped the phone against his hand. "Okay. We'll go to the hospital and ask for a woman doctor."

"Naseer said I wasn't to leave the house."

"Well, he didn't know how sick you are. I do. We're going."

Lying on her side with her head in her mother's lap, Shahnaz endured the bumps and turns of the trip. Another instance of disobedience. It seemed like she'd lost control of it all.

Once in the emergency room, Abu asked Dr. Humayan about a female obstetrician. There wasn't one on duty or on call. Following their wishes, Dr. Humayan summoned a nurse to check Shahnaz's vital signs. She confirmed the fever, probed Shahnaz's abdomen, and received a groan of pain in response. They would wait for Naseer before going further.

After a long look at Shahnaz and a shake of his head, Abu

phoned Naseer again. Still no success. He turned to the doctor. "What's going to happen to my daughter if she doesn't have this operation?"

"The most likely scenario is that she'll have a fever from the internal infection, off and on, for a while, maybe a day or two, and end up either unable to bear children or, in the worst case, she'll die." He slapped his clipboard against his leg.

Abu ran his hand through his hair. "My son-in-law will be here in two, three hours. Will Shahnaz be all right until then?"

Ammi started to cry and squeezed Shahnaz's hand.

"Why don't we admit her, and when he arrives, we'll be ready."

Shahnaz allowed herself to be wheeled to a room and settled into bed. Had she done the right thing, telling Abu? What if Naseer forbid the operation without a female doctor? Was she willing to die for the sake of obedience? She didn't want to die. It even seemed a little silly, to die from a treatable condition. But here she was, Naseer's wife. Another act of defiance could be the death of her marriage. She didn't want that either. Perhaps this was God's final test for her to see if she could be obedient. Would He do that?

—••—

Four hours later, Naseer appeared at the door of her hospital room and took in the presence of Shahnaz laid out, sweaty and pale, against the sheets, her mother at her side, and her father standing at the streaked window. "What's going on?"

Abu answered. "It's the miscarriage. She's developed a fever and needs an operation. There are no female doctors available."

Naseer glared at Shahnaz, arms folded. "I'm surprised you didn't use a male one. You don't seem to mind disobeying the rules. Why stop here?"

Abu stepped between Naseer and Shahnaz. "She may be bar-

249

ren or die without this operation, son. I'm asking you, for all of us, to relax this rule."

Naseer studied his relatives. "I'd like to be alone with my wife, please."

Abu looked him up and down, took Ammi's elbow, and they walked together into the corridor, she whimpering, he staring ahead.

Naseer shut the door. "I'm so angry with you. First it was staying in Islamabad, now you're pushing on this rule about doctors."

"I'm too sick to argue. I'm sorry all you can see is the trouble I've caused. I had to find Noshaba. I didn't want to lose our baby."

He waved his hand across the room. "Look what's happened from your disobedience. You did lose the baby and here you are—"

Dr. Humayan opened the door. Naseer stared at him, then turned slowly back to Shahnaz. "Who is this?" He spit out the words through gritted teeth.

Shahnaz pulled the sheet up to her chin. "This is Dr. Humayan. His wife is also a doctor, but she is in England now. Ammi spoke to him when she called last night for his wife."

Dr. Humayan stuffed his hands in the pockets of his white coat. "I understand that you prefer a female doctor. I have tried— unsuccessfully—to find one. Let me assure you I have only talked with your wife this morning. I won't go further without your approval."

"Doctor, I will speak to you in a few minutes. I'm sorry, but first I must speak to my wife alone."

"We have an imam on call, if it would help to speak with him."

"I don't need an imam."

The doctor nodded and left the room.

Naseer closed in on the bed and grasped the side rail. "You saw him last night?"

"He couldn't come. But I...I would have seen him to save

the baby."

The door opened and Ammi slipped in. "I have to speak."

Naseer turned toward her voice, startled. "Please give us a few more minutes."

"I can't. She's my daughter. I don't want her to die. You can't want her to die either. Please, this rule about female doctors, it's not in the Qur'an. My husband doesn't believe in it. Shahnaz hasn't been raised with it." She reached out both arms, pleading.

Naseer stood stock still, not approaching Shahnaz's mother and not turning to look at his wife. "I'm aware Shahnaz was not raised with these rules, but they are the rules of my house."

Ammi dropped her hands and sobbed. "Naseer, you can't, you can't let my child die."

Abu, who must have been listening outside the open door, walked in, and shook his head at his wife. "Come out here and wait with me."

Shahnaz watched her parents leave and shrank back into the pillows under her husband's glare. "I'm sorry I've been disobedient. I've tried to follow the rules, but they don't make sense to me. I had to stay to find Noshaba. I needed a doctor to save the baby. I haven't disobeyed for me. I've done it for our family."

Naseer eyes blazed. "I'm going to pray." He stalked from the room, his fingers closing into fists.

Ammi sidled past Naseer, back into the room, openly weeping, and wiped Shahnaz's sweaty and tear-stained face with her handkerchief. "Abu's gone with him. He'll talk to Naseer. Insh'allah—"

"Please, let's not talk anymore. I don't feel at all well."

Ammi pulled up a chair, sat down, and held one of Shahnaz's hands.

Shahnaz's eyes wandered from the bright light on the ceiling to the water damage streaking the wall next to the bed to the cracked floor tile by the door. So, this was the end of the road. This was what it had all come to. One angry husband. And this waiting. Rivulets of sweat wandered down her face and dropped to the sheets. She had no energy left to stop them. If he forbid the operation, so be it. She'd hold on to the love they'd shared in those months of happiness and grief. Naseer had to choose, as she had chosen.

Her eyes drifted shut, and she let her fevered body sink into sleep.

———•◦•———

Shahnaz woke to the quiet voices of Naseer, Abu, and the doctor. She forced her eyes to open, feeling drained of energy, yet also of tension. Ammi was at her side.

Dr. Humayan spoke. "So, we're agreed then. A female nurse will examine Shahnaz. Right?"

Naseer nodded.

"Then we'll decide what happens next."

A second nod. Naseer caught her eye for a moment without smiling and with no word of assurance. The men left the room.

She patted her mother's arm. "It's in God's hands, Ammi."

Her mother sagged in the chair, both hands covering her tear-stained face.

In just a few moments, a matronly woman in a white nurse's uniform arrived. Ammi stepped out, and the nurse carefully examined Shahnaz. "You're infected, I'm afraid."

Shahnaz smiled. "I thought so. Thank you."

As she lay alone in the bed, she listened to the men in the corridor decide her fate. It was a bit surreal, like a dream in which she tried to speak up but couldn't make any sound.

Dr. Humayan's soothing tones explained, "Naseer, the procedure is simple. A doctor scrapes the sides of the uterus, clearing out all of the infection and whatever was left from the pregnancy. But it must be done soon if she is to survive and live a full life."

Such a kind doctor. Thorough and understanding.

The doctor argued, "Is there a compromise available here? I can assure you that a woman will be present in the O.R. at all times."

"I don't know."

That was Naseer. She liked his voice, always had. Oh, but he sounded scared, poor man. Funny how dissociated she was from it all, like she was from another planet, curious about a novel situation but not really involved. Shahnaz shivered, her whole body cold. She pulled up the bed coverings and imagined being swaddled. Her teeth chattered.

Then it was Ammi, pleading with Abu to talk to Naseer, change his mind. Her Ammi. *You could always depend on her to stand up for you, protect you.* Shahnaz wanted to call out to her to bring a blanket but couldn't muster the strength.

Abu's angry words shook Shahnaz's eyes open. "We chose you for Shahnaz because of your modern ideas. This is a modern hospital. It's 2007. Dr. Humayan is a gentleman. He's not going to behave inappropriately in the operating room."

"My brother forbids male doctors."

"And he isn't here, Naseer. You are."

Bless Abu and his debate skills. Knows how to hit where it hurts, when he decides to. How nice to be loved so much that he uses those skills for me. Poor Naseer.

"I don't understand why there are no female doctors here."

Dr. Humayan cleared his throat. "There usually are, but with all the soldiers around, all the guns, the women have left for safer places or are staying home, as you want your wife to. I'm sorry."

"But one of them must be on call. This makes no sense."

"Please feel free to ask other doctors. I have taken as much time with you as I can spare. There are many others in this hospital in great need of my services."

Shahnaz flinched at the sound of his retreating footsteps. *Oh, Naseer. Don't blame this on the poor doctor. He was up most of last night, and he's been so kind.* "Naseer? Naseer? Come, please?"

There was some scuffing of feet, some exchange of quiet words, and Naseer came to her bed. "What?"

"Please, I need to clear things up." She took hold of one of his hands. "I want to thank you for being a kind husband and tell you I'm sorry, so very sorry for pestering you about the rules. We talked about bullying and agreed we wouldn't allow it. Yet here are all these people bullying you now. You do what you think is right."

She dropped his hand. "I need to sleep."

As she sank into a drowsy state, she heard her Ammi. "Don't let her die, Naseer."

—◀•▶—

Shahnaz woke in a small white room feeling decidedly queasy. She groaned. Naseer's face slid into view under a halo of fluorescent lights. Strangers' voices murmured in the background.

"You're going to be all right."

"I am?"

"You had the procedure. Dr. Humayan said your uterus was all cleaned out and you should feel better in a day or two." His eyes crinkled at the corners as he smiled at her.

"Can I have some water?" It was hard to string words together and make the right sounds. Her throat was scratchy, and her mind flitted from thought to thought.

"Not right now. In a few minutes, when the anesthesia has worn off."

"Why, Naseer?"

"Why no water?"

She rolled her head from side to side. "Why did you let

him do it?"

He leaned in until his mouth nearly touched her ear. "When I got over being angry, I got so worried. You looked deathly pale, lying in that bed. You were willing to give up your life for me. I...I couldn't let you do it."

He pulled back a little, his arms resting on the sheets. "I know Raja Haider made the rule to make sure you all behaved modestly, as the Qur'an requires. I talked to another doctor about modesty in surgery. He reassured me. They're good men, these doctors. I could tell they're good Muslims. Dr. Humayan told me God couldn't want women to die just to prove a point. That would be a waste of a being He created. It felt right. I only hope Raja Haider will forgive me." He rubbed his hand across his eyes.

Shahnaz felt her body relax, as it hadn't in months.

14

The following morning, several members of the family crowded into Shahnaz's hospital room. Abu, Ammi, Naseer, and Tanvir discussed plans for the day, leaving Noshaba to pat a fussy Riffat in the lone chair. Shahnaz lay back against the pillows, tired but free of her fever. "Have you recovered? Is Riffat all right?"

Noshaba pressed her cheek to the baby's head. "Yes, but we haven't found my husband."

"It'll happen. As Naseer and I have found each other again, so you'll find Raja Haider. As soon as I'm out of bed, we'll all be able to search."

Noshaba just shook her head.

Tanvir's phone jangled, and he immediately opened it. "General Abbas, do you have news?...Oh...Yes...Yes, I can join you in, say, twenty minutes?...Good." He clicked the phone shut and clapped a hand on Naseer's shoulder. "Might be another red herring, but I've gotta check. The Federal Constabulary has a couple of men from the mosque who aren't giving their names."

Naseer faced him. "Thank you so much, Tanvir Uncle, for all you're doing. Thank you from all the family."

Tanvir looked back at Shahnaz and then at Naseer. "Couldn't have done it all without your wife. She's one brave woman, son, a good person to have by your side."

"Yes, she is."

"Good lad." A pat on the shoulder.

"Uh, Tanvir Uncle, is there any place you haven't been? Anything I should take care of while I'm here?"

Tanvir rubbed first one of his cheeks and then the other. "Hate to do this to you, my boy, but I haven't been to the hospital's morgue. Just couldn't bring myself to go. Been putting it off. I mean, Raja Haider's name isn't on the list of the dead, so it didn't seem critical. I know it's a terrible thing to ask, but would you go?"

Naseer straightened to his full height. "Of course."

After Tanvir strode out, all eyes turned to Naseer. "I'll leave in a moment. I want to say something. I made up my mind yesterday that this rule about male doctors isn't right for the family, but I do intend to keep Raja Haider's other rules. I gave him my word." Naseer looked at Shahnaz and Noshaba, eyebrows raised, and they nodded. He headed for the door.

Shahnaz called out, "Wait, please. I'd like to go with you to the morgue."

He turned and stiffened. "Why?"

"Oh, Naseer, I don't want to be protected against the bad in the world. I want to face it with you." She knew she was pushing. It came with feeling better.

"But dead bodies? Who knows what condition they're in? And they'll be men, Shahnaz. It isn't right."

"Yet you let me be with women delivering children, including Noshaba. I've nursed any number of men, in my training."

Naseer glanced at the others, who looked expectant. "Well, yes, but women do those things. They don't seek out opportunities to see male bodies. Do we have to discuss this now, here?"

She sat up. "Please. So we understand each other, so we are a couple who help each other. I've been to morgues before. I'll know what questions to ask."

He stared at the ceiling for a few moments, then shook his head. "No. This is a man's job. I'll go alone."

Abu said, "I'll go, too, if you'd like."

"No, thank you. He's my brother. I should do it."

When Naseer came through the door a half hour later, his face was ashen. He grabbed the rail at the end of the bed. "I'm afraid I was sick. It was worse than I thought. That awful smell."

Noshaba was the first one to ask, "Was he there?"

"I don't know. Maybe, maybe not. There were two unidentified bodies, both burned so badly no one could identify a face or find a fingerprint."

He closed his eyes, and his body swayed. Shahnaz thought he might be sick again and spoke quietly. "We need to be sure."

"I can't go down there again. Besides, another look won't help."

Shahnaz turned to Noshaba, her eyebrows raised.

Noshaba nodded rapidly several times, a frightened look on her face.

"Naseer, Noshaba's told me that Raja Haider has, well, distinctive marks on his chest and back. Did you see any?"

"Marks?"

Noshaba nodded again.

Shahnaz bent toward him. "Noshaba will know if it's him. But she can't talk to the doctor. I can."

"I can't let the two of you go alone. I'm not sure I should let you go at all."

"Then come with us, or allow Abu to. Please, we have to know." Shahnaz took Noshaba's hand and squeezed it.

Naseer paced. "I don't know."

Abu cleared his throat. "I'm willing, Naseer, if it's all right with you."

Naseer stopped, taking another deep breath. "No, it'll have to be me. Bu you stay in a wheelchair, Shahnaz, and you both wait outside until I clear it with the attendant."

"Thank you."

Noshaba handed her baby to Ammi, her hands visibly shaking.

Silence enveloped the three of them as they made their way down to the hospital's basement. Naseer pushed the wheelchair; Noshaba walked at its side. The long basement corridor stank of cooked flesh, the odor more pungent as they neared the correct room. Naseer entered alone, leaving the women in the corridor, and when he returned, he was swallowing repeatedly. "The smell is much worse in there than out here. Are you sure you want to go in?"

Shahnaz felt Noshaba grip her arm and turned to see her sister-in-law's haunted eyes and nodding head. "Yes, we're sure."

Naseer opened the door and pushed the wheelchair inside. Noshaba followed, coming to Shahnaz's side. The room was a long rectangle. Corpses wrapped in white sheets lay in a row on the floor like giant cocooned caterpillars. Toe tags rested against their naked feet. Naseer pushed Shahnaz to the wrapped figures on the near end, the two without tags. The attendant, a nervous man in hospital scrubs, pulled back the sheets, showing first one man's head and then the other. Most of the skin had burned away, revealing naked bone, protruding teeth, and a few wisps of singed beard under the chin. Shahnaz ignored her nausea and squinted at the figure on the end. His forehead was broad, as Raja Haider's had been, and the beard hairs suggested he might have been curled up and not totally burned. She grimaced.

Noshaba gasped and fainted, sliding into Shahnaz's lap.

Naseer gently laid her on the floor, rolling Shahnaz's proffered dupatta into a pillow, and looked with raised eyebrows at his wife.

"She'll be okay, nothing injured, but before she wakes, tell me, how badly burned is this man's chest?" She pointed to the closest corpse.

The attendant looked at Naseer to see if he should answer.

Naseer gave a curt nod. Sweat was beading on his forehead. "He was in a fetal position. His chest isn't too bad."

Shahnaz nodded. "Then let me see it."

Naseer took a breath through his handkerchief, coughed, wiped his nose, and nodded again. The attendant unwrapped the body to expose a hairy chest, the thick curls singed.

Shahnaz reached down to part some hairs.

Naseer yelled, "No!" and caught her hand in mid-air.

Startled, she sat back. "Please, then, will you part the hairs so we can see his skin?"

Naseer's eyes widened in shock. "The marks?"

"Yes. You see, he was bullied—at the madrassa. They burned him with cigarettes."

Naseer clapped a hand over his mouth. "Are you sure?"

She nodded. "Noshaba told me. Please, will you do it?"

"All right." Naseer knelt and carefully pushed back one bunch of curled hair and then another. The scars of several round burn marks glistened under the fluorescent lights. He pulled his hand away and stared at Shahnaz, horror on his face. "My God."

She bit her lower lip. "I know, it's awful. Burned as a child and then dying like this."

Naseer stood, walked to the back of the wheelchair, and gripped both handles.

Shahnaz slewed her body around, feeling queasy herself. "We need Noshaba to tell us for certain it's him. I'm only guessing."

"I...I didn't know."

Noshaba stirred. Naseer bent over and jiggled her arm. Her eyes flickered open.

It was Shahnaz who spoke, leaning over the arm of the wheelchair. "Noshaba, you must be brave and look at this man's chest. Can you do that?"

She struggled to sit up, a hand to her head. "Yes, I must."

Naseer helped her to sit up straight and then crouched to push back some of the corpse's chest hair.

She looked at the exposed burns and sobbed.

Raja Haider was dead.

15

A subdued cortege plied the road to Muzaffarabad. Tanvir sat with the body of Raja Haider in a rented van; Shahnaz, Naseer, Noshaba, and the baby filled the family car. It was Monday, July 16, less than a week since the army moved against the mosque. The curfew had been lifted, and though the sandbags were still in place on many corners in G-6, few soldiers were visible on the streets. It was hot, dusty, and quiet.

Unsure how much more a distraught Noshaba could handle, Shahnaz wandered among her own thoughts. Her body was healing, she was certain, but her mind was fickle. It kept returning to an image of her rocking her baby, an image too sad to hold on to. She forced herself to think of Bibi and Kameela, or Irum, or the things she'd do if she could return to work.

She checked Naseer's face every few minutes. He was pale and looked lost.

Maryam met them in the driveway. Like a switch turned on, she talked non-stop, issuing orders to the men to put Raja Haider's body in her bedroom, and then to Noshaba and Shahnaz, demanding they rest.

An hour or so later, Maryam tapped on Shahnaz's door. "Are

you awake? I'd like to talk, if you're up to it. I've asked for tea to be brought into the garden. The men are with Raja Haider, and Noshaba's with her children."

As they walked down the path to the bench, Shahnaz took hold of Maryam's hand. "Did you know about the burns?"

"No, no. How could you think I would? Had I known, I'd have brought him home." She sniffed, her face gray and lined. "Oh, I watched him get quieter, more religious, but I thought he was just growing up. I know he was hard on Naseer, but, in my mind, that was what brothers did." Maryam wiped tears with her dupatta. "Why couldn't he tell us?"

Shahnaz pulled her mother-in-law down on the bench. "Ammi, I think not telling you was a part of the rules the boys were following, that worse would have happened to him if he'd appealed to you for help."

"Such a talented boy he was."

"Yes, and a determined man."

Maryam sighed, scraping her eyes with her dupatta and tucking its ends back into place. "Hmm, with too many ideas from that madrassa. And they got him killed."

The cook approached, carrying a small table which he set before the women. They remained silent for the few minutes it took for him to settle the tea tray on the table.

Shahnaz poured. "I think, Ammi, that he hated bullying and saw it in the men's making girls stay in the mosque complex. I think he came to appreciate what girls have to offer, and he saved many lives. Insh'allah, we can hold onto that."

Maryam took the teacup from Shahnaz's hand. "You have a good heart. Thank you."

As they sat back, lost in thought, Zainab appeared from Shahnaz's bedroom, a roll of papers stuck under her arm, striding forward as her father had done, an angry pout on her face.

Shahnaz tapped Maryam's arm. "Ammi, look what's coming." Then, clapping her hands, she called, "Come here, sweetie, show us what you have."

The little girl tripped down the dirt path to the tree and dropped the papers onto Shahnaz's lap. "Abu's. See?" She grinned, obviously pleased with herself.

"And you looked like your Abu, too. But where did you find them?"

Zainab pointed to Shahnaz's door.

"Yes, in my room." Shahnaz took the child's hands. "But where in the room? I haven't seen them in some time."

Zainab squatted down and pointed under the bench. "There."

"You mean they were under something? The bed? The chair?"

The child shook her head. "Guess more."

Shahnaz mentally reviewed her picture of the bedroom. "The dresser?"

With a vigorous nod, Zainab said, "Yes."

"How odd. I wonder why Naseer hid them away?"

Maryam answered the rhetorical question. "They're a burden to him. Perhaps along with all of us."

"Oh, Ammi. I don't want to be a burden."

"None of us do."

Shahnaz pressed out a fold in the papers and wound them more tightly within their bands. She'd put them back in a few minutes, maybe ask Naseer about them later. But when she lay them down on the bench, she found her hand drawn back to them as by a magnet. "Have you looked at these?"

Maryam shook her head. "They seemed to belong to the men."

"Well, I'm curious. Shall we?" And without waiting for an answer, she removed the rubber bands and unrolled the diagrams. "Look at this. He's drawn in the bench we're sitting on and our tree. And here," she pointed behind the penciled bedroom walls, "...he has twelve fruit trees, complete with the names of the varietals he wanted."

"Ah, a legacy for his father." She wiped her eyes again.

Shahnaz straightened Maryam's dupatta and then ran her hand over Zainab's hair. "Thank you for showing this to us. You brought us your Abu's dreams."

—•—

Only a smattering of work colleagues, near relatives, and a few unfamiliar men with long beards attended Raja Haider's funeral. It seemed to Shahnaz that most of the family was going through the outward motions of mourning without the depth of sadness they had felt for Sohail. Except, of course, for Noshaba, who was continuously near tears. Naseer and Jamil returned to work the day after the funeral.

In those first few days back in Muzaffarabad, Shahnaz took up her duties caring for Raja Haider's children and obsessed about her circumstances. So far, her husband had been adamant they all continue to cover, she not return to work, and no one think of changing the educational plans his brother had laid out. In whispered exchanges, the girls suggested arguments she might try with her husband to change his mind, like reminding him that he'd always been more like Sohail, liberal in his interpretation of Islam, and surely he couldn't be true to himself and continue these restrictions. Shahnaz agreed with the ideas but respected the integrity of Naseer's mourning process. She didn't want to push too hard. Each day she prayed he would wake to enlightenment.

In the morning, exactly a week after Raja Haider's funeral, Amir called. "I'm sorry to disturb your mourning, but I'm afraid I need to know if you'll be returning to us."

Shahnaz took a deep breath. "Insh'allah." She gritted her teeth at her audacity and then held to her promise of obedience. "But we're in mourning again. And my husband...well, he hasn't actually agreed. Can you give me until August 1 to let you know?" Her stomach knotted.

"August 1. Well, I guess so. We've waited this long, we can hold on another couple of weeks."

She bit her lip. "Thank you, Amir. It means so much to me, your generosity."

That afternoon, as she and Noshaba sat in the garden with the children, Maryam called to her. "Do you have a thousand rupees for the electric bill? I want to send Abdul out to pay it."

Shahnaz looked up from the blanket she had spread out for their play. "Sorry, I don't think I even have a hundred."

Noshaba blushed. "I'm afraid I don't either."

Maryam pursed her lips. "I'll have to ask Naseer to go to the bank." She turned and disappeared back into the house.

"I seem to contribute very little." Noshaba stared at the ground. "To anyone, really." She straightened the folds of her dupatta. "I owe you so much for caring for my children." Tears rolled from her eyes.

Shahnaz rubbed her sister-in-law's arm. "I love them both, and you need your time to mourn."

Noshaba looked up. "I want you to know that when you have babies, insh'allah, I'll be here to care for them." The flow of her tears increased.

"Oh, Noshaba, that is so kind of you. Thank you. Insh'allah, I will have a baby one of these days. You...you aren't worried that Naseer will send you away, are you? Because he won't. He's said you may stay here always."

She showed a tremulous smile. "He's said so, I know. Praise Allah. But it's you I wish to serve. There is so little I can do and so much you want to do. You can count on me."

Shahnaz leaned over to hug her. "Sisters, always."

Noshaba sniffed, staring with a tilted head at Zainab, who was using a trowel to dig a hole. "I think my daughters—and yours—should grow up without the hijab."

"Oh, Noshaba. Do you think you could let go of it, if Naseer says we can?"

She smoothed her brown tunic. "No, not me. But for them, yes."

—•—

After dinner, Maryam called Naseer, Shahnaz, and Jamil into her bedroom and encouraged them to "sit, sit, sit." The men took the room's chairs, and Shahnaz sat at the end of the bed, angling her body toward her mother-in-law, who sat at the corner table, a sheaf of notepapers in front of her. Maryam spelled out her worry. "I've made a list of our expenses, and in the next couple of weeks, we'll need to pay the school fees for all three girls, Qadir, and you, too, Jamil. While we have enough money for that, we're using our savings, which means we haven't a lot of free cash and probably won't be able to renovate the house without help—from somewhere."

Jamil spoke up, "I could take a break from the accountancy course." He looked remarkably pleased at the thought.

Maryam shook her head, peering at him over the top of her glasses. "That's a very temporary solution, and you must get fully qualified. Thank goodness you're working, but to move along in the field you must pass the next exams."

Shahnaz glanced at her husband and plunged ahead. "I could return to work. Peace wants me back, and you know I love what I do." There, she'd thrown down the glove.

"I'm not prepared to allow that." His voice faded. He looked at his fingers and knotted them together.

Maryam steepled her hands against her mouth and then dropped them to her lap. "Let's put the facts on the table." She started to tick off items, raising a finger with each declaration. "One, Sohail left us enough money for perhaps a year. Two, there are bound to be legal fees for Raja Haider's activities and probably a large fine to pay. Three, the bedroom wing has been condemned, and we must renovate soon or move out of it. Four, my brothers and Sohail's will help us but they also face extensive house renovations." She looked at each face in turn.

Naseer answered, "These are issues that men should decide, Ammi. I had meant to lift this burden from you already, but there's been so much to do, I haven't had the time. I'll discuss our finances with my uncles."

Maryam looked again over the top of her spectacles, turning intelligent eyes on this son. "Sohail always shared financial realities with me. I probably know more about this family's expenses than any of you, and I think it's time for us to work together on these problems."

Shahnaz was caught between her agreement with Ammi's proposal and her need to protect Naseer. She turned to her husband. "I have a few ideas. You've talked about doing special teacher training for groups like UNICEF. That would bring in extra income. Ammi can speed up her writing, and, if you agree, I can return to my job. Even with that, we'll still need help that you men can negotiate with the uncles. Perhaps they'll help us renovate now and, insh'allah, we can help them out later, when Nooran is working and we all get raises."

The room was silent with all eyes on Naseer.

"You've continued your writing, Ammi?"

Glancing at Shahnaz, who mouthed "sorry" toward her, Maryam folded her hands and looked levelly at her son. "Yes, I have. I find writing a healthy reprieve from our sadness and a way for me to repay the blessings I've been given."

Naseer glared back at her. Then he rose and paced the room,

back and forth, anger clear in the bang of each heel on the wooden floor. His teeth sank into his bottom lip. At the door, he took hold of the frame and turned to face the others. "I won't be railroaded into such a complicated decision. I'm going to talk with the uncles."

—••—

As Shahnaz brushed her teeth, she heard the bedroom door open. "Naseer?"

"Yes."

She rinsed her mouth and dried her face before slipping into the bedroom.

Naseer collapsed into the chair. "Why did Raja Haider have to take our religion to such an extreme?"

Shahnaz sat back against the pillows, oddly comforted. They were talking again. "I wonder if he saw this jihad as a test of his faith? Maybe he felt he'd been able to defend his beliefs when it was easy, but at the Red Mosque, it would be hard and he needed something hard. Or maybe he was tired of listening to our objections. Well, to the girls' objections. He could have wanted to be with others who'd reinforce his ideas instead of denigrate them."

Naseer stood, walked to the window, and stared out, hand on the sill. "It sure would be more comfortable not to have your family argue with you at every turn."

Shahnaz allowed him a few moments of private thoughts and then patted the bed at her side. "Come over here, please. Sit next to me."

He ambled back to the bed and sat down on its edge.

"I want to tell you a story. See, when I was in the sports arena, I met several girls who told me about a man who helped them leave the mosque area. One girl said she thought his name was Haider. I believe it was your brother. I think he objected to forcing the girls to stay and to some of the other jihadists' actions."

"He said once he didn't like using the girls for cannon fodder."

"So, it makes sense he'd hate ordering the girls to refuse amnesty, with the likelihood they'd die. He'd hate all that."

Naseer ran his hand through his hair. "True."

She fiddled with the edge of the sheet. "It makes me wonder what other ideas he questioned, toward the end. I mean, we're sure he stayed. That could have been out of loyalty to the people he'd joined—"

"Or commitment to his belief that Pakistan needs Sharia law."

"Right. But look at what he said to the girls. By letting them go, urging them to go, he wanted them to live, to be with their families, to have full lives."

Naseer sagged forward, forearms resting on his thighs. "Full lives."

"We'll never know whether he'd have taken that any further, changed his ideas about other things women should or shouldn't do, but that's not really the point."

"I'm not sure I want to hear the point."

"You already know what it is."

He struggled to sit up, pushing one forearm at a time. "Yeah, I suppose I do. If my extremist of a brother could question his ideas and change them, why can't I?"

"If we don't know what his ideas were, at the end, how can we say that the rules he set for us are the ones he would have continued?"

Naseer shook his head. "You really think he'd have tolerated Nooran working as a doctor?"

"Do you think he would have watched those young girls die while a male doctor stood by?"

Naseer sighed. "I don't know."

She touched his arm. "I'm not trying to force changes down

your throat, but I am asking that you think about the rules of a modern Islam, find the ones that make sense to you. That's what Sohail did, what Raja Haider was in the process of doing."

Slowly, Naseer stood, put his hands behind his hips, and stretched. "The uncles can help, some, but they think I should let you and Ammi work."

He threw his body into the overstuffed chair. "You don't know what you're asking, all of you. I feel like I've failed. I should have been able to get Raja Haider to come home. I should have stopped you seeing a male doctor. I promised my brother I'd keep his rules. It's all I can give him now."

Shahnaz held her breath through a long pause.

"If I countermand his orders, it's like I'm killing him again." He stared squarely at her face. "I...I look at you and think of my sisters and Qadir, and I want to give you what you're asking for, but what about my promises to Raja Haider?"

Shahnaz knelt at his knee. "I saw his blueprints today. If we work together, all of us, we can make his dream for our home a reality. We can allow him to give us a lifelong gift. Please, listen to your heart."

Naseer stared at her and ran a finger down the side of her face.

—◆•◆—

Two days, full of anxiety and hope, passed without any sign of a decision from Naseer. Shahnaz tried to relax, worked at filling her time with tasks instead of worry. On the third evening, as the family got ready to go to Tanvir's for dinner, she saw Naseer staring at her and smiled. "What is it?"

He pulled a pin from her hijab, freeing it to fall from her face. "I'd like to see your face this evening." And as the echo of his voice faded away, one edge of his lip curled into a half-smile.

GLOSSARY

Abu: Father; used to address one's father or father-in-law

Aloo chole: Potatoes and chickpeas in a spicy sauce

Ammi: Mother; used to address one's mother or mother-in-law

Azaan: Call to prayer

Azad Kashmir: "Free" Kashmir; the section of this state within the borders of Pakistan

Biryani: Spicy rice, usually made with chicken, lamb, or vegetables

Bismillah ar-Rahman ar-Raheem: In the name of God, the compassionate, the merciful

Chappati: Thin round of unleavened bread cooked in a hot skillet; also known as roti

Charpoy: A bed consisting of a frame strung with tapes or light rope

Chowkidar: Caretaker

Diaspora: A group of people, such as those sharing a national, religious, and/or ethnic identity, living away from an established or ancestral homeland

Double cabin: A truck with four doors, two bucket seats in front, and a bench seat behind

Dupatta: Shawl, generally used as a head covering

EidFeast or festival: Eid al-Fitr is a three-day feast to celebrate the end of the fasting month of Ramazan (Ramadan)

Goshtaba: Balls of minced lamb with ginger, fennel, chili, and other spices, served in a sauce

Gulab jamun: A dessert of balls of dough, deep fried, and soaked in sugar syrup

Halwa: A sweet dessert; carrot halwa is made of fresh carrots, milk, and ghee, garnished with nuts and raisins

Hijab: Covering for the face leaving only the eyes showing; often made from a portion of the dupatta or shawl, using pins to secure the material at either side of the face

Insh'allah: God willing; an expression used whenever referring to an event in the future

Islamabad: The capital of Pakistan, a planned city begun in the 1960s and still growing. It is set out as a grid with each sector identified by a letter and a number (e.g., F-7)

Jalfrezi: A spicy curry, often made with chicken and green peppers

Jumma prayer: The extended Muslim religious service held on Fridays about 1 p.m. and containing a sermon and communal prayer

Keema: Ground lamb cooked with curry spices and green peas

Kofta: Deep-fried balls of lamb in a curry sauce

Kohala Bridge: The two-lane road bridge that separates the North West Frontier Province from Azad Kashmir

Kohl: A stick or soft powder used to outline the eyes

Ladyfingers: Okra, often used in stews

Lal Masjid: The Red Mosque, a large Sunni Muslim place of worship in Islamabad

Load shedding: The practice of rotating electricity outages across a city to conserve a scarce resource

Mahar: A wedding gift provided to the bride on the night of the ceremony

Mangni: Engagement party

Mehndi: Celebration of henna; generally the day before the wedding contract is signed

Muzaffarabad: The capital of Azad Kashmir, a state within the boundaries of Pakistan

Naan: A yeast-raised oven-baked puffy flat bread containing wheat flour, oil, sugar, and salt

Nikah: Celebration of the signing of the wedding contract

Ramazan: As used in Pakistan, the name for the holy month of fasting in Islam; also known as Ramadan

Roti: Round flat of unleavened bread made with wheat flour and water; also known as chappati

Sahiba: An honorific for a married woman

Shaitan: Satan

Shalwar kameez: Clothing worn by both men and women, consisting of a tunic top that extends to the back of the knees with a slit up the sides and baggy pants cinched at the waist by elastic or a drawstring

Sura: A chapter of the Qur'an

Takht: Dais on which the wedding couple sits during the celebration after signing their marriage contract

Taqiyah: A short rounded cap, often worn for religious purposes. In the United States and Britain, vendors often call these caps *kufi*

Walima: Hosted by the groom's family, a celebration on the day after the signing of the wedding contract

Zakat: Charity, one of the five pillars of Islam which requires that each Muslim give away a percentage of his wealth each year

Author's Note

The Khan family and friends portrayed in this book are fictional characters inspired by the many people I met while working in northwestern Pakistan from 2006 to 2008. My Islamabad office was only a couple of blocks from Lal Masjid and its associated girls' madrassa, Jamia Hafsa. For several days in July 2007, the curfew forbade anyone going into the sector, and we set up temporary quarters in the basement of a hotel and my dining room. When we were allowed to return, I passed the burned-out mosque each day and turned into our street past the stacked sandbags and soldiers with guns ready. My driver told me caskets with sixty-six children's bodies had been returned to his village, though the government had reported the total killed to be not many more.

Quotes from the *Holy Qur'an* are taken from the following English translation: *Quran: The Final Testament, Authorized English Version.* Translated from the Original by Rashad Khalifa, Ph.D. (Revised Edition III). Fremont: Universal Unity, 2001. Any historical or interpretive mistakes in the manuscript are mine.

About the Author

Lorelei Brush holds two doctoral degrees, a Ph.D. in Developmental Psychology and a Doctor of Ministry focusing on Islam and Christianity. Since 1996, she has worked in international education. From 2006 to 2008 she managed a large US-AID-funded education project in northwestern Pakistan, an area seriously affected by the earthquake of October 2005. *Uncovering* is her first novel, a work of love arising from her time among so many gifted people committed to Islam as a religion of peace and helping others.

Along with two beloved cats, she lives outside of Washington, D.C. in a community of good neighbors, friends, and fellow writers. In her spare time she sings, hikes, and shows up for those healthy work-outs at the gym. Learn more about her at www.loreleibrush.com.

Acknowledgments

So many people have supported me in the preparation of this novel that I'm afraid I may have forgotten them all. If so, please forgive me and know that I appreciated your comments and critiques. My thanks must begin with the many Pakistani staff with whom I worked in the North West Frontier Province and Azad Kashmir. Let me use the names by which I know them: Naeem Sohail Butt, Tanvir Latif, Salima Malik, Asad Khan, Noshaba Zafar Mir, Raja Mohammad Qadir Khan, Manzer Abbas, Tahira Syed, Riaz Khan, Khadim Hussain, Mehnaz Chaudhry, Mohammad Haroon Ahmed, Rizwana Aqeel, Raja Naseer, Syed Shafait Gardazi, Jamil Ahmed, Nayyar Malik, and Sofiya Afzal. I so appreciated the welcome you accorded to me and the passion with which you joined together to improve children's education. For their careful reading of the manuscript and corrections regarding Pakistani customs, I particularly want to thank Babar Mufti, Talaat Moreau, Naeem Sohail Butt, and Shabnam Arora Afsah. And for reading the manuscript and making helpful suggestions, I sincerely thank members of my writers' groups: Hildie Block, Patricia Morningstar, Sandy Coburn, Kaaren Christopherson, Raima Larter, Melanie Griffiths, Pragna Soni, Susan Lynch, Christine Jackson, and Margaret Rodenberg.

Finally, to all the staff at Mascot Books, I extend my thanks for a smooth process of escorting my manuscript into publication.

Book Club Questions

1. What was your reaction to Shahnaz entering a marriage that had been arranged by her parents? Such marriages are not common in the West, but can you see advantages for her and for society in this type of marriage? Disadvantages?

2. Christianity has a traditional wedding vow including the word "obey." Did any of you promise that? If you didn't, think of someone who did (e.g., perhaps a parent or grandparent). What did it mean to you or your relative? How does that meaning compare to Shahnaz's idea of the obedience she owed her parents, her husband, and her husband's family?

3. Who was your favorite character and why? Whose motives did you understand best? Whose were just not clear to you?

4. Shahnaz makes a momentous decision when she says Naseer must decide if a male doctor can operate on her. Why do you think she made this decision? Does it seem out of character for her? Could you see yourself making such a decision? Why or why not?

5. How would you describe the character of Naseer? Think about his dilemma—trying to remain faithful to what he had promised his brother and yet also staying true to his love for his wife. What does his decision say about his character and the strength of his beliefs?

6. The jihad described in the book, which demanded the government to replace its rule of law with Sharia law (that which is written in the Qur'an), is based on a series of events that occurred in Islamabad in the spring of 2007. [To read more about the events, refer to "Lal Masjid, Islamabad" in Wikipedia.] Pakistan government officials were in a difficult position when the occupiers of the Red Mosque declared the jihad and intensified their demands. What do you see as the government's options for response, what were the advantages and disadvantages of each, and what do you think the government should have done to address this crisis?

7. This book is steeped in Islam. What similarities did you find among Islam, Christianity, and Judaism? How are these religions different? How does the Islam described in this book compare to your own beliefs?

8. Shahnaz's parents worry that Raja Haider is a "fundamentalist." What do they see in him that suggests that title? What beliefs place a person, of any religion, in that category? Is a fundamentalist always a radical?

9. As the story climaxes, Raja Haider slips from a fundamentalist into a terrorist. Did this seem a "natural" progression? How could his family have stopped him—or was that impossible? Had he survived, how could he have been brought back from that brink?

10. What is the importance of pregnancy, miscarriage, birth, and nursing to this story? What surprised you about Shahnaz's health work?

11. Just what has been "uncovered" in this book?

12. What information or ideas suggested in this book would you like to learn more about? Think about Pakistan as a country and its governance; religion, education, and health in developing countries; the differences between rural and urban environments and the beliefs of people from these areas.